TERRA

GEORGE PLOUMIDIS

Dedication

To my parents, Spiro and Chryssoula, and my in-laws, Pasquale and Anna. This book is dedicated to your pursuit of a better life; not knowing the obstacles in your way.

Acknowledgements

This book is fictional. While snippets of conversation, transactions, anecdotes and phrases I have had the privilege of hearing have snuck their way in, the characters bear no resemblance to any person living or deceased.

Following up *Koraki*, a story written in the present-day Melbourne I know, to write about events that took place in the 1960s in small towns of Sicily and Crete was a difficult task. I am fortunate to have had brilliant brains to pick to make this book a reality.

In the first instance, I was curious as to why immigration (for some) carried an almost romantic connotation. The passing of decades will do that to an experience as the memories of hardships fade, but it takes very little to be convinced otherwise.

While studying Italian in the pre-internet 1990's, a man once said something profound to me while we were discussing his life story.

"La decisione di immigrare, di lasciare il tuo paese, non è sempre stata romantica. A volte era una scelta forzata e affrettata, ma non mi pento nulla. Amo Australia, ed è diventata la mia casa."

The decision to immigrate, to leave your homeland, it was not always a romantic one. Sometimes it was a forced and hurried choice, but I regret nothing. I love Australia and it has become my home.

My Father and many immigrant Greeks have said:

"Δεν ξέραμε τι θα βρίσκαμε όταν φτάσουμε εκεί. Δουλέψαμε σκληρά, μάθαμε την αγγλική γλώσσα και τα έθιμα όσο καλύτερα μπορούσαμε. Έτσι να δώσουμε στα παιδιά μας μια καλύτερη ζωή από αυτή που περάσαμε εμείς."

How did we know what we would find when we arrived? We worked hard, learned the language and local customs as best we could; all to give our kids a better life than we endured.

These are just the two reflections that come immediately to my mind, two I suspect of many that reflect immigrants' experiences in this wonderful country; the feelings a mix of the essential sentiments in both quotes; the duress and fear mixed with the bloody-minded determination to make it work for their children, with little regard for themselves. Some of the stories of the work my parents and in-laws did to get by are truly eye-watering and awe-inspiring in their nature.

And like any large sample size, their experiences naturally varied. Despite some racial intolerances that burned at the time, most managed to maintain their cultural beliefs and rituals while integrating into their communities, servicing their communities through cafes, fish and chip shops like the one I grew up in. With time, they became butchers, mechanics, teachers, scientists, doctors, lawyers, politicians and many shone on the sporting stage and television.

Eventually the immigrants mirrored the communities they moved into as strangers, a jewel in the crown of Australian multiculturalism, one that (insert declaration of inherent bias) remains unmatched in the world. It is because of their hard work in the shadow of uncertainty that I have the privilege of writing about the fictional characters like those in this book. I will be forever grateful for this sacrifice.

I wish to thank some people for their contributions to *Terra*;

Evan Binos, for suggesting, sorry, demanding that the backstories of the elderly parents in *Koraki* be fleshed out and told as a story in its own right. It's your fault – you goaded me into it. Thank you for fulfilling your part in catalysing this project by taking frequent phone calls at obscene hours of the day. Your suggestions, feedback and historical perspectives were crucial.

Sandy Togias, the speed-reading Queen of the comma, for her eagle eye, feedback, encouragement, constantly telling me 'what did I tell you?' when I finally got published, and her fabulous cover art on both *Koraki* and now, *Terra*.

Dina Gerolymou, Senior Producer at SBS Radio; for taking an interest in my story and her expertise in Athenian geography, both social and physical, that painted a vivid picture of the landscape occupied by only a small yet important part of this book.

The many Greeks and Italians, whose idioms, mannerisms, crude aphorisms, phrases, encounters and stories true and apocryphal have filled my memory bank to overflowing; these have been the richest of fertiliser for the garden I pick from. And we all know how you like your gardens.
My fabulous Mother, Chryssoula; humble, yet so knowledgeable, selfless and generous. Thank you for your

self-appointed advisory role in answering questions that Google algorithms could not get close to; the minutiae of Greek life, questions of food, priests, wedding dresses and expressions that helped shape the story.

"But beneath it all will run that Sicilian understanding that the underside of joy is grief, that the face of sacrifice and suffering is the dark mirror image of pleasure and enjoyment, that every moment of arrival is to be treasured and enjoyed in the full knowledge that it has brought us a moment closer to the moment of departure."

Francine Prose, Sicilian Odyssey

"Love of liberty, the refusal to accept your soul's enslavement, not even in exchange for paradise; stalwart games over and above love and pain, over and above death; smashing even the most sacrosanct of the moulds when they are unable to contain you any longer - these are the great cries of Crete."

Nikos Kazantzakis

CHAPTER 1

Sicily, 1967

The *scirocco* came early, its hot bluster drawing a ring of sweat under the cap of the man rowing against it. Renzo Scardamo's bag was full, bulging with mackerel and squid, the live ones squirming in vain amongst the dead. He wanted to fish on into the afternoon, and five years ago, as a single man, he might have pushed his luck. *No chance with this*, he said to himself. His wife would hound him in the afterlife and punish him mercilessly if he perished here. He rounded the Mazzaro headland and cursed the wind for the burning in his shoulders.

As he passed the Grotta Azzurra, a movement of bright white from the rocks caught his eye. His hands followed his eyes and operated the oars with urgency. The fabric flapped in the wind above the body's belly. The rigid arm jutted out of it, bent at an unnatural angle, the hand resting against a rock, raised up in the air like a signal for help, fingers stiff. The waves lapped over the man's lifeless legs, trying to draw him away from rocks smooth and rough but reaching only as far as his knees. After two days, the cuts on his body were covered by the bloating of separated skin in the heat. Birds approached and observed from a distance.

Scardamo rowed with great effort to get closer, the wind blowing him further offshore as a warning. If he was sufficiently close, he would have seen a mottled head, dead eyes and a crooked mouth bent away on the other side of the white shirt, neck broken.

Rowing the last of it round the headland to the jetty at Villagonia was agony, but he walked his way up the hill to the police station. Still breathless and sopping with sweat from his efforts, he recounted the scene, his catch bag dripping on the marble floor to the irritation of the station master.

CHAPTER 2

Sicily, 1961

At six-foot-three, Augustino 'Tino' Liverani stood tall over the area of broken fence line at the edge of his farmland outside Zafferia. Twelve kilometres northeast from where he stood was the city of Messina. Though technically part of Provincia Messina, their bayside neighbours considered them simple mountain folk, *maleducati.*

The corpse of a fox lay half-decayed on the other side of the river that divided his land and that of Filipo Maresca, the Mayor of Zafferia. If not for the recent bloom of wildflowers and the prevailing wind negating the foul odour, he may have put off the task for another day.

Claudio Liverani, aged fourteen, sat as his Father winced with each downward blow of the new post into the ground. For the first time there was a slackness about him, a lag in his movement that he interpreted as ageing. He often compared his body with his Father's, resenting his Mother's genes for tempering his height to average. He wanted so much to be tall and gave up on any impending growth spurt. But where he was average in height, he was unusually strong. At thirteen, he lifted a pig freshly killed by Tino over his shoulder from the pen to the barn and onto the hook, much to his Father's amazement. *Always keep your strength silent,* Tino told his son often, gesturing with his palm close against his chest.

"Are you Ok, Father?"

"Yes, Claudio. Just tired."

"You're never tired."

Tino smiled at his son. "Comes a time, my boy. For everyone."

The fence repaired, they sat together and shared the last of the bread, cheese and figs they brought along. The green land this side of the river was dotted with wild orchids at their peak, soon to perish. Maresca's land rose to a hill, becoming barer the higher it went, receiving little benefit from the dividing stream. Looking at the land either side of the river was like looking through different lenses.

Tino's forebears carved irrigation furrows to maximise access to the water, producing sufficient crops and feed for their pigs, sheep and goats. The animals roamed without need for shepherding over rough terrain and the land provided for them in excess of subsistence. Tino and Vanna Liverani were well liked by their neighbours, who traded food according to their needs; meat, milk, honey, rosemary seedlings, eggs and other necessities. *Maleducati* they were not; transactions was quickly calculated without need for currency and agreed with goodwill and appreciation.

"Why is our land greener than Mayor Maresca's?"

"Luck of geography Claudio, nothing more."

"Do you think he is jealous of us?"

"Probably, but I am not concerned with him and his jealousies. Being Mayor means you are well paid." code for having fingers in many pies.

"How do we own so much land?"

"Long story, Claudio. Latifundia. It belonged to my Father,
his Father, and so on, back and back since early times."
Claudio had no concept of how early his Father meant.

Latifundia was a custom from different times and under
different powers but the land passed onto the next generation
and the one after. World War Two replaced the perennial
jealousy and resentment, the need to pull together taking
priority, landowner or not. But as memories of the conflict
faded, these envies resurfaced.

The feudal arrangements of *latifundia* that drew the land up
centuries ago were no reflection on their current owners.
Some who worked hard and could look after the land given
the chance had no claim, while others of an indolent nature
had it handed to them on a plate.

Tino's Father, Domenico, took full advantage of both a
strong body and the good fortune to be descended from
landowner after landowner, before emphysema ate him out
from the inside, taking him at fifty-nine. Tino shadowed him
from a young age, and took over without missing a beat, the
hard work left behind making grieving easier.

The majority of Sicilians who did not own land suffered from
poor or no infrastructure, had menial or no work, and wished
for problems such as those of Mayor Maresca.

CHAPTER 3

Crete, 1961

Nikos Petrakis cursed as the needle he struggled to pass through the thick leather hide broke through and pierced his left index finger.

"Ρε πουτάνα του σατανά!" Whore of the devil!

"Niko!" yelled Fotini. "Do you want all the neighbourhood to enjoy your cursing?"

"Leave me be, woman. Stelios and his fucking saddles. I'm a shoe repairer, not a saddler."

"Yet you smile like a gentleman when he pays. And he pays well, so either take his money and be nice or refuse his business."

As the sole shoe repairer in Tavroniti, Nikos was in high demand. Fotini was an accomplished seamstress, doing the odd dress alteration but most of the work fell to Nikos. His Father, Alexandros, started the business in the thirties and passed the shop and house to him. The front room was wide, well lit, benches running along each wall. The room behind deeper, where the family cooked, sat, ate and talked. In the corner was a small curtained off area, where the eldest boy, Nectarios, slept. Two small bedrooms rooms fed off a small hallway, where his parents and younger sister, Rita, slept. The toilet and a small shower were outside in a small brick room Nikos built with his Father.

The shop was located on *Odos Theoharos*, one of the few streets left unscathed by the brutal German assault of 1941. No one expected paratroopers to land on the beaches. The heads of the four men who provided initial resistance rolled down the street within days of the invasion as a warning, their funerals forbidden by the Nazis to prevent any resistance from galvanising. The island was frozen into submission before a bloody revenge brewed. Selfless bravery and fury drove them off the island with the help of Allied troops, stemming the Nazi march and denying them the base in the Mediterranean they craved.

As long as the Church of Saint Nikolaos remained standing, Alexandros was going nowhere. He was proud to help erect the monument that exemplified the Cretan spirit; a pair of spent German torpedoes set in concrete, pointed back at Germany. The tourists that returned after the war to enjoy the crystal blue water had to walk past the imposing metal twins, Tavroniti's defiant *fuck you* to the Nazis. Alexandros died ten years after the monument was erected, and Margarita passed a month later.

Fotini was a slender waif, but at twenty weeks, she was starting to show, her tired hips widening from memory to accommodate their third child. Her face contorted for a moment as pain shot through her lower back.

"Where is Nectarios?" asked Nikos.

"Delivering. He should be back by now. Getting food as a tip slows you down."

"Ah, here he is." said Nikos, a large hand softly ruffling his son's short brown hair as he walked in. He handed over the cash to his Father. Nectarios was a wiry boy with brown eyes with flecks of green and a smile that all women loved. He attracted offers to take some food with him as he made his deliveries after school, which he burnt off quickly with his fast metabolism. He walked front to back to use the outside toilet. Rita was skipping outside, and she poked her tongue out at him. Nectarios pulled his ears wide in return and Rita chased him, but Nectarios was always too fast for her.

CHAPTER 4

Sicily, 1961

Claudio's parents were religious, not in the pious sense but through respect for their neighbours and helping anyone out with excess food. "It always comes back." said his Mother often. No tabs were kept, nor written nor mental. They attended the church of San Niccoló most Sundays and Tino helped out with its maintenance works, his considerable handyman skills much appreciated.

Father Antonio Di Pardo took over after Father Grossani passed away, aged eighty-five. At forty-three, Di Pardo softened the tone from his predecessor's hard-line message and drew more of the local community back to church. The female parishioners warmed to his soft nature and he came across as approachable to the men. Di Pardo could read faces well and took pride in being able to mould his tone and message according to the audience. After a year, he began bible lessons for the children after church, which became popular, especially when he offered cannoli and soft drink at the end to make sure they stayed.

Claudio was reluctant but his Father insisted he go with his younger sister, Lidia, twelve. The first bible lesson attracted thirteen children. The boy opposite kept staring at Lidia, distracted by her blonde hair and bright blue eyes. He had never seen eyes this blue before. He shifted awkwardly in a chair too small for his large, round form. He ran his index finger down the perfect part his Mother had combed for him and scratched an itch as Claudio's stare caught his attention. He averted his gaze, staring down at the floor. Di Pardo noticed and closed his book with an audible snap that raised the children's heads.

"Is something wrong, Claudio?"

"No, Father."

"Has something about the Miracle of Lazarus raised caused offence?"

"No, Father. Truly miraculous that Jesus could raise a man dead for four days back to life." Two or three children laughed, the others joining in, further irritating the priest.

Impressed yet suspicious of irony, Father Di Pardo smiled politely and praised Claudio for his appreciation in an effort to garner some enthusiasm from the other children. The boy staring at the floor, Matteo Maresca, excused himself but only made it halfway before the warm trickle spread over his trousers. He rushed to the bathroom and splashed water over his front, so it looked like he had an accident with the sink, but Claudio knew and speared him with a glance as parents arrived back from their coffee to collect their children.

In the car, Lidia squeezed Claudio's hand and whispered *why?*

Claudio mouthed *shh* and squeezed her hand in return.

The next lesson revolved around The Hidden Treasure and the Pearl.

"Matthew 13:44, children," said Di Pardo. "Ready to listen?"

He continued. "The Kingdom of Heaven is like treasure hidden in a field. When a man found it, he hid it again, and then in his joy went and sold all he had and bought that field." He watched the eyes and saw only emptiness, except for Caterina, a girl not yet eleven, who had her hand up, eager to share.

"Caterina?"

"Yes, Father. If we sow our goodness into the land by doing good things, we can hope it pays us back for being a good person?"

"Very good, child. Can anyone add to Caterina's excellent observation?"

"You reap what you sow." said Claudio in a flat voice.

"Go on." said Di Pardo.

"In a world which is right, good things come back to people who do the right thing, without any expectation of credit."

Di Pardo's pulse quickened. Unusual for a child this age to form such a coherent argument. He decided to indulge him.

"And bad things?"

"They are punished by God. Unless-"

"Yes?"

"Someone gets in first."

The children began murmuring and the chatter became
louder until Di Pardo tapped the book on the table, the noise
clearing the air. "Let us remain respectful in this holy
building, children. That will be all for today. Go in peace and
be kind."

The Priest caught Claudio's eye. Claudio gave him nothing,
which troubled Di Pardo no end as he walked back to his
residence behind the church. At the next lesson he divided
the children onto two groups and asked Sister Malena to take
the younger children. Claudio made sure to avoid eye contact
with Di Pardo and contributed enough to settle his nerves.

CHAPTER 5

Sicily, 1961

Du' su' i putenti, cu avi assa' e cun nun avi nenti.
There are two kinds of powerful, those who own too much
and those who don't own anything.
- Sicilian proverb

Mayor Filipo Maresca wiped his bald head as he stepped off
the bus. The ride back from Palermo was long, the frequent
stops for the incontinent man in the front seat stretching his
patience. His mayoral status meant stomaching the
inconvenience, smiling politely as the man hopped off and
back on. He waved the greetings of his wife and son aside
when he got home, dumped his suitcase and suit jacket to the
floor and lay on his bed.

"What are you doing? I haven't seen you for three days."
said his wife, Concetta.

"What do you fucking think? I'm tired. The bus took five
hours from Palermo, five hours. I need to sleep. Please, don't
break my balls."

"Ok, Ok. Go to sleep."

He loosened his belt, let out an angry fart and fell asleep.

He woke late in the afternoon. made himself an espresso,
took some dry biscuits from the pantry and walked up to the
highest point of his farm, where he could see over his three
farming neighbours' properties. He bristled at the green of

their land and the relative pallor of his. He spat at the ground, the mucous refusing to seep into the dusty hardness beneath.

He concluded that the meeting with all the provincial leaders in Palermo was worth the inconvenience of the bus trip, the unsupportive bed of the hotel and the relative anonymity he felt as a small-town mayor. The promise of the north to throw more than loose change at the south was real, real enough to give him a warm feeling about the future.

The Government officials revealed plans to enrich the south with infrastructure; roads, irrigation, mining, new buildings, hydroelectric works and power for those without it. Companies setting up in the south would be given tax concessions and mills producing steel and sulphur were promised.

If Sicily wanted to move into the modern age, it had to let go of the past. By the past, they meant the end of *latifundia*, the end of expanses of land being passed onto the next generation. Land was needed for industry, roads and dams, give and take.

Maresca saw opportunity in the three properties. How the Sidero family of Messina found out about the meeting was anyone's guess, but they insisted on sending one of their men to Palermo. When he knocked on Maresca's hotel door, the man introduced himself as 'your secretary for the meeting', promptly sat himself on the bed and lit up without shaking Maresca's outstretched hand.

"I recognise you." said Maresca, scared but trying to sound assured.

"You know of my family, do you?"

"Yes."

"That will save some time. We understand that after years of
the north spitting on us, some money will be devoted to our
noble island. I imagine you have been coveting that fertile
land to your south for some time, correct?"

"Yes." *How the fuck did he know?*

"Ok. And let me thank you for being so honest and cordial.
That is much appreciated. What we want is some access to
the construction companies, mills and mines so we can
protect them from nasty criminals who might want to steal
their materials. Your electoral fortunes would be enhanced
by works benefitting your town, no?"

"Of course." said Maresca, eyes open with anticipation, wide
enough for the man to realise how pliable and ambitious
Maresca was.

"Tell me how much of each property you would like us to
acquire for you. Don't be too greedy. We want to acquire
land under a proposal to harvest the woodlands. The
pinewood will be needed for new housing. And then we can
pass some of that land to you - once we have everything in
place."

"How do we define that point in time?"

"We'll tell you. Now, my room is the last one on the left,
number eighteen. My name is Pasquale Brinto. Remind me,
what is my role?"

"You are my secretary."

"That's the way. Now, I'm off to sleep. I'll come and get you for breakfast at seven. Make sure I have plenty of paper and a pen to take notes."

Pasquale Brinto, or whoever he was, left, this time shaking his hand, brief and firm.

Maresca was no stranger to affairs that veered outside the respectable, but this excited and scared him at the same time.

He panned across the land again. He said the names aloud from left to right; *Rossi, Crudelli, Liverani.* He estimated that the wooded area fell roughly forty-sixty between the Crudelli and Liverani farms. The clouds began to make their afternoon passage overhead, and with it, the cool sea breeze. He watched the shadows pass over the land below and imagined houses there, houses he would rent and live off. He wouldn't be Mayor forever. He was able to influence the last two elections, and a third term was likely, but nothing was forever.

CHAPTER 6

Crete, 1962

"In the name of God, Niko, close the window."

Fotini shivered. A week after Christmas, the northern gale from the Atlantic reached Crete. Cold winds and rain lashed hard against windows, breaking those unprotected by shutters or improvised wooden planks hurriedly arranged and fastened. Nikos pulled the window shut and stopped dead as he turned to look at his wife. Even in this dim light she was bright yellow. He felt her back and she grimaced at his touch. He didn't bother grabbing a coat, instead waking Nectarios with something between a whisper and a premonition.

"Watch your Mother. I'll be back with Arvanitakis."

Nectarios lay down next to his Mother, shivering but on fire. An eternity passed before his Father came back with the Doctor, still in his striped pyjamas. He only lived a two-minute walk away but was difficult to rouse after a long day. He refused to believe the metallic clang of his doorbell was real until the persistent peals got him up. The Doctor ushered them out of the room and within a minute burst back out.

"Hospital, now. We need to deliver the baby, or they will both die. We'll take my car."

"No time." said Nikos, already walking. He banged on the door opposite. Mr Pandelis, the general store owner opened, gruff and hairy, waking up fast at the urgency on Nikos' face.

"Pandeli, I need your car."

"I'll drive." he said

"No, stay here."

Nikos took the keys off Pandelis and turned to Nectarios.

"Stay here with your sister."

Nectarios went back inside but not until he watched the car disappear, wheels slipping against the mud as Nikos drove the three-wheel truck. The wipers were inadequate for the sheets of rain being dumped on the windscreen. The Doctor sat in the back, cradling Fotini's head across his lap, ice blocks under a towel across her head.

"Is a boy or a girl?" came Fotini's unearthly voice, eyes closed.

"We will know soon." said the Doctor, straining to be as calm as possible with Nikos' lead foot and his Fotini's shaking.

The road to Chania was quiet, the rain still heavy but easing until the police car stopped them at Daratsos, the officious manner of the policeman dissolving when he saw the woman in the back seat. He drove in front of them with his siren on, giving them clear passage to the emergency entrance, Nikos carrying Fotini running in, Arvanitakis yelling *baby inside, liver failing.* Another doctor came out and had a rapid-fire conversation with Arvanitakis in language that Nikos didn't understand and carried Fotini in. The policeman ushered

Nikos to a quiet corner of the waiting area. He sat with him and offered a cigarette, which he took with shaking hands.

"Your first?" asked the policeman, his helmet still in place.

"Third. You?"

"Four." said the policeman, tapping his head. "I haven't learnt." he said with a smile under a thick moustache. He removed his helmet. "Courage, brother. I'll wait here until…we know what is happening."

"I'm Nikos." he said, shaking the officer's hand.

"Vangelis. Vangelis Dourakis."

They sat and smoked, waited and made small talk. Nikos' ears pricked up at every noise. A nurse rushed out after an hour and called him in. His wet shoes slipped on the smooth floor before he composed himself to walk alongside the nurse. The door opened. Straight ahead, a baby crying under a bright lamp; to his left, Fotini lifeless but still yellow.

"She's alive but critical. She almost died during the delivery, but we are trying to get her temperature down. She was boiling. We had to get the baby out before they both died."

Nikos turned from Fotini to the baby, its limbs making small movements and the room whooshed around him. He fell and hit the back of his head on the floor, the rain against the window the last thing he heard before he blacked out. The nurse called for help and Nikos was settled in the room next door.

The nurse adjusted the ice pack on Fotini's head and remeasured her temperature: 38.5°C. She was past the worst and her skin was settling back to normal, the yellow now paler. She opened her eyes.

"Where am I?"

"In hospital. You were very sick, but your baby is Ok."

Fotini's eyes opened wide with horror as she tried to move, her legs and lower back unresponsive, still numbed from the anaesthesia of the emergency Caesarean.

"We had to knock you out, otherwise you both would have died."

"Where is-"

"She." The nurse pointed to the bright lamp a few metres away. "Your baby is over there under the lamp to keep her warm."

"Your name?"

"Aspasia. But my friends call me Sia."

"I thought I was dead. Bring little Sia to me, please." The nurse stood still, confused.

"Please. Bring her to me."

Aspasia lay little Sia in Fotini's arms and she cradled her, whispering in a low voice. Her hair was sparse, her cheeks still swollen. *Sia, Sia shh, Sia, Sia, shh, mama's here.* The nurse wiped the tears from her eyes and walked out into the corridor to compose herself. She went next door to check on Nikos, waking him with a gentle rub of the arm. He woke, lifting his head and opening then closing his eyes as sharp pain in the back of his head forced him to lie back. She placed a fresh ice pack under his head and shoved another aspirin in his mouth, forcing him to swallow it with a sip of water. *These Cretan men, so invincible.* thought Sia. In a half hour, she returned.

"What happened?" groaned Nikos, now sitting up in bed.

"You fell on your head."

"Not me, Fotini." he said, irritated.

"Shh, your girls are next door. I will take you in a little while."

"Girls?"

"You have a daughter and your wife is past the worst."

"Take me now."

"Ok but slowly. I'll wheel you in."

"No, I'll walk." he said, swinging his legs around.

"No." she said in a firm tone, pushing him back onto his bed. "Wheelchair or nothing. You hit your head hard." He gave in and nodded.

She wheeled him in. Nikos saw Fotini lying down, little Sia draped across her breast, barely sucking. Fotini's eyes opened a small slit and she mouthed 'Sia'.

Nikos leapt out of the wheelchair and fell into the chair by her side.

"My Fotini, you are alive. And this angel, yes, Sia. It is a lovely name."

"Aspasia saved us, Nikos."

He turned to the nurse with tears in his eyes and held her hand, drawing her in and whispering *thank you Angel* as he hugged her. They would become good friends and five months later, she became Sia's Godmother.

CHAPTER 7

Sicily, 1963

Claudio walked in for the bible lesson and was surprised to see only Matteo Maresca seated. Matteo started at Claudio's footsteps, but Claudio raised his hand in a pacifying gesture.

"Matteo, relax."

Matteo's shoulders dropped but he was still nervous as he turned to face him.

"That day I scared you. You pissed your pants, didn't you?"

"Yes." said Matteo, his face red with embarrassment.

"I'm sorry." He put his hand out and Matteo grabbed it in an eager handshake. Sister Malena walked through the side door towards them; a short, thin woman with a stopped posture, thick rimmed glasses magnifying her dark brown eyes.

"There is no class today, boys. Claudio, is your sister unwell?"

"Yes, Sister Malena."

"Wish her well for me, will you?"

"I will. Thank you, Sister."

The boys walked up one hill and down another. Zafferia was a series of land plates on different slopes to each other, with the only the piazza situated on a small, flat plateau. Claudio observed how difficult Matteo found the inclines and declines, his balance uneasy.

"Funny how we are neighbours but only see each other at church or school."

"My Father doesn't let me go too far from the house." Matteo squirmed. "He thinks I'm weak and might get lost or hurt myself."

They reached the piazza and found their parents drinking coffee.

"What, no class today, Claudio?" said Tino.

"No."

Filipo Marecsa shook Claudio's hand.

"Hello Claudio. I'm-"

"Mayor Maresca; nice to meet you."
Maresca had a feeling of *other* about Claudio's voice that made him uneasy. He convinced himself he was reading too much into it and smiled back.

"Gelato, boys? On me."

"No, thank you." said Claudio.

"Claudio please don't offend the Mayor What would you like?"

"Chocolate please. Thank you, Mr Mayor."

Claudio did not question how he could read faces. He just could. Matteo was innocent, just immature. The Mayor though was *cattivo* from his eyes, the fake assurance in his voice. He just knew.

The next morning, he walked into town and bought the *Gazzetta Del Sud*.

LATIFUNDIA SOTTO MINACCIA
Latifundia under threat.

He read down, scanned and stopped when he found what he was looking for:

To accommodate La Cassa del Mezzogiorno, the immense range of infrastructure intended to stimulate economic growth and prosperity for Sicily and other regions of the south, the Italian government will require significant land reclamation.

It is promised that this process will be through proper consultation and due compensation to the landowners releasing some of their land for the greater good of the great island of Sicily.

Proper consultation, the greater good, words that made Claudio scoff as he read them, unable to get the image of Mayor Maresca taking their land out of his head. He did not think that Mayor Maresca had ever done anything proper in his life, yet here he was, Mayor of Zafferia.

He walked home and hugged his Mother. Vanna Liverani was a small to average sized woman, with mousey brown hair that curled and draped over her shoulders. Her dark brown eyes, dimples and the small beauty spot on the left side of her face rose and fell with every smile attracted many men, but she fell for the gentle giant in Tino.

"You bought the paper, Claudio, since when?" she asked.

"Since this, Mother. Read it, both of you."

He presented the story, tapping the paper hard against the wooden table to make his point.

"And?" said Tino.

"Our beloved Mayor will try and take our land, even if it is only part of it. Do you look at him and see proper consultation?"

"Claudio, my boy. *Latifundia* is an old relic. Your Mother and I expected this would happen eventually. If it says we will be compensated, we will be compensated, and we will downsize and move on. It is not as if we need every square metre to hold thousands and thousands of animals. Most of our crops and animals are on less than half of our land."

"What if even part if what Claudio is saying is right? Maresca is a cunning man. How else has he stayed for two terms?"

"Maybe because he's popular?"

"So popular he had the last votes counted by his accountant nephew? So popular that his front door was covered in eggs for days afterwards? People know when they are being screwed."

"Language, Vanna."

"Don't worry about my language. Worry about our land. Any offer we discuss together."

"You are too suspicious, both of you."

The Mayor of Messina, Andrea Palumbo puffed out at the chaos in his office. Piles of folders lay stacked on his desk and along the long table against the wall, paperwork rising like the buildings promised by *La Cassa del Mezzogiorno*; plans and proposals for mills, council buildings, power stations, post offices and roads. He removed his suit jacket and hung it over his chair, his shirt still bulging slightly from the recent overindulgence in Palermo.

The Palermo gathering was a crammed event; lots of speeches, back slapping, food and camaraderie, but behind the northern generosity Palumbo detected an aloofness of spirit accompanying the transaction of north handing over money to the south. Many of the factories required skilled labour and some automation - *so much for increased jobs in the south,* he thought, but he was resigned to the irresistible wave of mandated works and had to move things along.

Accompanying each region's stack was a red folder with the cartographer's layout of land and the recommended areas to be absorbed by the government for works. He counted each stack and stopped at twenty-five before his big eyes bulged larger than usual. He loosened his tie, undid the top button and started at the end of the alphabetically stacked series - Zafferia.

"*Uffa'.*" he said and called out "Beatrice!"

"Yes, Mayor." came the reply from her tiny office in the next room.

"We need to make a start on all this. Call in that *cretino* Maresca from Zafferia. This afternoon at four. Tell him to cancel whatever he has organised."

"Yes, Mayor."

Maresca called Pasquale Brinto and collected him on route to Messina at the roadside mailbox Brinto specified. He sat without eye contact the whole ten minutes and Maresca tried his best to stay calm.

Palumbo loomed over his Zafferia counterpart, pushed his impressive wave of white hair aside and shook his hand with force. "And you are?" he asked Brinto.

"Pasquale Brinto, secretary to Mayor Maresca."

"Pleasure to meet you. Come through. Caffé Beatrice!"

"Shortly, Mayor."

After a brief outline from Palumbo, Maresca sat back, underwhelmed. "That's it?"

"That's it."

Maresca was disheartened by the smile on Palumbo's face.

"Come on, Maresca. Beyond some roadworks and revamping your piazza what were you expecting?"

"If I may," said Brinto, "Mayor Maresca wanted to propose harvesting timber, here-" pointing out the Rossi, Crudelli and Liverani properties, designated here only by land codes. A jolt of excitement shot through Maresca as Palumbo's large eyes opened wide.

"A timber plant?"

"It would employ many local people. There is more than adequate natural irrigation right there."

"Area?"

"Between twelve and thirteen thousand hectares. Dense forest, a lot of hardwood for the east of Sicily. No need to drive trucks all the way from the west of the island.

"We were proposing to refurbish the *baracca* districts to our south, and this timber would greatly help. I'll add it to your list of works. You have to make it sustainable, Ok? No dumping waste to piss off the locals. Look at all these different regions and towns I have to oversee. If you could make this work and not give me a headache, I would be grateful to you both."

The *baracche* were shacks erected in haste after the earthquake and floods of 1908 that housed people who had lost everything. Far from people wanting to move away from these now dilapidated structures, they were their only connection to the old city. Over seventy-five thousand people perished after plates under the Strait of Messina clashed, sending earthquakes, landslides and a tsunami into an unsuspecting Messina at five-twenty a.m. The rebuilding created a virtual new city, with the population replaced by those who helped the survivors and survivors whose stories died with them.

Maresca made eye contact with Palumbo and nodded with confidence.

"You can count on us."

"The government will tender out works to different companies. We will find you a suitable timber milling company and send you the finalised paperwork so you can make the necessary preparations; land acquisition and the like." He shook Maresca's hand.

"Lovely to meet you, Mayor Palumbo." smiled Brinto.

Brinto turned to Maresca in the car. "Well played, Mr Mayor." Giving Maresca the impression of competence and being in charge was essential for Brinto and the Sidero family to get what they wanted. Possessing soft skills allowed them to move under the radar and only use force where necessary, not as an opening gambit. That Mayor Palumbo was also on their books just smoothed the way. That Maresca had no inkling of this was even more advantageous.

A week later, Claudio hunted for quail with his Father. The busy, furtive birds ducked in and out of the trees for safety from foxes and hawks but lived off the grass where they fed on small insects and grass seeds carried across the wind. Claudio walked without a sound, adjusted his aim and breathing before pulling the trigger, his direct hit scattering the surrounding birds back into the safety of the forest. Tino patted his son on the back for an excellent shot. It took him at least til the age of eighteen to master the art of spotting the birds and getting into position without scaring them with his footfall on the ground or missing the moment. At fifteen, Claudio had acquired this skill with little teaching. As they approached the dead quail, Claudio saw blood a further twenty metres away.

A dull ache spread somewhere between Claudio's stomach and his sternum as he approached the area, the geometric striping of red, four strokes making a crude square made him dry retch. *Maresca*, he said to himself.

"That's not blood, that's paint." said Claudio as he leant down, smelling the fumes, now in no doubt. Tino pointed out another marking twenty metres away.

Things had moved quickly since the meeting with Palumbo; men were dispatched to mark out the woodlands, but Maresca did not expect Tino Liverani or Marcisio Crudelli to confront him this soon, and definitely not together. He froze as he saw them walk up the long road to his house, the acorn tree canopy making their presence even more ominous. *Liverani was reasonable,* thought Maresca. It was Crudelli he was worried about.

He worded up Concetta and waited out the back of his house so he could hear their arrival. Concetta opened the door and greeted the pair.

A beast of a man, broad shouldered, heavy-bearded with long hair, Crudelli intimidated those unknown to him. Maresca knew him and remained intimidated regardless. Brinto told him not to worry about him or Tino.

"Has the Mayor been expecting us?" asked Crudelli.

"No, but he is here. Walk around the side and you'll find him out the back."

He *was* expecting us, thought Tino.

"Let me talk first Marcisio." suggested Tino as they walked alongside the house.

"Ok."

Maresca set himself as he heard their feet against the dirt. He aimed his rifle at the square piece of wood hanging from the tree about fifty yards away. As they turned the corner, he fired and hit the target's right side. He tried to hide the pain the recoil gave his shoulder.

"That's the first time I've seen you with a shotgun in your hand, Mr Mayor." said Crudelli, enjoying the Mayor's discomfort.

"Can we talk?" asked Tino.

"Sure." said Maresca, showing them to the chairs surrounding a round firepit. Maresca took care to sit closer to Tino than Crudelli. Tino leaned in and opened his hands.

"I went hunting for quail yesterday. Do you know why there would be red painted squares at intervals of twenty metres outside the forest on my land?"

"On your land?" asked Maresca.

"Why would he be talking about someone else's land?" asked Crudelli, leaning forward.

Maresca leant back and put his hands up in defence. "Sorry, silly question; of course, it's your land."

"So?" asked Tino.

"*La Cassa del Mezzogiorno*. Messina Council decided last month to acquire land to develop a timber processing plant. I didn't think it was going to happen so close to us, or so soon." Maresca raised his eyebrows and stroked his chin to feign surprise.

"There isn't a forest as big as the one on our properties in the Messina area. Where did you think they would go?" said Crudelli.

"As I say-"

"As you say, Mayor. You were aware of this *possibly* happening and as a true neighbour you decided not to tell us?"

"You're right, I should have. But you will be compensated."

"Compensated?" said Crudelli, spit collecting at the margins of his mouth. Tino held his hand above his leg as a moderating gesture.

"Is the acquisition compulsory?"

"Yes." said Maresca.

Both men dropped their heads in resignation and Maresca breathed slightly easier. Some moments passed before Tino spoke again.

"We need to know now how much land is intended for this acquisition. As Mayor, you should have no trouble finding that out for us, correct?"

Crudelli picked up Maresca's gun, checked it still had a cartridge left, and aimed at the wooden target. The shot broke the wire suspending the target, sending the lump of wood somersaulting backwards.

He handed the rifle back to Maresca and patted his tender shoulder, his baby sized teeth showing through a menacing smile.

CHAPTER 8

Sicily, 1963

Days passed with no word on how much land was needed or when the government wanted it. After riding the initial anger, Tino and Crudelli waited and waited, and the thought came to them both that it may not happen at all. Winter passed and on the third day of spring, Pasquale Brinto and Mayor Maresca arrived at the Liverani farmhouse.

Vanna ushered them into their sitting room, where Tino sat with Marcisio Crudelli and his wife, Filomena. Tino got up and shook their hands while Crudelli shook without getting up. Tino sent Claudio out to feed the sheep with Lidia.

Lidia was fifteen now. Claudio looked at how boys watched her, admiring her taller, fuller figure, strawberry blonde hair and eyes that mirrored the sea; sometimes blue, sometimes aqua. She skipped along the grass and laughed at Claudio telling her to slow down. As a child, as late as eight years of age, she ran off from Claudio; in town or on the farm, just for the thrill of being found by him, watching his expression flipping between panic, relief and anger, but always loving.

"You are a bit old for that trick now Lidia."

"Ha ha," she laughed back. "Will you always be my big strong brother, Claudio?"

"Always; now help me please. Feed the six sheep over to the left and I'll handle these troublemakers."

Lidia spoke to the sheep over the fence, their strong collective *baaah* relenting as they ate with gusto. Two of the group edged back with a start, followed by the others, the two rams being fed by Claudio also running without warning. The sound flew through the air, a loud crack, a whoosh then a loud thud that Lidia thought she felt through the ground. Claudio grabbed Lidia's hand and walked fast back to the house. The adults were already outside.

"What was that, children?"

"Sounds like trees falling, Father." said Claudio, looking at Mayor Maresca.

Tino turned to Maresca with a withering look and asked for an answer.

"It was always a compulsory acquisition, Tino."

"So why the charade with the paperwork?!" yelled Crudelli, his wife trying to hold him back.

"The price is a fair one, but it is not subject to negotiation as per the regulations provided by government. Shall we go inside?"

"Claudio. Stay here with Lidia." said Tino.

My Father being shown into his own house by this criminal, thought Claudio. He looked at his secretary and observed his composed manner, the way he oversaw things. *Secretary my culo*, he said to himself.

Inside, Maresca showed both men the areas of woodland on the maps.

"These are the acquired areas-"

"Acquired?" boomed Crudelli. "Just say robbed and be honest about it."

"If we wanted to, we could apply for compulsory acquisition without compensation, a measure reserved where an agreement cannot be reached. The help from the government is not something we want to dither about with. Our great island needs this infrastructure." Maresca placed the paper in front of them.

Property: LIVERANI
Area of forest and farmland: 4,300 hectares
Amount of compensation: 5 lira per hectare
Total transaction: 21.500 lira

Property: CRUDELLI
Area of forest and farmland: 3,000 hectares
Amount of compensation: 5 lira per hectare
Total transaction: 15,000 lira

Terms
Period of acquisition: 3 months
10% payment upon signing
Balance upon departure from property

"The acquisition will be in two stages; first we close off the forest area, and then the farmland in a reasonable period of time. Three months; although an earlier settlement would be greatly appreciated."

"And Rossi?" asked Tino.

"Rossi has already settled and has decided to leave his farm." Ottorino and Vera Rossi were getting on in years and had no children Their farm was closest to the nearest main road and had the best irrigation of the three. It made sense to build the plant there. Any obstruction could be mitigated by restricting the water flow downstream and force their hand. Tino took it all in and decided in his mind to settle, already thinking about how to maximise his value by sale of stock and equipment. If push came to shove, both Crudelli and Liverani would leave with nothing if they wanted to play for the long game, a slow strangulation.

"Can we meet with you at your office tomorrow to discuss?" asked Tino.

"If you need to, of course." said Maresca. "Nothing will change - what you see on paper will be the same, but I understand you need to take this all in and plan for the future. This does not have to happen today or tomorrow."

Vanna saw them out and came back inside. Crudelli's face was bright red and his eyes narrowed.

"You're caving in, aren't you?" he asked.

"What choice do we have?" said Vanna. Tino opened his hands, unable to respond.

"I admit that we have never been as productive with the land as you, but it was ours, our Fathers' land, our Grandfathers' before that, and on and on."

"This land being passed down had nothing to do with us, Marcisio."

"That is not the point, Tino. It is the *principle*."

"I agree, but what power do we have? The government despises the south, and if they are going to give us money to take us out of the stone age, they won't want little people like us blocking the way."

"Ok, so say we sign, no problem, Take the money and move on. What comes next? What other compulsory acquisition will there be, my balls?" Crudelli left the last statement hanging in the air, grabbing his own balls as he walked out with Filomena.

Vanna turned back and pushed her finger into Tino's breastbone. "To be clear, I agree with you, but you promised me we would talk before signing."

"I have not signed a thing. What are we doing now? Talking. Don't break my balls as well."

"That is my job. That is what this means." she said, pointing to her ring.

"Ok, love. I'm sorry. This is a difficult situation. We are being wedged here."

Vanna slapped Tino's face with a playful pat and smiled at him. Claudio peered from the window at the side of the house.

"I love you, Vanna."

"Better you keep it that way, my gentle giant."

Lidia clipped her brother around the ears.

"Stop eavesdropping, Claudio."

"It's my house too, little sister."

"Don't ever call me little again."
Claudio arranged everything in his head and concluded that the timber mill was just the start. The number was a lot of money to a boy his age to process, but he guessed that it would not go far for a family of four. He wondered how others down the line would be treated if Maresca and his corrupt friends decided they didn't have to pay anything for the land and just take it.

Crudelli signed five days after they met, the sleepless nights rolling into each other and the normally placid Filomena exploding and pleading with her husband to take the fucking money and get on with life. While the deal cost the government 15,000 lira, it could not have been more of a blank cheque. First the forest, then the wide expanse of land for real estate. After his bluster, Crudelli couldn't bring himself to front up to Tino and tell him.

In other parts of Sicily, organised crime families were successful in opposing some reforms that came with *La Cassa del Mezzogiorno*. Where their aims and those of the local community aligned, they were hailed as heroes, which cemented their power.

The Sidero family though were a different beast, working like termites. They insisted, with Mayor Palumbo's

imprimatur, that they go into the mill as equal partners with a
northern company *Mulino*, promising local jobs to soothe
local tensions.

If need be, the new entity would throttle the water supply,
starve the landowners slowly and force them to leave on
terms they wanted. Rossi read the message and moved with
his wife to Catania to be close to her sister, and chose not to
stop by his neighbours to say goodbye.

CHAPTER 9

Crete, 1964

Nikos puffed his last morning cigarette into the air before opening up for business. The winter was brutal but there was always a day around late March where the locals knew it was on the turn, the knowing nods a collective assurance that the worst was over. Children started playing on the narrow streets, a group of boys kicking a tattered ball against the white concrete walls, stopping only to let the occasional car pass.

He turned and heard the patter of Sia waddling outside to join him, calling out *Niko*. She had taken an eternity to walk, cradled as she was by all and sundry, the feted miracle baby of the town. However, she spoke months ahead of her time, learning names early, calling her parents *Niko* and *'tini* instead of *Baba* and *Mama*. She called Rita *Ita* and Nectarios *'tario*. Nikos gathered her into his strong arms and stamped out the cigarette. Sia gazed into his Father's eyes, green sparks scattered around the edge of her large brown eyes.

"God saved you, my little Sia."

Sia laughed and buried her face into his hairy chest. Rita, now eleven, scowled as she brought out her Father's coffee. Nikos scooped her into his embrace with his free arm.

"What face is that, Rita? You have a beautiful smile when you want to. When you were three, everyone spoilt you the same way. Don't be jealous, gorgeous girl." He gave her a gentle tickle and got the laugh he was after. She tickled Sia and the three of them laughed.

Nectarios ran regular deliveries while school was out. As a favour to Mr Pandelis for use of his car that fateful day, Nectarios added his deliveries to the shoes, belts and bags of his Father. After a few months, Mr Pandelis insisted on paying him.

"A favour is a favour. I can't kill the pig on this forever." *Killing the pig* was the local idiom for taking generosity too far.

Nikos protested, as was the gentlemanly norm, but accepted. But he insisted that he work him as hard as he needed to be worked. After all, Nectarios was fifteen and though not as tall as his peers, he was wiry, strong and had good endurance. He occasionally took his time to smoke a Camel cigarette that fell out of a packet and took longer to get home for even modest deliveries. Nikos caught him stamping one out and shoved him against a wall behind the school, slapping him on both cheeks.

"I have made my mistake – it is too late for me! Don't you dare start this young. Do you think you are cool because you smoke?" He shook his head and slapped him again. "No more, OK?!"

Nectarios wished for a breeze to cool his face, unable to look away from his Father, stunned as his cheeks burned red, the waves of pain not easing with each pulse. "I'm sorry, Father."
Nikos traded on the fear in his eyes. "If I catch you at it again, well, I can't even think of what I will do." He stormed

off, turning back after a few seconds. "Are you coming or not?"

Nectarios caught up and walked in silence the way home, his Father's meaty hand resting on his shoulder. His chest tightened up and the stinging of his cheeks was replaced by a giddiness he couldn't explain.

A minute from home, Nikos stopped and leant in. "Nothing to your Mother, otherwise I'm in more trouble than you. Now go rinse your mouth out and chew some gum."

Nectarios saw his reflection in the mirror blur for a split second. He tried to put a name to the light-headedness. He had smoked before and didn't feel lightheaded then, so what was this? He walked over to Mr Pandelis and asked if he had any more deliveries for the afternoon.

"What afternoon? It's nearly six, my boy. Mrs Vouliadakis usually gets her delivery of cheese and salami every Tuesday, but if you have no arse to sit on, take them to her now."

Mr Pandelis watched the boy from behind the counter as he wrapped up the order and looked over his shoulder to whisper to his wife, Anthoula.

"I know that face; the boy has been stung by a girl and he doesn't know it."

"Because you forgot your idiot days," Anthoula whispered back. "Leave the kid alone and give him the order, you idiot."

"Here you go, Nectarios. Be safe."

"Yes, thank you."

He made short work of the trip and became impatient at Mrs Vouliadakis' chatter. She was elderly sure, and he was tolerant of older people more than most his age, but tonight he fidgeted and scratched; until she sensed his irritation and bid him a curt goodnight, shutting the door in his face. He walked a fast pace the way back from where his Father had slapped him senseless and slowed as he approached the spot where the lightheaded feeling kicked in.

Up to his right, there she was: Litsa Sfirakis. Tall and eighteen, her blonde hair was tied up in a bun, and below it, blue eyes, thick lips, exposed shoulders, her cleavage visible. He couldn't tell for sure, but she didn't look like she had a bra on.

"Hello, Nectarios. Are we doing laps?"

"Deliveries. Nice night to be calling out to people in the street."

"Only the ones that look up, Nectarios." Slow on the *a* in Nectarios and he became aware of his erection. He looked towards the cross of the Church over the houses on the other side and felt relief as it subsided.

"Be safe, Nectarios," said Litsa in a higher voice. "Come past any time."

Litsa's Father, Stelios walked out to the balcony to see who his daughter was talking to. A squat man, shorter than his

45

daughter, he angled his big head around the side of the balcony to get a better view but only caught the sound of fast footsteps as Nectarios turned the corner.

"Who were you talking to, Litsa?"

"Auntie Pipina, Father."

"You don't invite your Aunt inside?"

"She had to go."

Nectarios crept the last metres home and jumped when his Father came out from inside the door.

"You found the way home from Mrs Vouliadakis did you?"

"She talks a lot."

He leant in and smelled Nectarios' breath. "We have been waiting for you so we can all eat."

"Sorry, Father."

"Leave him, Nikos." said Fotini. Her sense of discipline slowly ebbed away with the birth of Sia, her appreciation for letting kids just be kids taking over. They sat and ate snapper with potatoes and wild greens.

After dinner, Nectarios stepped into the outdoor shower, twice checking to make sure the door was latched. He started the water, the steam making him hard again. He thought of Litsa, her nipples poking through the thin material, her face and blue eyes. He imagined her riding him and within a

minute found sweet relief, almost blacking out as he came for
an eternity, bracing himself on the sink with his free hand.
He thought about her as he fell asleep. He walked in a daze
for the next week making deliveries, hurrying past her house
at fast pace, trying not to look up. It took a further week for
the fluttering in his chest and the hardness of his groin to stop
interrupting his thoughts.

CHAPTER 10

Sicily, 1964

Claudio smiled at Matteo Maresca on the first day back at school. Matteo smiled back and Claudio knew he had no idea. *Poor kid*, he thought to himself. He was better off without a Father than the fat greedy bastard whose fat greedy defective genes were his sole paternal contribution. He hoped Matteo would become his own person and not be trapped in this existence forever.

Father Di Pardo blessed the school assembly after the forty students sang the national anthem. *Il Canto degli Italiani* was sung with gusto on the first day back every year. Halfway through the second verse, Claudio saw Di Pardo staring intently across the room, his focus on Caterina from bible class. Di Pardo turned to look at him, and hairs on his neck stood stiff like quills. To distract himself, he sang louder:

> *"Uniamoci, amiamoci,*
> *l'unione e l'amore*
> *rivelano ai popoli*
> *le vie del Signore,"*

> *"Let us unite, let us love one another,*
> *union and love*
> *reveal to the people*
> *the ways of the Lord."*

Di Pardo addressed the children before they dispersed into their respective classrooms. Claudio watched Caterina, her hands fidgeting; nails scratching skin, nails picking nails until a teacher shot her a glance for her to stay still. At lunch, she sat on her own under a tree and he sat two metres away from her. The wind kicked up dust and she sneezed.

"Bless you."

"Thank you, Claudio."

"Are you Ok, Caterina?"

"What do you mean?"

"Because you used to be smiling and happy. What happened?"

"You wouldn't understand."

"Does Father Di Pardo understand?"

"What do you mean?" *A-ha*. He took no pleasure from his instinct, but the signs were clear; her higher tone of voice, colour draining from the face, eyes darting, brain searching for a way to end the conversation as her body leant backwards in defensive posture.

"I'm not making fun of you, Caterina. Please, believe me."

"Father Di Pardo has helped us since my Father became sick. He has come over every second day to check in on us."

I bet he wouldn't dare come if Pietro La Spina was home, thought Claudio. A self-declared agnostic, he waged war against the Catholic church many times, pointing out hypocrisy with a fervour bordering on, well, religious. Rosina La Spina was a quiet woman who appreciated the religious support, drawing on it to deliver her husband a swift recovery from the emphysema that addled him, blind to the years of smoking unfiltered cigarettes.

Caterina composed herself and her body leaned forward, her finger pointing at Claudio.

"Don't you dare speak ill of the man who has given my Mother strength in these times. I hope you never have to go through this, ever!" She turned on her heels and walked away, pausing only once she confined herself to the toilet, collapsing to her knees and sobbing.

Claudio heard stories about priests being moved away from parishes from snippets of conversation when adults were talking after church.

Did you hear about the priest from San Delfino?
They should let them marry.
It is the way it has always been.
Thank God ours is not damaged.
This one is upstanding and has excellent character.

How would they know? thought Claudio.

He found it strange that the bible portrayed Jesus as a man among men, but a unique man. Yet the Priests who were supposed to be God's conduits on earth were expected to live an artificial existence, without the love of a woman and children. He accepted the majority of priests were of excellent character, free of aberrant desires, but was troubled Father Di Pardo was not one of them.

Of that he was sure.

CHAPTER 11

Crete, 1965

Rita became more tolerant of her little sister. Sia's attention shifted from her Father to her and she became her shadow. They played together much of the day as their Mother was needed to alter and sew as the population grew and tourism increased with the better weather.

Dresses hung neatly on a long metal pole, Fotini working on each with meticulous care on her foot-operated sewing machine.

Nikos worked at the other end of the wide workroom, strewn with shoes, belts and fishing nets. Stelios no longer brought in his saddles, having achieved the craved status symbol of a car from his new tourist business of boat tours for tourist couples. He took his wife and Litsa to Chania to live and rented his house out to tourists. Everyone in Tavroniti knew when he was back to visit from the hearty honk of the horn as he drove down the main street.

Fotini had long given up on the scattered mayhem of Nikos' bench. As chaotic as his bench looked at eight a.m., by six in the evening every item was repaired, tagged and in order the items being brought in. They had enough work to feed themselves and be reliant on no one else. Fotini smiled at her husband as they sat for dinner.

God has been kind, thought Nikos.

<h1 style="text-align:center">CHAPTER 12</h1>

<h2 style="text-align:center">Crete, 1965</h2>

A month after his sixteenth birthday, Nectarios began making more regular deliveries for both his parents and Mr Pandelis. He knew the town's every nook and cranny and became popular with the locals. Tourists tipped him generously and he always gave the money to either his parents or Mr Pandelis. Nikos was relieved that his hiccup was behind him.

Nectarios often thought about the image of Litsa Sfirakis but was relieved not to see her anymore since they moved to Chania. He returned after a long day of deliveries, numerous trips with his bike his Father bought him as a birthday present. He dropped off the money to his Mother and told her he was just going to buy some chewing gum from Mr Pandelis. He walked in and was aware of Litsa before he saw her, ignoring Mr Pandeli as he made a beeline for the other side of the aisle.

"Oh hello, Nectarios. Where do they keep the almonds? My Mother wants to make a cake for dessert."

She stood up and smiled at his expression, Nectarios ogling at her tanned body.

"No?"

"I couldn't tell you where the almonds are."

Litsa smiled again, her mouth curled up on her left side. "We moved back yesterday. My Father's crazy idea to fleece tourists for boat rides around Chania backfired when two other companies offered the same thing for half the price; and with food too. So, we are back. Back here in fucking Tavroniti."

"Back. For good?"

"Until my Father's next stupid idea. Hopefully I can get out of this dump one day."

"Tavroniti is not so bad."

"Keep telling yourself that. One day you'll convince yourself. At least Chania had other people our- I mean, my age to hang around with." She took a step closer and connected with her blue eyes. "So, do you have a girlfriend?"

"No."

"Really? I find that hard to believe."

"There are not- many around, and anyway, I'm busy with-"

"Listen, after lunch tomorrow, I'm going for a bike ride to the Vaulted Tombs at Maleme. Want to come?"

"Just us two?" Nectarios pinched his nose to stop the room from spinning.

Litsa smirked and rested a hand on her breast. "Would you not come if there were others?"

"No, of course."

"Then why offend me by asking?"

Nectarios struggled for words, his mouth dry and his head a mess. "I just meant-"

"Relax, I am messing with you. It will just be us. If you can come, leave a single stone next to the door of my house and I will see you at the bridge at half-past three. Can you get your deliveries done by then?"

"Sure." he said without hesitation.

Litsa put out her hand and Nectarios kissed it, inhaling her scent. Then she turned and bid Mr Pandelis good evening.

As the door shut, Mr Pandelis turned to him with a grin.

"Η μουνότριχα τραβάει καράβι, αγόρι μου." A pussy hair can pull an ocean liner.

"Pandeli!" yelled Anthoula. "How do you talk to a boy like that?!"

He turned to his wife; palms upturned. "He's sixteen."

"Shut up, you idiot!"

"I'm only-"

Anthoula shut down her husband with a withering stare.

"Go and grab the flour from the storeroom!"

She slapped him hard on the back of the neck as he went

past. Nectarios wondered how a woman so small
could deliver such a blow.

"When you say stupidities like that, your wife will give you
one too, don't worry. Come and sit, Nectarios." she said, her
voice softening.

"How long have you and Mr Pandelis been married?"

"Thirty-five years. He is not the man I fell in love with, but
he was for long enough. That keeps you going, until he says
stupid things like that."

She offered him a tea towel. "You're sweating." He wiped his
forehead and sucked in a deep breath. "My boy, do not do
anything you may regret."

"I'm just-"

"You're just doing nothing," she said. "She is eighteen and
bored. Teasing you and driving you crazy is the only thing
that is in her head at this moment. Just filling in time."

"It is just a bike ride."

"Very well; do not say you have not been warned."

He walked back to his house and grabbed a rock from outside
his door. He rode to Litsa's house and left it near the front
gate.

The next morning, Nectarios woke early and walked into the
front workroom. He was perplexed to see no dresses hung to

the left and only a few shoes on the long bench to his right. He made himself some toast and lathered soft cheese over it.

"Up early, aren't we?" asked Fotini as she walked into the room. Nectarios dropped the knife onto the concrete floor.

"What is with you?" asked Fotini.

"Nothing, Mother."

"Do you have deliveries?"

"Yes, I am about to start now."

"Get them out of the way quick. Your Father wants to take us to the beach after lunch."

"I can't."

"What do you mean you can't?"

"Deliveries."

"Ok then, we will wait until you are finished, then we will go as a family."

Fuck, thought Nectarios. "Ok."

"Nectarios."

"Yes Mother?"

"Your shoes are the wrong way on. Silly boy." she said, ruffling his hair and kissing his ear.

He collected the sum total of three deliveries from Anthoula. Without a word from her, he set off for Dr Arvanitakis. He walked into the surgery and checked the clock on his surgery wall.

"Yes, can I help you?" asked the clinic nurse, impatient at Nectarios' blank stare.

"An order for Dr Arvanitakis." he said, handing over the doctor's order of cheese, salami and halva.

"We won't have him for too much longer if he eats that stuff every day." said a patient under the window.

"Mind your own business." said the Doctor, handing over the money to Nectarios with a generous tip. "How is my miracle girl going?"

"Very well, thank you. Must go." said Nectarios, trying his best not to run out of the room.

He ran his eye over the last two orders; the usual order of olive oil for the lovely Mrs Livanakis and one marked Sfirakis. Anthoula found the almonds and hoped Nectarios would read the note. He unravelled the scrap of paper and read:

One warning can be ignored by anyone, only donkeys ignore two.

He pedalled slowly to Mrs Livanakis, even taking time to sit and talk while she produced a spoonful of vanilla mastic in cold water. He thanked her for the treat and made his way to

Litsa's house. The rock was gone. He rang the bell and Litsa came to the front door, eyes open is disbelief.

"What the hell are you doing here?"

"Your Mother wanted almonds?"

Litsa snatched the bag off him, grabbed his arm and walked him to the front gate.

"What is wrong, Litsa?"

"My Father can't see you here."

"I can't come at three-thirty. My Father wants us to go to the beach after lunch and I could not make it work."

"My Father comes back from Chania around lunch time. Can you go now if I tell my Mother I'm going back to the shop?"

Nectarios enjoyed the shifting of power and waited for three seconds before saying yes.

"Ok, it is ten-thirty. You go ahead and I will deal with my Mother. I will tell her I have to go and get the almonds. I told her I forgot to check last night." She stuffed the almonds in a shaded spot behind a pot plant.

"Ok, see you there."

Nectarios rode quickly. He lay his bike in the long grass about twenty metres off the road and sat there, the wind picking up. He heard the ding of her bell fifteen minutes later. They rode across the river, Nectarios leading the way, staying low to negate the headwind. They pedalled the short uphill distance to the tombs and hopped off. They walked their bikes up the path hidden under thick, old vines, left them there and walked, slightly hunched until the brick entrance came into view. Litsa took Nectarios' hand and looked him in the eye.

"Are you Ok?"

"Yes."

The wind funnelled through the tomb structures and made a low humming noise. Nectarios led Litsa inside the entrance and chose the right corridor as it came to a T. Another ten metres on, Litsa stopped.

"Here." she said.

"Here what?"

"Here." she repeated, her eyes boring into his, equal amounts fear and the cockiness she showed the night before. He smiled at her.

"Is this a good idea?"

"No. But we are here, and I won't take no for an answer." She pulled his face close to hers, before freezing up, her movement tentative. Nectarios closed the gap, meeting her lips with a gentle kiss before she took his tongue inside her mouth. She broke off, the wind whistling to a high pitch, then pulled him into the grassy alcove. She kissed his nose and moved back down to his mouth, his hand moving through her blonde hair, unconscious of it moving in time with their kissing, the other across her shoulder. A warmth spread from her thighs, moving up to her breasts and then across her whole body. She stopped and he moved back.

"Is everything Ok?"

"Yes. Can we try?" The momentum was carrying them onto the inevitable but Nectarios read uncertainty in her face.

"Are you a virgin, Litsa?"

"Y-yes." she said, eyes looking downwards.

"It doesn't matter, so am I," he said, bringing her chin up with his index finger. "We'll find out together."

"Are you sure?"

"Of course. I thought you were-"

"Experienced."

"Yes, the way you teased me and spoke to me. But that is Ok."

"Actually, can we just do everything except…that, today?"

"I'm Ok with that."

She reached for his hand and kissed him hard on the mouth. "Touch me." she said.

Neactarios kissed back and let her guide his hand slowly down her belly, an intake of breath as he reached her pubic hair, then a trace of warm moisture. She moved his hand as if it were her own and mouthed *leave it to me* in his ear. Her tempo slowly increased, and she let out a high yelp as she came, her hand holding him there, tight. She had brought herself to climax before, but her body shook and convulsed with a force she had never experienced. She gently pushed Nectarios' hand up from her pussy as her breathing returned to normal, her eyes glazing over as she watched his face.

"Now, your turn."

She unzipped his trousers and freed his erect cock, rubbing herself again and using the moisture to glide her hand down his shaft, kissing him hard as she used her free hand to bring herself to orgasm again. As her body tightened once more, she came. Nectarios felt the surge and took over, minding not to come over her clothes while he could think straight in the milliseconds before the blood flow left his brain. He came over the ancient brickwork, Litsa kissing him as she held his face hard against hers.

They lay together, the ancient breeze passing over them, both paranoid that someone may have heard them. But they needn't have worried. They were alone, alone with their thoughts, their expended bodies slumped against one another, the tomb adding this act to the many it had witnessed since the Minoans built it.

"You ride back first," said Nectarios. "I'll follow from afar."

"Such a gentleman." said Litsa, leaning in to kiss his forehead. "Tell me, how are we going to hide this from everyone?"

"I won't say anything."

"Neither will I," said Litsa, rolling her eyes. "I mean, we are young, and we may give it away without saying anything. You're a male and you're more likely to give it away. The more you try to act normal, the less normal you will appear to others. Our parents' generation are so suspicious."

"What do you think we should do?"

"Pretend we are back at Mr Pandeli's. I'll tease you; you act awkward and Anthoula will think nothing has happened. She spoke to you after I left, didn't she?"

She's psychic, thought Nectarios.

"I thought so. Now, go."

Nectarios waited a minute before following at a safe distance with no cars around. He waited until Litsa turned right at the T intersection of the town before turning left then right. He stopped at Mr Pandelis, handing over the money from his deliveries, then walked around the back, taking a towel and heading straight for the shower.

Fotini spotted him from the kitchen and called out.

"Why bother? We are going to the beach, remember?"

"Of course, Mother."

Litsa grabbed the almonds, snuck in and started the shower just as her Father walked into the house.

CHAPTER 13

Sicily, 1965

Casa quantu stai e tirrinu quantu viri
Home as long as you need to be and land as far as the eye can
see.
- Sicilian proverb

Tino stood over one of his irrigation furrows. Mud, weeds
and debris needed to be cleared to allow water to flow. He
smelled the air and screwed his face up at the faint odour of
gasoline, one he hated getting used to. Trucks stopped and
started, then silence. He worked up a hot sweat as he cleared
the crude yet effective opening that allowed water to flow to
his crops and livestock. Four hours later, he stood back and
forced a tired smile as water flowed through the furrow
again. He waited an hour and checked down the line to make
sure the water was getting through. He needed Claudio's help
for this job. He was strong and getting stronger, but this fever
he picked up from God knows where had laid him up for
over a week.

When he arrived home, Father Di Pardo was holding court
with Vanna and Lidia.

"Progress is always good, but - oh, carissimo Tino, how are
you?"

"Father. Nice of you to drop in."

"I was worried about Claudio. Such a strong young man
diminished by this...virus or whatever it is. It is awful."

"Thank you for your concern, Father. If you will excuse me, I need to wash up."

Tino walked past Claudio's room and peeked in. "Is he still there?" Claudio whispered. Tino nodded and made a *shh* gesture as he walked in. He sat and placed the underside of his forearm on Claudio's forehead.

"That's better. Are you feeling better? "

"I think so."

"Go back to sleep."

Claudio turned to the wall and fell asleep.

The room, humid, smelling of incense with a hot wind banging against the door, a draft whooshing in. In the room opposite, a small space, Father Di Pardo held Caterina's head tight against his groin, his robes a crude tent over her head, suffocating her as he came, her release from his tight hold only coming as he walked out of the room.

Claudio woke with a start and washed his face with cold water. He looked in the mirror and squeezed his eyes hard. Afraid to sleep again and revisit the scene, he checked to make sure Father Di Pardo was gone.

"Father Di Pardo? He was here yesterday, Claudio," laughed his Mother. "You slept a long time, my boy."

Claudio found Lidia as soon as she arrived home
from school.

"You're up?"

"I am much better," said Claudio. "Is Caterina Ok?"

"Caterina? Why do you ask about her?" asked Lidia with a curious smile.

"She seemed very unhappy last time I spoke to her."

"She told me you were rude to her."

"No, I asked if she was Ok. She wasn't as happy as she usually was, and she got upset and walked away."

"Well her Father has only just come home from hospital. He has an oxygen tank he has to carry everywhere with him, like a metal tube. Of course she is upset. I would be if Father was unwell."

"Me too."

CHAPTER 14

Sicily, 1965

*Cu' duna pi prima, duna a'ncarzari, cu duna d'appresu duna
cu tuttu u verse.*
Those who harm first can expect greater harm in return.
- Sicilian proverb

The congregation was full for the celebration of San Niccoló.
The air was cold but dry. Many people came from Messina
and surrounding small towns and villages. Father Di Pardo
was joined by priests from surrounding areas and they
conducted a joint liturgy to bless the town and its neighbours.

Everyone walked to the piazza, where restaurants and side
stalls opened up, the local culinary delights on full display.
Di Pardo strolled, arms behind his back, stopping to talk to
parishioners and visitors to wax lyrical about Zafferia's local
charm. Tino and Vanna walked the piazza with Claudio and
Lidia. They sat with their food, which Claudio ate with a
renewed appetite. Across the piazza he spotted Caterina, and
she waved with a smile. Claudio waved and smiled back,
calling her over.

"Are you well Claudio?" asked Caterina.

"Yes, thank you. How are you, and your Father?"

"Well, thanks. My Father is feeling better. He may get off the
oxygen tank soon."

"That is great news."

"Ok, I'm off to play. Come with us, Lidia."

Lidia turned to her parents. They nodded and insisted she take a last mouthful before she ran off with the group to the swings on the other side.

"Remember how she used to run off on us, Tino?"

"*Uffi* do I ever. She will be trouble for whoever marries her."

"I'll make sure she marries the right one." said Claudio.

"That's my job, no?" said Tino with a laugh.

"Another opinion never hurt anyone, Father."

"Always the protective one. Bravo, son." said Vanna.

Father Di Pardo approached the children playing and asked them if they wanted gelato. They flocked to him as he walked like the Pied Piper to the gelato counter.

"Caro Salvino, gelato for all the girl and boys, please. I do have an ulterior motive, children. Once you have finished your gelato, I need you all to come to the church and bring the effigy of San Niccolo to the piazza for people to pin their donations."

Claudio rolled his eyes. Father Grossani pulled the same stunt every year, the lure of gelato fresh every time. A small collective groan escaped the group, but they nodded in recognition of the fair trade as they slurped on their gelato. Ten minutes later, they returned from the church with the effigy. Once positioned on the platform. Mayor Maresca whistled and asked the crowd for their attention.

"Ladies and gentlemen, children, and of course Father Di Pardo and visiting priests. Thank you for this grand turn out to our humble town to celebrate our beloved San Niccoló. Please show your appreciation by donating whatever is acceptable to you at the foot of his effigy. If you have paper notes, please pin these to the tunic."

"God bless you all for your generosity!" exclaimed Di Pardo.

People made their way as they passed and left, leaving generous donations. Mayor Maresca made a point of waiting until bystanders were watching before pinning a ten lira note, drawing muted applause.

As the crowd dwindled, Father Di Pardo asked a group of girls and boys to help carry the effigy back to the church and to help count the money collected. The dark was falling fast, and they had to hurry. The children were efficient in unpinning the notes, retrieving the coins from collection bags and stacking them in their respective nominations for counting.

Di Pardo addressed the seven children and thanked them for their help. As they walked away, he made eye contact with Caterina. She hesitated to see if he needed any further help. He beckoned her to come and sit with him.

She sat next to him. He felt her shoulders and she tensed, his fingers squeezing gently. "Relax, child, relax."

"Come inside for a moment. I want to show you something."

"Inside, where?"

"The vestry. You have not seen the vestry before?"

"I thought that was only for priests."

"Well, priests are allowed to show special people the
vestry. We communicate there exclusively with the Lord. Do
you want to see?"

"My Mother will be waiting for me. I don't want to worry
her."

"She knows you're with me. Does she not trust me?"

"Of course she does."

"Do *you* trust me, Caterina?"

"Yes."

"Ok then. Let us go inside."

His grip was not firm but persuaded her to follow him. She
saw the icons inside, the big brass statue of the Lord Jesus
Christ, tall, nailed into the wall, HE IS RISEN inscribed
along the top. Caterina looked around in awe at these things
no one else saw, before turning to see Father Di Pardo's eyes
change, narrowing as his cheeks rose, the smile below not the
gentle smile she knew from his visits to her home but that of
a monster snarling, his white teeth showing. She was mute,
paralysed by the person she did not recognise, seeing only
danger.

"Come here, child."

"What are you going to do to me, have I sinned?"

"No, child."

"What are you going to do to me."

"Not to you, *with* you."

Di Pardo removed his robes and reached out to her, Caterina
already inching herself back to the wall furthest from him.
She imagined there would be a table in this room,
hoped there was one to keep distance from him but only air
separated her from harm and the only way out. He lunged
and covered her mouth with one hand, holding the back of
her head with the other. He held her head against the wall
and used his free hand to unfasten his trousers, his erect penis
straining to escape. He managed to pull down his trousers,
Caterina crying yet mute, her eyes looking past him. A sharp
force struck his head, the blood flow to his brain interrupted,
unbalanced, before resuming. Before the second blow,
Claudio's face to his left, the last thing Di Pardo saw, then
his eyes rolled back as a harder blow caught him on the left
side above his ear, shattering his skull at its most vulnerable
spot. *These are the ways of the Lord*, the last words he heard
and even then, he couldn't be sure as his consciousness
fractured, blood streaming onto the feet of Jesus.

Claudio grabbed Caterina's hand and led her outside, opening
the vestry door. His mind moved fast; a new moon, pitch-
black outside and his first priority - ditch the rock. Just larger
than his full grip, the rock didn't drip as Claudio expected, or
at least he couldn't feel any blood dripping in the dark. He

walked with Caterina around the back of the church and climbed the fence to see the faint outline of the rocky hillside. He lobbed the rock in a looping arc and let the slope do the rest, listening for the tumbling, soft and hard sounds against the dirt and stones before the welcome *plop* into the stream below. He turned to Caterina.

"Are you Ok?"

Caterina strained to speak but nothing would come out. *No time for a debrief, get her home calm* he told himself.

"I won't say anything." she finally whispered as they approached her house.

"You need to calm down before you go inside, or your parents may suspect something."

"Ok, tell me a joke, anything, Claudio, please." she said. He had an idea. Not a joke, but something mundane and therefore believable.

"This may hurt," he said. "I'll make a little scratch on your knee. Say that Father Di Pardo walked you home but he had to go back to the church. You tripped and fell. Here. Ok?"

"Ok."

For the second time that evening, Claudio grabbed a rock and drew blood, a smaller one, and made a small glancing motion across Caterina's knee, nicking the skin and a trickle of blood came out. He pinched the edges so it would bleed more. She winced and cried, for only for a few seconds.

"I'm sorry but I had to do that. Let it run." said Claudio. "Now are you alright?"

"I think so. Thank you, Claudio, thank you. I-"

"I'm sorry he did that to you."

"How did you know?"

"I just did. Now go, please. And remember one thing."

"What?"

"None of this is your fault."

Claudio washed his hands at the school on the way back to the piazza. His parents danced as Lidia watched them a few metres away at their table. The band was playing *Rose Rosse Per Te*, Tino and Vanna cuddling as they slowly moved. He nodded towards the couples dancing and took his sister by the hand. They danced next to their parents.

The news spread fast the next day that Father Di Pardo was dead. Two monks found him just after lunch when Di Pardo failed to meet them for prayer and morning tea, his bloodied head leaning against Jesus' feet. One of them hitched the deceased's pants up to avoid any embarrassment and the other debated the ethics of contaminating the scene with leaving the scene as it was. They panicked and repositioned the pants as they were and walked quickly to the sole officer at the station. The police arrived from Messina the next morning, self-important in their garb and puffed chests. The church was locked up, the sign *closed until further notice* nailed to the front door. The officer in charge insisted in being called *Dottore*, Doctor, a term extended to a figure of authority in the Sicilian police force. Dottore Dario Fulmino, a tall man with short hair and an impressive V-shaped body, sat waiting for Mayor Maresca to brief him. He twirled his handlebar moustache while he waited and unused to being bored, became impatient.

"Dottore Fiumino."

"*Ful-mino.*"

"My apologies, call me Filipo."

"How can you enlighten me?"

Maresca shrugged his small shoulders. "Hard to believe this could happen. Here of all places."

Fulmino rolled his eyes. "Do me a favour and spare me the surprise, Filipo. Nothing shocks me anymore. We need to get on with this. So, we have a forty-three-year-old priest killed by blunt force, two blows to the head after the celebration of San Niccoló?"

"That is correct."

"I need to interview the teachers of your local school; I presume you only have the one school?"

"Yes."

"Close the school for tomorrow, a mark of respect for the priest. Schedule interviews of all school staff there tomorrow at seven. I am an early riser."

He left without salutation and walked to the church.

CHAPTER 15

Crete, 1965

Αν ήμουν νιφάδα χιονιού,
η ζωή μου θα ήταν ευτυχία
Θα βρεθώ στα χείλη σου
Και να λιώνω στο φιλί σας

If I were a snowflake,
my life would be bliss
I'd lie on your lips
And melt in your kiss
- Cretan lyric

Half of Chania is here, thought Nikos to himself. He was in good humour having closed for the day of the celebration of Saint Nikolaos. People gathered everywhere, the few cafes and tavernas bursting at the seams, and Mr Pandelis running out of small goods, breads and cheeses as people made lunches wherever they could find a spot. Locals set up stalls of local cakes which disappeared fast as parents tried to keep their kids happy.

Hariklia Sfirakis stood proudly behind her renowned *amygdalopita*, an almond torte moist enough survive the trip back home. Dwarfed by her tall, angular Mother, Litsa stood arms crossed, wishing she was anywhere else but here, only stepping forward to give people change and box up cakes as her Mother talked about her recipe to those interested. *Boring*, thought Litsa, a bit more honey, a bit less cinnamon, a bit more semolina, who cares? Her thoughts were interrupted by a flash of light that blinded her for a second before she regained sight and recognised the form of

Nectarios on the rooftop of the building across the street.

"Litsa!" implored her Mother, "please give this lovely lady her torte and pay attention. Where are you today?"

"Here where I've always been, Mother."

"Cut the sarcasm and be nice."

In another half hour, they sold out and carried the tables back to their house. Pleased with herself, Hariklia strode with long steps, Litsa wary in case Nectarios was following.

The *esperinó*, the evening church service was full, people spilling out onto the concrete perimeter of the church, mostly men in their groups of three and four swinging their beads and talking until people in the doorway shushed them every five minutes, their volume creeping back until the next glare.

Nectarios stood by the back with his Father as Fotini did her best to keep Rita and Sia from erupting from boredom, finally letting Rita take her sister outside to play. "Stay close." she said.

The church caretaker, overheated, opened the nearest window. Litsa turned her head at the sound of the window resisting then sliding up, catching sight of Nectarios' face, smiling then turning to face forward again before her Father caught her. The crowd followed the priest, Pater Manousso's short form leading the seven strong group of priests and the icon of Saint Nikolaos from the church to the main town square. Families separated by the gender divide of the church pews reunited and walked together. Nectarios dawdled behind waiting for Litsa to do likewise. He turned when she

76

kissed him behind his ear.

"Worried you couldn't see me?"

"Yes."

"So, having a great time?"

"Not yet."

"Once the dancing starts, let's try and sneak away. In the meantime, if we are around people, be your usual awkward self, Ok?"

"Happy to be your clown. Thanks, Litsa."

"No problem." She winked and was gone, back with her parents before they realised she was even gone. *She's quick*, he said to himself.

Father Manousso tapped the microphone and with St Nikolaos looming over him, blessed the community of Tavroniti and all the visitors who had made the trip. He recited the Lord's Prayer and blessed the food prepared by the community. Long half barrels of coal and wood burned and glowed into the darkening light, the goats and lambs rotating slowly above them, their fat dripping and sizzling on the heat. The aroma of oregano, garlic and lemon hung in the air as the meat was cut by community members for the public. Bottles of high octane *raki* sat on tables sprawled across the large concrete area near the beach. The sounds of conversation, greetings, laughter and eating filled the air. Nectarios felt a tug on his trousers.

"Help me."

Sia was yet to master cutting her meat so Nectarios sat her on
his lap, making her think she was doing all the work as he cut
while Sia held his hands. "Bravo, Sia." he said, and kissed
her on the head. Three tables across, Litsa smiled. Nectarios
caught her and smiled back.

"Who are you smiling at, Nectarios?" whispered the man to
his right with a grin.

"No one." he said to the man. Sifi Polendakis was a local
fisherman, a hulk of a man with a thick mop of hair and a
gentle nature, well loved by everyone in Tavroniti. He leant
in closer.

"It is natural, don't worry. Just-"

"Don't do anything I might regret?"

Sifi smiled, his teeth showing under his broad, thick
moustache. He tapped his nose. "Bravo, my child." Sifi
turned to his right and playfully slapped Nikos across the
cheek.

"You've raised a smart boy here, Nikos."

"We try, Sifi. He's Ok." Nikos smiled at his son and winked.

As the dessert and fruit platters came out, a microphone
crackled, giving way to the sound of a *lagouto* being
tuned, then a *violi*. The interplay of the two instruments
defined the Cretan musical sound, the rhythm setting the
pace for the traditional *sirtó*. The floor soon filled, young and

old celebrating the evening. It was cool outside but with the coals persisting and the *raki*, no one noticed. Nectarios held his Mother's hand on one side and Rita's on the other, Rita smiling at her brother. Sia sat on Nikos' shoulders as he led the group. They sat as the musicians took a break. A man staggered across the concrete, assisted by the local policeman to a seat.

"Stelios is finished." said Nectarios to Nikos.

"It appears so." said Nikos.

"Go help the policeman take him home will you?" said Nikos, pushing his son towards them.

He approached them, Stelios looking up, his eyes peering, his hand raised. He pointed his finger at him.

"You were talking to my Litsa that night, weren't you?"

"Sorry?"

"I know," he said, tapping his nose with his index finger. "You can't fool me-". A guttural retching sound, vomiting, and a loud belch escaped from his mouth. Hariklia walked up and admonished her husband.

"Stelios, if you can't control yourself, we can never come out. Stop embarrassing us. Let's go home."

"This boy." said Stelios as he wiped his mouth, trying to stand up, slipping comically then grabbing a chair and falling on his stomach to the amusement of onlookers.

"Let's go, Stelios." said the policeman.

They tried various methods to carry him to the police vehicle before the policeman told them to stay put until he brought his car around. Stelios opened his eyes and smiled at Nectarios.

"If you were five years older, maybe. Such a pity you're so young." He lurched to his side and threw up again, narrowly missing Nectarios.

"I'm so sorry, Nectarios." said Hariklia, red with embarrassment.

"No need, Mrs Sfirakis."

The car came, without the siren, much to Hariklia's relief. She bundled him in and tapped the policeman's shoulder. Hariklia leant out the the window. "Could you tell Litsa we're going home? Tell her she can stay out with her friends but to be home by midnight. Make sure, will you?"

"Of course, Mrs Sfirakis."

Another rasping sound came as the car took off, the irritated policeman stopping for Stelios to throw up again.

"Is everything Ok with Stelios?" Fotini asked Nectarios.

"He has gone home with his wife. She asked me to make sure Litsa gets home safe by midnight."

"It is ten past ten, so no problem." asked Fotini.

"Yes, no problem."

"Such a gentleman, my boy." said Fotini, kissing him on the head. "Now go and tell her what is going on."

Nectarios couldn't believe his luck. He approached Litsa and her group of friends. She winked at him and turned to her two friends, both a year older than herself. Litsa's face changed to a snarl.

"Oh, look. Here's little Nectarios, the delivery boy." she said in a mocking tone.

Her friends laughed. "What are you delivering, Nectarios?" asked the taller of the two friends.

"How about a new nose to replace your beak, Stavroula?" said Nectarios, tapping his own nose, shock on all three faces.

"How do you insult my friend, Nectarios?" said Litsa.

Nectarios smiled and shrugged. "She asked, I answered."

"Let's go," said Stavroula, touching her nose. *Wait here* Litsa mouthed as she walked past.

Ten minutes later, Litsa startled him. "Truth is her nose is a beak." She snorted as she laughed.

"Sorry. you asked me to be my usual awkward self."

"You were, don't worry."

"I actually came across to tell you your Father is blind drunk. Your Mother went home with him in a police car."

She smiled. "What an idiot. I'm sure Hariklia wished the ground would swallow her up."

"She asked me to tell you to be home by midnight."

"And?"

"I said I would make sure."

"And you're going to, aren't you?"

"I'm a gentleman of my word."

"Your Mother is walking over. Go." said Litsa.

"Nectarios, we are going home."

"Ok, Mother."

"Stay in the area, Ok?"

"Of course, Mother." He waved goodbye to his Father waiting across the other side, Sia asleep on his shoulder and kissed his Mother on the cheek. Fotini kissed Litsa goodnight and walked away.

"They suspect nothing," whispered Litsa, "Nor my parents nor yours."

"What do we do with this unexpected opportunity?"

"Let's not analyse too much then, let's go."

"Where?"

"My Father has a small vineyard a few minutes' walk away."

"Vineyards?"

"We can't rent a hotel room and we can't go back to your place or mine. Have any better suggestions?"

"Vineyards. Let's go."

The remaining people were either dancing or watching those dancing while drinking. He turned and Litsa was moving quickly down the small lane between two shops. He caught up to her. He was more nervous now than the first time. But *this* was the first time, he said to himself.

"What are you thinking about?" said Litsa.

"You, what else?"

"You have no idea what I'm thinking about. I'm thinking about what happens if, tonight, we do it for real, what happens if I get pregnant. Has that not crossed your mind?" She stopped and squared up to him.

"Well, yes. It's possible."

"Yes, it is possible, and no you hadn't thought of it. What happens if I end up carrying your baby?"

"I'll pull out?"

"It's your, I mean our first time. I'm not sure if I can rely on you pulling out. How will you be sure?"

Nectarios wasn't sure if the cool sea breeze made him shudder or this new pressure, but his semi-erection receded fast.

"Come on," she said, "Time is against us."

They walked in silence for the next ten minutes. "Over there." pointed Litsa to a small building at the end of a row of withered vines. Spikes, rakes and other metal tools rested against the side of the building. Litsa pushed the door open and found the kerosene lamp by the door. She struck a match from next to the lamp and the small space slowly glowed' a concrete floor, a bed with only a quilt slung across sideways, some hay piled into a corner and two barrels against the wall. A high solitary window to let light in spanned the wall above the bed.

"So…" said Litsa, removing her dress.

Nectarios leant in and kissed her on the neck reaching around the back to unfasten her bra. She pushed his hand away and whispered *slow down*. She pushed him against the cobbled wall, unbuttoning his shirt and taking off his undershirt, before unbuckling him. She reached down, touching his erection and kissed him harder, biting his tongue for an instant. He dropped to his knees and kissed her through her panties, her scent filling his nostrils before he slowly pulled them off, Litsa nodding, placing a hand behind his head. He kissed her mound and she pulled his head in closer, her hips slowly moving. *Use your tongue.* He took out his tongue and licked tentatively, her groans telling him he was doing the

84

right thing. She covered her mouth with her free hand, and she came, waiting a minute before pulling Nectarios away from her by the hair. Eyes wide open, she led him to the bed and sat him down, kissing his penis and unsure of herself, she glided her mouth down it, Nectarios leaning back with a guttural *oh my God*. He stopped her after a minute and lay her on her back.

She looked up at him and said *let me*. She used her hand to guide him in, less awkward and uncomfortable than she expected. She slowly moved in towards him and whispered *push gently* to him.

They moved together, first in countering rhythms, then in sync, neither sure when Nectarios should pull out. He decided for them, even though he could have gone on for longer, pulling out and sitting on the edge of the bed stroking himself. She sat next to him and took over and looked him in the eye. *Come, baby, come for me, let go*, which he did, thinking it would never end. He sat back, lightheaded as Litsa got dressed.

"Come here, Litsa." said Nectarios, his arm outstretched.

"No time for cuddles, friend. Twenty past eleven. Best we go back. We can talk on the way."

He dressed and Litsa threw water onto the kerosene lamp on the way out. They navigated their way out of the vineyard, the sky much darker than when they arrived.

"What happens now?" asked Nectarios as they walked along the road.

"You, we were fantastic. I would like to do this again, but opportunities won't come along often like this. Tonight, all the stars, moons aligned for us. Life isn't always like that."

"So that's it?"

She stopped and faced him, irritated. "What do you mean, *so that's it?*"

"You were so keen for this to happen and now, you only want to if a clear opportunity comes up like tonight? What about getting away with it, the bike ride, sneaking away tonight without people knowing, wasn't that part of the thrill?"

"Yes, but be realistic - chances to sneak away won't come easy, will they?"

"Only if we don't try."

She stayed silent until they got into town, the music continuing strong and unabated in the public area. They arrived at the intersection where she would turn right and he left and she turned to him.

"Look, I thought you were an awkward boy, but you proved you were a man."

"I will walk you home to your house as I promised your Mother." He tried not to sound resentful, but he did.

"Ok, let's go."

She kissed him on the cheek when they got to her front gate.

She walked up the path and he waited until her bedroom light came on. She waved from her bedroom window, then shooed him away.

He walked home, confused. He strained to think about why and helpless, grabbed a rock on the ground and threw it down a lane. It skipped up and narrowly missed a window along the side of a house.

"Be careful where you throw rocks, my boy." The figure silhouetted in the pale light spoke. "It's Sifi. What's going on, my little friend?"

"Nothing."

"It appears bad enough to throw a rock. Only a female can cause that much anger, or happiness. Believe me."

"And? What is there to do?"

"Some things start, and some go on beyond the start, depends on the way of the heart, Nectarios. Litsa then, eh?"

"What makes you say that?"

"You're walking back from her house, you kept looking at her at dinner and you walked to her after her idiot of a Father got drunk. I may look stupid, but I take in everything."

"I never found you stupid, Mr Polendakis."

"Call me Sifi, you're old enough.This girl, is she leading you on?"

"Yes."

"My compliments for your honesty. In return, I am not going to mention this to your parents, as close as I am to them. This stays between us, ok?"

"Ok."

"Now, come and sit with me." He led Nectarios to his house and told him to wait. He brought out a bottle and two glasses.

"No, no, Sifi."

"Wine, not *raki*. I'm not irresponsible. A small nip of wine. *In vino veritas* the Latin say. In wine lies the truth." He handed Nectarios his glass.

"To our health." said Sifi.

Nectarios nodded.

"Have you have already had relations with the girl?"

"Yes."

"Again you impress me with your honesty. Did you pull out?" He winced as he asked the question.

"Yes."

"Let's hope for the best, my friend."

"Don't scare me, Sifi."

"Well, apart from Stelios being an unbearable idiot among idiots, you would be obliged to marry the girl. You are both too young."

"People married young before."

"During the occupation, during the war yes, I agree. I was one of them. Penelope and I are married fifty-five years. But these are different times. People live longer, we are not threatened by war, there is more prosperity. You can't seriously be contemplating fatherhood at your age."

"No, you're right."

"But if you pulled out, you pulled out, right?" He slapped him on the shoulder. "Go home, my boy. And remember, this is between us, my promise."

"Thank you Sifi."

Up to nature now said Sifi as he swirled the last of the wine in his glass.

CHAPTER 16

Sicily, 1966

Chiu neri ti mezzanotte nun po fari
It cannot get darker than midnight
- Sicilian proverb

Christmas was subdued this year, owing to no church service and many reluctant to brave the cold and travel to another church. Dottore Fulmino was in no festive mood, becoming increasingly frustrated at the lack of cooperation from locals, most of whom, after the initial shock, presumed Father Di Pardo had ticked off the wrong person from the wrong family. They were happy to move on.

The body was transported back to Di Pardo's native town of Brindisi once an autopsy had been performed. The cause of death was obvious to Dottore Fulmino; but he was perturbed by the effectiveness and efficiency of it being caused by only two blows, which told him he was dealing with a dangerous man. He presumed the murderer to be a man because of the sheer force of the blows. The first was to the occipital area, stunning and unbalancing the departed, giving the murderer time to watch his last living moments then deliver the fatal blow to the point above the ear where the sutures or borders of five bones of the skull at the same point. The blows were precise and not frenzied, and Fulmino thought the murderer was not a first timer. But he was keenly aware of the pressure on him, the time he had to spend on this case was fast running out. Killings and revenge killings between rival families in Sicily and Calabria needed more resources and soon he would be pressured to write this off as unsolved. Interviews with the teachers, parents and nuns yielded nothing to proceed with. No weapon was found, no blood outside of the room. Nothing.

In the month after the murder, Claudio waited for a sense of remorse to visit him, some guilt to descend, but nothing came. He saw Caterina on two occasions; both times she appeared happier. She looked at Claudio a different way, but they did not get the opportunity to talk so he tried not to read too much into it. But tonight was *capodanno*, New Year's Eve, where in spite of the cold, the whole town gathered to welcome a better year in. They sat with candles as Mayor Maresca let Matteo light the fuse to the fireworks in the piazza. As the new year clicked over, Claudio stood himself next to Caterina and asked if she was Ok.

"Yes, Claudio. And no, I have not said anything."

"I am happy you are feeling better."

"I am, thank you." she said with a smile, before re-joining her parents.

As the fireworks fizzled out, they clapped along with everyone else. The Mayor made a short statement, wishing everyone a prosperous and healthy New Year. He cleared his throat and announced the Vatican was sending a new priest to the town in the coming month, drawing subdued clapping and more of an exhalation of relief than a cheer from the crowd.

"Welcome news, wouldn't you say Claudio?" said Sister Malena over his shoulder.

"Yes, Sister Malena. How are you?"

"Well, thank you. Happy New Year to you and your family."

"And to you."

She walked off, speaking to no one else as she left the piazza. Claudio had heard her speak before, but now found her voice flat, strange without any of the local rise and fall in tone. Though not taking a vow of silence, the nuns' voices often flattened and metallic from relative disuse.

Nuns at the Monastery in Badiazza co-habited with a group of five monks, their living quarters at opposite ends from each other. In keeping with a tradition of over three hundred years, the nuns left first at the end of services and the monks returned to their quarters after a respectable period of time.

If her tone made Claudio feel uneasy, he was more unsettled to see her not stop to talk to anyone else. *You're being paranoid,* he told himself.

Five seconds later, at the edge of the piazza, Sister Malena turned and caught his attention. A wave and she resumed her fast pace.

CHAPTER 17

Sicily, 1966

Cu lassa u vecchio cu u nova, sa chi lassa ma nun sa chi trova
Whoever decides to change is aware of not knowing what the changes may bring.
- Sicilian proverb

January and February were unusually cold in Zafferia. The felling of the trees was in full swing, the logging starting from the furthest point, on the Liverani farm where Tino had hunted quail year after year. Their habitat disappearing, the birds flew confused and vulnerable to makeshift homes to stay out of the reach of foxes, wild cats and larger birds like hawks.

The fencing dividing the Liverani farm and the *Mulino Sud* (South Mill) land was a rudimentary length of chicken wire punctuated by steel posts ever twenty metres. Pasquale Brinto added the role of council liaison to the mill to his position of Mayor Maresca's secretary, and found himself prominently walking around the building in hard hat, which he removed as he sat with his feet up in his office, a three by four metre space with a view to the valley and across to the forest being pillaged. The Sidero family owned a sizeable share of the mill, sizeable enough to demand protection through a security business under another name also owned by the Sidero family. They earned profits on timber sales, on protection and on the construction side of the *baracca* rebuild. As long as progress was seen, no one complained. And if no one complained, no one got hurt.

Except Marcisio Crudelli. Despite promising Filomena he would sign and move on, he found too hard to leave it alone. He walked to the edge of his property, now defined by fenceposts a few metres in from the red markings, paler but still visible. An explosion went off in his head. He gathered firewood and as much combustible material as possible, stuffing everything under a tractor parked under a tree, lighting the bundle, smiling as smoke rose, giving way to flame. He walked back without a care and laughed at the loud pop of the fuel tank exploding. Two hours later, Pasquale Brinto arrived with three men, all with cloth caps and overalls. Only Brinto spoke once Filomena let them in, Crudelli not bothering to get up from his lunch meal of pasta fagioli.

"Signor Crudelli?"

"Yes?"

"Can we talk outside, like men?" asked Brinto.

"What is this about, your little tractor?"

"We signed a deal - we already own that portion of land. Touching the tractor means you are trespassing."

"Trespassing? I have hunted on this land before you had balls." He got up and caught Brinto by surprise with a right hook on the jaw. The other men rushed him as he offered no resistance, his arms down by his side, watching Brinto hold his jaw. They dragged him outside, closing the front door, one coming back in to stop Filomena from watching the other two men break her husband's jaw, crack five ribs and leave him face down in the mud, the blood gushing from his broken nose and a cut above his eye flowing into the cavities formed by the stomping feet and slowly seeping into the ground.

Brinto placed a blank piece of paper on the dining table next to Crudelli's unfinished pasta.

"Do I have your attention, Filomena?"

"Yes." she said, shaking.

He held up five fingers. "Your husband's act of stupidity just cost you five thousand lira."

"Watch." said Brinto, pointing at the paper as he wrote fifteen, placing a line through the figure and writing ten. "Now I am sure despite your loyalty, you won't tolerate this, so let me tell you what we are going to do. I have organised a small apartment in the south of Messina which we own. Your husband will work in construction for us until he has paid off the tractor. Then we will talk. Ok?"

"Yes."

"Now please sign this amended sale contract." he said, producing the original one and initialling the amended figure and guiding Filomena to do the same.

"The figure will drop significantly if you have to leave a widow. Do you understand?"

Filomena nodded; her eyes red from worry. She rushed outside to check on her husband. She knelt at his side, turning him over before he groaned and asked to be left where he was, pointing to his ribs.

"I'll be back in three days. I hope your husband feels better."
said Brinto.

The men got into their car and drove away. Ten minutes
later, Filomena, still outside in the cold, cradled her husband
until he could breathe properly and got up, taking a further
hour to bathe him and lay him in bed, applying an ice pack to
his jaw and ribs.

"I've never seen you like this, amore." said Filomena.

Crudelli struggled to speak, between his breathing being so
shallow and half his face swollen beyond recognition, the left
eye swollen shut. He shook his head as a question, and
Filomena grabbed the paper Brinto left behind. She showed
him the figure.

"That's everything." she said.

He began to cry. The next day, the local doctor checked his
lungs were not punctured.

"No puncture, but you must rest Marcisio, do you
understand? Rest, proper rest."

Crudelli nodded.

The meeting with Brinto was brief and cordial. They signed
and Brinto surprised them with a year's free rent on a first-
floor apartment in Messina. But he still had to work off the
debt incurred by his recklessness.

"We'll make sure everything is healed before you move,"
said Brinto in a gentle tone. "We're not unreasonable. We'll
take care of the move. Your neighbourhood is a very safe
one, too. Filomena, I believe your sister lives nearby, a three-
minute walk."

"Thank you." said Filomena, the hairs on her arm standing
up.

Crudelli shook Brinto's hand and thanked him. For the next
four weeks, they sat around the house, without motivation to
go outside. Tino and Vanna visited with Claudio and Lidia,
having heard the news.

"Don't do what I did." said Crudelli, his speech now affected
by the beating.

"Tino isn't going to provoke them." said Filomena.

"It's not that. Think - why push so hard for two-thirds of the
land and leave you alone? Don't let what happened to me -
us, happen to you. And you have more forest area than us.
Work it out for yourself, Tino. Find an easy way to get out
with something."

Crudelli didn't have to convince him, but with the idea
floating in his head, Tino went to check on his fences along
the river. The rainfall on his land was if anything greater this
year than last, yet the river levels were low, half a metre of
mud starting to dry out on the opposite bank, the river
eddying more than flowing. He lifted his head at the whirring
and buzzing of trees being sawn through, the whoosh of the
trees falling through the air, the thump and the cracking of
branches.

He brought Vanna down to the river and showed her.

"I take no pleasure in being right, Tino. If you were on your own, all the best trying to keep these wolves at bay. But you've got two children."

"And you."

"And me. So, what do we do?"

"I'm going in next week to visit Maresca. I will ask for thirty days. I'm not happy, but what other options do we have?"

"Whatever happens, we need to make sure Claudio and Lidia have a future; before anything else."

Claudio observed the swallowing up of land and took their exit as inevitable. His parents having no bargaining chip to keep their farm nagged at him; their land, the earth parents and their descendants had walked upon and cared for. But he was realistic. He had no idea how the land was handed down on the first place and no one living did either. His parents sat him down with Lidia to talk about the changes. Claudio and Lidia spent much time talking about the family farm.

"Father, Mother, we know you will be selling the farm to these people, whoever they are." said Lidia.

"We know you are not stupid," said Tino. "We are being squeezed and do not want to ruin your future. So, we are going to sign and move on."

"Claudio, you were right." said Vanna, smiling at him.

He shrugged. "We'll do what we have to do." he said.

Tino worked fast, contacting farmers he dealt with to sell off most of his livestock and already harvested crops. He didn't want to be too greedy and he left about a fifth of each behind. He stored the cash away, happy he had been proactive, but angry he had to be furtive about selling his own possessions and produce.

Tino walked into town and meet Maresca. He waited half an hour as Maresca's secretary said he had official business to attend to. Maresca sat at his desk and drew out the wait, struggling to stifle a smirk as he emerged from his office.

"Hello neighbour, what do you I owe the pleasure for your visit?"

"You know why I'm here. Shall we talk in your office? These aren't matters for hallways."

Maresca showed him to a seat in his office.

"So what have you decided to do, Tino?"

"What valuation do you give for our land?"

"Valuation? The one you we gave you. You are misinformed if you think I am influential enough to change the figure. I will have a representative of *Mulino Sud* come and confirm the valuation so both parties are happy."

"You were always able to talk with a mouth full of your shit, couldn't you?"

"I believe we are finished here."

Two days later, Brinto, this time alone, came with a briefcase
to speak to Tino and Vanna. At 25,000 lire and an apartment
for the four of them, Vanna nodded in the affirmative.

"We reassessed the value of your land. I hope you are happy
with the revised figure."

"My wife and I thank you. How much is the rent?" asked
Tino as he read the paperwork.

"Tino, do you see any rent on the paperwork in front of
you?"

He scanned the page, his eyes stopping when he read the
words: *Augustino and Vanna Liverani appointed as trustee of
apartment 2C for Mulino Industries.*

"*Mulino Sud* owns the apartment. You will merely be
responsible to maintain it for us. It is a nice area. Feel free to
sign when you are ready."

Tino's signature was shakier than usual. He handed the
paperwork back to Brinto, his whole body shaking.

"If I may ask, can you give us a week to say goodbye to our
land?"

"Take a month Tino," said Brinto wth a smile. "I will arrange
the removal and transport for you as a gesture of thanks for
your cordiality in this matter."

"Thank you, Mr Brinto." said Tino.

A week later, Crudelli was in far less pain, able to walk unaided and breathing more easily. Brinto sent three men to help them pack and drove them to their new address in Quartiere Lombardo, Messina, another man driving a truck with their belongings. Inherent in the deal was the relinquishing of all farm equipment, livestock, crops and anything else Marcisio and Filomena Crudelli would not reasonably see as essential in their new abode. Unlike Tino, Crudelli was a broken man, and the thought of recouping what he could didn't come to mind. The termites went to work, selling anything of value not nailed down within a week.

Tino and Vanna took some time to accept they were alone in the area, even if only for a month. While visits between the Rossi, Crudelli and Liverani families were not frequent or regular, it was reassuring that they were nearby. They had helped each other in difficult times and celebrated good times.

Being alone in a farming community was one thing. Feeling alone surrounded by people would be quite another.

CHAPTER 18

Crete, 1966

Η αγάπη και η εγκυμοσύνη είναι σαν βήχας - δύσκολο να
κρυφτεί.
Love and pregnancy are like a cough - difficult to hide.
- Greek proverb

Fotini walked outside and enjoyed the slight warmth on her
face. It was the last week of February and the worst of the
cold was gone, pushed north by the mild but persuasive
pounentes, the gentle western wind heralding spring. She
opened the windows and attacked her racks of repairs, Nikos
sipping his coffee in between his shoe repairs. He drank more
coffee and ate more biscuits with it since giving up smoking
and the workroom smelled better since. Sia, coached by
Nectarios and Rita, tugged on his guilt, and managed to make
him go cold turkey. The coughing stopped within a week and
so did the irritability Mr Pandelis warned him about.

Nectarios continued with his deliveries, also helping Sifi
Polendakis with fish deliveries once his Father's and Mr
Pandelis' were done.

He returned after delivering a bounty catch of snapper.
Handing over the money, Nectarios braced himself for
Sifi's meaty hand on his shoulder.

"Sit with me." he said.

Nectarios sat and took a wine from him, Nectarios confused
until Sifi composed himself and explained.

"Penelope had four miscarriages. We gave up after the last one. What she went through, no one should have to endure. Having you around has made me wonder what a son of my own would have been like."

"Thank you, Sifi."

"How long since you saw Stelios' daughter?"

"Ten, eleven weeks?"

"So no news then?"

"Nothing."

"Thank God. I mean, for where you are in life right now."

Nectarios nodded. "I'm sorry you could not have children, Sifi."

"Nature is nature and what the Lord wants." said Sifi, palms upturned. "Go home and give your parents my love."

He was approaching his house when Rita ran out from the house. She was looking through the window, ready to warn him about the tension he was coming home to.

"What's going on, Rita."

"The girl, Litsa. She is here with her parents. What did you do?"

The colour drained from Nectarios' face and he had to lean against a wall to compose himself.

"Come on," said Rita, with no idea of what was happening and what kind of bomb was about to drop on their family. "I was looking out for you. They sent me out to my room, but I wanted to warn you."

"Thank you Rita." said Nectarios. He braced himself and pushed the front door with a soft hand. "In here." said his Father.

Around the kitchen table, his parents sat on one side; Stelios, Hariklia and Litsa opposite.

"Sit." said Nikos, pulling out the chair between him and his Mother. He sat directly opposite Stelios, his small, beady eyes close together, his fat head with no neck perched on his squat, fat body. He tried to distract himself by wondering what Hariklia found attractive in him, and how Litsa turned out so beautiful. Litsa couldn't look him or anyone else in the eye, her head was bent downwards to the floor.

"Do I have your attention, boy?" asked Stelios.

Nikos leant in. "Stelios, he has a name. Nectarios. Whatever and however serious this is, give him the courtesy of calling him by his name." Fotini held him back with a firm hand on his forearm.

"Very well, Nectarios; my daughter Litsa is, *was* pregnant. She miscarried three weeks ago. Tell me when and where you did this to her."

"On the night of Saint Nikolaos, Sir." said Nectarios.

"What did you do?" yelled Nikos, slamming the table.

104

Fotini watched Litsa stare at the floor; Hariklia, Stelios and Nikos glaring at Nectarios. It was over a minute before Nectarios broke the silence.

"I, I pulled out. I didn't think Litsa would get pregnant."

"Well you are correct - you didn't think." said Hariklia.

"It takes two, Hariklia," said Fotini, her eyes narrowing at her.

Nikos raised his finger to his lips to Nectarios, and turned to Stelios. "I am ashamed and sorry this happened. How can we-"

"Stop!" said Litsa, lifting her head. "Has anyone even bothered to talk to me about this? What I went through, having then losing a baby? Yes, there were two of us, and the blame belongs to the *two of us*, Father, so drop your self-importance and let us try and move on from this."

Stelios smiled. "Move on, move on you say? Barely eighteen and you say move on as if this was a small thing. This is a tremendous insult to our family, our honour-"

"What honour?" interjected Nikos. "Who the devil do you think you are to make the mistake of these two children all about you? What gives you the right?" Nikos looked to Hariklia for support, but from her pursed lips told him she backed her husband.

"My husband is right. We need to decide how this should be made right."

"Made right?" asked Fotini. "What do you suggest, castrate him? Or brush a symbol in red paint above our door so the whole community knows?"

Stelios got up, buttoned his jacket with an exaggerated motion. "Believe me, I will think of something."

"And what, we should stew here and wait?" asked Nikos.

"As the sinning party here what do you expect me to say?" said Stelios, puffing out his chest. "We will meet again in three days."

Stelios left the room. Litsa stopped to face Nectarios, but Hariklia muscled her towards the front door with her long arms.

"Hariklia, please ask your husband to be reasonable about this. No child should be punished for a lifetime for an error of a moment." said Fotini in a smooth but pleading voice.

"When I married Stelios, we had Litsa after a year. I promised to support him as we raised her. We have one child, one, and your son has treated her as some kind of game. Reverse the roles and tell me how reasonable you would be."

Nikos, still seated, turned to his son. Nectarios told *himself do not cry, do not give anyone the excuse to hit you for being weak.* When Fotini re-joined them, they sat and stared at the table before Nikos put his hand on Nectarios' shoulder.

"I was not going to give Stelios the satisfaction of seeing me tear you in half in front of him, but now you are going to hear some things and some words you may not like, and you will wait until I am finished, Ok?"

"Yes, Father."

"I can see what happened here. One day, after deliveries, Litsa, and she is a lovely girl, she got your attention and drove you crazy. I blame myself in part for not educating you about these ways. But the responsibility lies with you. You must have known the storm something like this would cause if she got pregnant. How could you let your dick rule your head? Now, we are all in the shit because of you." Nectarios went to speak but was cut short by a backhander from his Father.

"I did say not to speak. I am not finished. Catching you smoking was one thing-"

"He was smoking?" asked Fotini, "and neither of you told me? What a situation this is!"

"I caught him, slapped him around and he has not lit one up since, believe me."

"I should slap you both around." said Fotini.

"Can we stick to more urgent questions? Did you not think getting her pregnant was a possibility? Are you that stupid? Now you can speak."

"I, we talked it before we did it. I promised to pull out, and I did, I DID."

"Poor girl; the colour was gone from her body. To miscarry

at that age." said Fotini.

"And now," said Nikos. "Whether you pulled out or not, here we are. Here at the mercy of the greediest man in Tavroniti and his heartless pelican of a wife. We are at their mercy, after everything we have managed to achieve here. What will be, will be. I have work to do. Get out of my sight."

CHAPTER 19

Sicily, 1966

Father Damiano was somewhere between his departed predecessors. At fifty-six and born in Messina, his appointment brought a level of calm and familiarity to the town. His soft-spoken nature endeared him to the nuns and monks, and the congregation as a whole. He continued the bible classes and requested the nuns run them with his oversight.

Claudio and Lidia had less than a week to go before their parents were taking them to Messina, making this their last bible class. Their classmates were equal parts jealous and curious as they spoke to them.

"Are you going to live in a mansion?"

"Can I have one of your lambs as a pet?"

"Can we stay at your place and go to the beach?"

Only Caterina was silent among them. Claudio was not concerned about Caterina, but his mind was still on Sister Malena and whether she knew or was just odd. The children hugged them goodbye, Sister Malena smiling when Caterina hugged Claudio.

"I will never be able be able to thank you." she whispered into his ear.

"Live a good life. I will be pleased with that." he replied.

Over Caterina's shoulder, he saw Sister Malena's expression change. *Like a hawk waiting for the quail to become distracted by food* he said to himself. He walked to her, keeping eye contact the whole ten steps.

"Sister Malena, I wanted to thank you for your biblical instructions."

"My pleasure, Claudio. Don't say goodbye though. I have arranged to visit you and your parents before you leave, tomorrow morning actually, for coffee. Your lovely Mother offered lunch, but I didn't want to put her out with all the packing."

Claudio kept his face vanilla through her attempt to flush out a change. She waited but got nothing. *She knows.*

"So, until tomorrow, Sister."

"And Lidia," she said, as she approached them, "how you have grown. You will need your strong brother to protect you when you live in that apartment in Messina, won't you?"

"I suppose so. But I am sixteen."

"It is indeed a dangerous world out there, child." she said, watching Claudio's face in her peripheral vision. His impassive face maddened her.

"Thank you, Sister."

Lidia turned to Claudio as they walked back to their parents in the piazza.

"You, Caterina, Sister Malena. What strangeness has happened?"

"Nothing-"

"Do not insult me, Claudio. You may be my older brother, but I know something is going on. What happened?"

"Did Father Di Pardo ever come across to you as-"

"Strange?"

"He liked young girls, Lidia."

"Caterina?"

"Yes. Caterina. I am sure he devoted so much support to Rosina to spend time with Caterina. Her Mother probably had no idea he was showing her so much attention. Neither did Caterina."

"And what, her Father found out and killed him?"

"What I am going to tell you is between us for as long as we live, do you understand?"

Oh dear God, no Claudio. After a long silence, she looked at him. "I understand."

"Father Di Pardo asked Caterina and some other children to carry the effigy back to the church. When all of them came out of the church except Caterina, I grabbed a rock and went inside. I caught him in the vestry. He had her pinned against the wall. His pants were-"

"Stop!" Lidia put her hands to her ears and squeezed her eyes shut, crying.

"You cannot tell-" began Claudio, before Lidia lashed out, not even realising she was beating Claudio's chest. Claudio grabbed her frenzied arms. She broke off from him, turning away before returning to confront him.

"How could you do this, kill a man, Claudio? Do you live alone in this life?"

Claudio looked around to make sure no one was watching them and tried to explain himself.

"Lidia, from the moment it happened, I have been waiting for remorse to come, but the truth is, he would have killed Caterina. Even if she remained alive, she would have been dead inside. Now she can move on."

"We move to Messina, and what? You decide someone deserves to die and you do this again? Do you think you will get away with it there?"

"Life does not always give justice, Lidia."

"Fine. Avoid the question. But promise me-"

"I cannot promise what you are about to ask. I cannot tell you now, here as I stand, how I will react to something I cannot predict, especially if it puts someone I love in danger. That would not be sincere."

"Better to be a truthful killer than a lying citizen like the rest of us?"

"You choose to put it any way you like."

Lidia walked away. This time, Claudio let her go. He balanced the situation in the ledger of his mind and decided he could not have done anything different. He also concluded he would travel life alone, the heaviest thought of all.

When he re-joined his parents, Lidia was transformed, happy and wondering what took Claudio so long, forcing him to lie and say he was saying goodbye to Matteo. Most nights before bed, he chatted to Lidia from his room to hers through their open doors.

Tonight, she closed hers.

CHAPTER 20

Sicily, 1966

Sister Malena woke refreshed. After a brisk walk into town, she took her assortment of pastries and began the thirty-minute walk to the Liverani farm. She smelt the air as the houses thinned out and screwed her nose up with disapproval. The timber mill emitted a foul odour, sawdust mixed with fuel smoke which disagreed with her sinuses, making her eyes water and triggering a cough. She gargled and spat out some water from her flask once she was sure no one was around.

As she passed what was previously the Crudelli front gate, a cracking noise came from a tree about twenty metres off the road. She went to investigate, looking around then upwards, seeing nothing but three trees. *Wind* she said aloud. The branch fell on the other side of the tree from her, startling her as it thumped into the ground. She held her chest and got her breathing back to a regular rhythm. *I'm no good today* she said to herself and sat down on a stump. She glanced at her watch and saw she had plenty of time. She peeked at the pastries, a slightly burnt almond *pasticcino* catching her eye and told herself *what a shame to offer this to company*. She took the offending biscuit out and shuffled the other pastries around the box to spread them evenly. It was moist and sweet, sickly sweet as she wasn't used to such extravagances in the monastery. After swallowing, her breath shortened, her airway narrowing and she forced with all her energy to take a breath, only choking further, her vision blackening at the edges before a high pitched wheeze like a kettle escaped her throat and the box of pastries hit the ground before she did.

"What time was Sister Malena supposed to be here?" asked Tino.

"Fifteen mines ago," said Vanna. "I hope she is Ok."

Tino went back outside to take a final inventory of the equipment he did not sell. Between the livestock and equipment, he managed to recoup a significant amount of money. He estimated it would get them through four, maybe five months without having to work. Some transactions he would not have entertained if he was to remain on the farm, but the money was better in his pocket. He even toyed with the idea of a holiday, before dismissing it as fanciful and a waste; barely half an hour away the beaches of Naxos and Taormina could be reached anytime they wanted to.

"She's an hour late, Tino. Send Claudio to meet her halfway, just in case." yelled Vanna from inside the house.

"I'll take Lidia for company." said Claudio, emerging from the house, before going back inside.

"No," whispered Lidia. "I'm not going with you."

"This way you can make sure I don't kill her as well."

"You are not funny."

"I know and I am sorry. Come on - our last farm walk before we leave. "

She hesitated and relented, putting her shoes on.

"Father did the right thing." said Lidia.

"Would he have left without broken ribs if his farm was closer than Crudelli's?"

"We will never know. Would Father Di Pardo be alive if he did this awful thing to another girl or boy in another parish?"

Claudio shrugged. "Why are you more worried about him being in my path instead of the children he molested being put in his path? What I did prevented lives from being ruined."

"I thought that was God's role. You are mortal and have no right. I heard you in bible class from the other side of the room when you said sometimes someone gets in first. Father Di Pardo's body changed even before he slammed the book on the table. Something was wrong."

"Wrong with him or me?"

"In general; wrong. When I heard he was dead, I did not want to believe my first thought - you."

They walked in silence for the next ten minutes. Lidia pointed out a black shape in the distance and ran towards it.

"Sister Malena!" she called out, patting her cheeks as she bent over her body, repeating her name louder, wiping the crumbs from her dry lips, seeing her eyes seeing but not seeing, her glasses on the ground beside her.

Lidia turned to Claudio, who had not changed pace.

"She's dead." said Lidia.

Claudio raised his hands to the sky. "This one is on God."

"Claudio!"

"Well, the crumbs and pastry around her mouth." Claudio opened Sister Malena's mouth and sniffed. He picked up the unfinished *pasticcino* on the ground next to her "Almonds. She must have had an allergy to almonds."

"What now?" asked Lidia.

"Well, we are halfway between home and the town, and she's going nowhere. Better we tell the police then they can give us lift back home."

"Sfogliatelle?" asked Claudio, sliding the box out of the paper bag, "or cannoli?"

Lidia shot him a look of disgust. "How can you think about pastries at a time like this?"

"Easy, she was bringing them to us anyway." said Claudio, making a satisfying crunch as he bit into a crisp cannoli, the softness of the ricotta and glazed fruit making him go mmm.

"Give me one." said Lidia.

She sucked out the ricotta filling and crunched the casing in one bite. "Oh, they are divine."

Claudio shuffled the remaining pastries in the box and placed the paper bag exactly where it was. "Ok, we better walk fast into town."

As they passed the school, Lidia took Claudio's hand and led him to the tap on the side of the building. "Wash the dusting off your face, *cretino*. Do you want to get caught?"

Claudio smiled at her.

She smiled and slapped him on the cheek. "Yes, I love you too, stupid. Let's go."

The solitary policeman made a call to Messina Police before driving the pair back to the scene, asking them the usual questions, Lidia letting Claudio do the talking. Tino and Vanna's anger turned to shock as the children recounted the finding, leaving out the cannoli. It was their final night, Lidia left her door open, smiling at her brother as he fell asleep.

The next day they placed their packed belongings in front of their house. Pasquale Brinto and his three men loaded up a truck with a hessian tarpaulin, insisting Tino and Vanna stand aside and let them work. Once loaded, the truck left.

"Are we ready?' asked Brinto.

Tino looked back across the land his Father had left him.

"I didn't take you as a nostalgic man, Tino." said Brinto.

Tino smiled, a rueful smile

"You only feel nostalgia well after you say goodbye to something, not as you say goodbye."

He got in and remained silent the whole drive to Messina.

CHAPTER 21

Crete, 1966

Ένας σταυρός στο στήθος και ο διάβολος στην καρδιά
A cross on the chest and the devil in the heart.
- Greek proverb

Litsa lay with her blanket rolled up between her thighs. Nearly four weeks after her miscarriage, it was the only position that gave her relief from the dull ache around her stomach down to her pelvis. The baby would have been twelve weeks old now if not for the hurricane of changes that passed through her body. She was five weeks along when the giddiness started, which soon progressed to nausea. It settled for three days, a cruel joke and she put it down to a virus. Then she passed blood with a pain she was helpless to stop, rushing to the only toilet in the house, clots like small red stones, the sound of them hitting the water loud in her ears, hoping her parents would not see the trails she left. Her discomfort was worsened as she bent down every time to clean up behind, managing to avoid detection until Stelios slipped on a small blood stain.

"Sort that out." Stelios said to Hariklia.

"Sort what out?"

"That." he said, pointing to a blood stain on the floor in the hallway. "I slipped on it."

Hariklia only pieced it together when she caught Litsa throwing up in the middle of the night, blood on the bathroom floor, her daughter shivering with a fever.

"What's wrong with Litsa?" asked Stelios, standing by her door, afraid to go in. *You weak, squeamish bastard,* thought Hariklia.

"She has a virus, don't go in there in case you catch it."

She waited until she was alone with her before asking the obvious question.

"Who is he?" she said, as calmly as possible.

Litsa hesitated.

"Don't invent a lie, you were pregnant child, and you are having a miscarriage. Who is it?"

"Nectarios."

"The shoe repairer's boy?"

"Do you know any other Nectarios, Mother?"

"Right." Hariklia got up and shut the door behind her. She returned in five minutes with pain tablets, towels, an ice bucket and another bucket in case she vomited and left without a word. She dithered about telling Stelios for two days, until Litsa told him herself as he attempted to show some fatherly love, sitting at her bedside. He sat at a distance from her but at least he showed *some* compassion, thought Litsa, that notion dispelled as Stelios called his wife and daughter deceitful and underhand for not telling him sooner, the saga now transforming into his honour being insulted, Litsa confined to her bed and Hariklia keeping to herself. The

family of three lived as strangers for a week until Stelios
gathered them together and led them to the Petrakis house.

Mr Pandelis sat for breakfast with Anthoula. He sipped his
coffee and did his cross as he ate the omelette Anthoula made
for him. She sat down and shook her head.

"A horrible business, this thing with Stelios and Nikos." she
said.

"You did warn the boy. Twice."

"Hormones ruled his head. "

"We have to try and help them."

"The only help would be to arrange a nasty accident for that
greedy bastard. How did Nikos accept his terms?"
"He knows the way things work here."

"When Stelios comes here, you will have to serve him. On
principle I won't."

On the day of the second meeting, Anthoula minded Rita and
Sia. Pater Manousso sat the parents, Litsa and Nectarios in
his small office beside the church. Nikos insisted on a neutral
location and Stelios agreed.

Pater Manousso asked them to move the table against the
wall and arranged the chairs in a circle.
"This is not a court, my children." he said. "Whatever has
happened, let us sit and talk in a rational way with each other
and show respect."

"The way this monster showed respect to my daughter?!"
spluttered Stelios, pointing at Nectarios.

"Stelios," said the priest, his finger pointing upwards, "be
careful what you say. Everyone take a deep breath." He
turned to Nectarios and Litsa. "How about you tell us what
happened. Take your time."

Litsa began crying. "It's partly my fault," she said, her
Mother reaching for her hand, Litsa pushing her away. "No,
you can blame Nectarios all you want, but this was the two of
us exploring."

"Go on, child." cajoled Pater Manousso.

"One day, Nectarios was walking past with his Father. He
didn't see me but later, he walked back past the same spot
and I was on the balcony looking down to him. I, I spoke to
him in a way..."

"Go on." said Pater Manousso.

Litsa shrugged. "I was flirting with him."

"And after?" asked Pater Manousso.

"In Mr Pandelis' shop a couple of months later, he was rattled
when he saw me. He liked me, which I played on. I invited
him to go on a bike ride the next day, just to see what would
happen." She breathed in and glanced at Nectarios. He
nodded. "We rode to the Tombs at Maleme and kissed a
little."

"The second time," said Nectarios, "was on the night of the festival of Saint Nikolaos, when your wife went home with you, on the account of you being-"

"Drunk." said Hariklia.

"Beyond drunk." said Litsa.

"Yes. Litsa and I walked to your vineyard and took things a bit further." said Nectarios.

"You're lucky I don't shoot you right here and now you little bastard." said Stelios through gritted teeth, standing up. Nikos stood up before Pater stood between them, urging them both to sit and relax.

"This is an extraordinary situation, but we all need to be calm, please." said Pater Manousso in a more frustrated tone, firmly pushing the men back to their seats. "It seems you went more than a bit further, my son." said Pater Manousso. He turned to Litsa. "Are you pregnant, my child?"

"No Father,"

"She suffered a miscarriage, a natural one." said Hariklia.

Pater Manousso wiped his brow and did his cross. "I am sorry for how you must have felt. We are God's representatives, but we are not black and white. We are nothing as humans if we cannot express sympathy and show understanding. May the Lord bring you strength, child."

"Thank you, Pater."

He tried to anticipate what was to come. "So, how do we progress from here? None of you can stop what has happened. I'm listening. Stelios?"

Stelios cleared his throat and stood up. Pater Manousso rolled his eyes. "Sit down please, you are not running for mayor here!" said Pater Manousso.

"Pater, my wife and I insist that Nectarios must marry Litsa as soon as is practical. In addition, I wish to receive your approval of ten percent of his Father's takings from his shop a year in arrears as compensation for the trauma my daughter has suffered, and for the dishonour this episode has caused for my family."

"For you, you mean." said Fotini.

"Fotini-" said Nikos.

"No, no, Nikos. For an act, a consensual act - wrong and sinful? Yes. But must we be condemned as we raise our three children? You have plenty, Stelios. And we do not have the money you ask lying around. You are like the bird flying with a full belly, but sees a glint, a reflection in the sand and thinks I must have that, because I can. I object to this with every part of my being."

"Hariklia?' asked Pater Manousso.

"What my husband said is my position also."

"Nikos?"

"I have to agree with my wife. We are raising three children; we are busy with small jobs and we provide modestly for them. How can they marry at this age?"

"How can they not?" asked Stelios. "This is the way things have always been done in this land."

"Have any of you asked Nectarios if he wants to marry me?" asked Litsa, looking at Nectarios. All eyes converged on Nectarios. *Be a man,* he told himself.

"Do you remember what you were like and what you when you were sixteen, seventeen, Mr Sfirakis? Did you ever do anything you regretted? What we did was wrong but at the time was something we both were helpless to stop. I am sorry beyond belief Litsa became pregnant when she did not expect to be, and how traumatic having a miscarriage must have been. But penalising us in this way only poisons all of our hearts, especially my little sisters. How can I call you Father after your words, how can I, as a man, respect myself for agreeing to be under your feet, day to day? I still have feelings for Litsa. But I cannot accept this vice you wish to put us in. I cannot."

Bravo son for showing some balls, thought Nikos to himself. In spite of the situation, he was proud of his response.

Hariklia buried her face in her hands, quietly crying. Litsa shook her head. "Did it happen to you or me, Mother?"

Nikos pointed at Stelios' chest. "You wear the cross on your hairy chest, but what you propose comes from the devil in your heart. Maybe a walk of shame through the town before the wedding day would appease you. But whatever Pater

Manousso determines is what we, as reasonable people will abide by." The colour drained from Stelios face, his heart pounding as Nikos' dark stare bore into him.

"Children," said Pater Manousso, "this is difficult. I have sat here to resolve many things in my time, but on this I cannot provide any counsel, direction, nor any judgement. These two questions of marriage and financial compensation must be settled by you." he said, laying out his hands to everyone. "All I ask is you come to a respectful position everyone is happy with, under the circumstances."
"What?" asked Stelios.

"You mean," said Nikos, "you will not help us settle this, as a neutral person of authority?"

Pater Manousso waved the notion away. "Neutral is a fantasy in this scenario. I would hardly be neutral if I offered a position one way or the other. One or both of you would be aggrieved. God asks you to show respect in your dealings with each other. What I ask you to do is listen to your children, be guided by them."

"Children," said Pater Manousso, "what are your feelings for each other?"

Litsa began to cry and shrugged. "I was close to Nectarios at the time but after, something changed, like we both reached a point and said 'what next?' I started feeling sick, and I could not tell my Mother. I had to wait until it was too obvious even for her."

"What do you mean, even for me?" asked Hariklia.

"We have never been close, Mother, don't pretend we have some special bond. And you, Father, you with your eye always after taking advantage of anything you can. This is all about you and your 'honour'. Nectarios is a nice boy, smart, funny and sweet, but how is it possible to be sure how a life together would be like?"

"How did any of us who married young know what to expect, child?" asked Hariklia.

Fotini nodded. "Many of us were lined up before we experienced anything of the world, Litsa. I was lucky. But you have to go by your feelings-"

"Do not try and corrupt my daughter's feelings with your maternal myths. They must marry. All the rest is nonsense." said Stelios, getting up. He kissed Pater Manousso's hand. "Pater, thank you for your time and valuable advice. Hariklia, Litsa, let's go." He turned to Nikos. "As the head of your family, tell me now what your decision is."

Nikos used the time listening to weigh everything up; the threat to his family, how he would tear Stelios with his bare hands if they were alone in a room, community perceptions. His compass swayed before he quietly responded.

"We ask for thirty days to prepare for the wedding. As for ten per-cent, this is unrealistic and disrespectful given that we are about to be related by marriage through our children. We do not have this kind of money. We will offer a dowry of an amount we can put together and discuss before the wedding day. Fotini is an excellent seamstress and will create Litsa's bridal gown. Is this satisfactory?" he asked, putting his hand out.

Fotini looked wide-eyed at her husband. Nectarios slumped in his chair, dull. Hariklia hesitant, watching the gears grinding over in her opportunistic husband's mind. Litsa looked at Nectarios, unsure but also dull.

"I accept your offer," said Stelios. We will visit you in three days, so-"

"Sunday." said Nikos.

"Sunday." said Stelios, beaming. "Come on Hariklia, Litsa, let's go."

Nikos let them leave first, turning to Pater Manousso and kissing his hand. "Thank you, Pater."

"Nikos, man to man: he is greedy beyond belief. Do not let him suck you dry, Ok?"

"Yes, Pater."

As they walked away, Pater Manousso did his cross again and hoped for either a wedding ceremony or nothing; anything but a funeral.

Nothing suited him fine.

CHAPTER 22

Crete, 1966

Περιμένετε για τους σοφότερους συμβούλους, χρόνο.
Wait for the wisest of all counsellors - time.
- Pericles

Mr Pandelis and Anthoula were not the only ones bemused by the demands or Nikos' willingness to accept them. Many offered their best wishes, awkward about the situation. Nikos though pressed on with his repairs, likewise Fotini, charged with measuring Litsa up for her wedding dress. Nectarios was prohibited from being in the house when she was being measured, although for better or worse he needed none of his Mother's tapes to remember her form.

Fotini did not question her husband when he agreed to the children marrying, and Nectarios was too dulled to raise a protest. They spent the rest of the day in silence, everyone absorbing what happened and what was to come. The next morning, as the girls played outside, Nikos sat Fotini and Nectarios down.

"You are both bewildered about my decision. My objection to all of his demands are as strong as they were yesterday, but you have to trust me on this. Do you both trust me?"

"Of course, Father." said Nectarios.

"I do, my love, but-"

"Fotini, I will always do what is best for our family. Believe me this is the first thing on my mind in all of this, Ok? Please say you trust me."

"I trust you."

The Sunday meeting was awkward, half the town peering out their windows as Stelios, walking ten metres ahead of Hariklia and Litsa, led the way to the Petrakis house. They exchanged gifts and allowed Rita and Sia to sit alongside them at the table, their innocent banter breaking the tension.

"I am glad we can make the best of this situation, Nikos." said Stelios, beaming.

"As we are." said Nikos, placing his arm around Fotini.

"Kiss her, kiss her," said Sia, running around the table. "Please, 'Ectario, for me."

Nectarios leaned over and kissed Litsa on the cheek, sat back and saw the smile spread over her face, an uneasy feeling in his chest. Sia clapped with joy, embracing Litsa who hugged her back. After a round of *raki*, Stelios got up and slapped Nikos on the back, walking out with him as Hariklia spoke with Fotini about the dress. Sia sat on Litsa's lap, playing with the strands of her hair.

"Are you going to have a baby?"

Litsa tried holding her tears back but cried, Sia jumping off her and running to Fotini's arms, also crying.

"I'm sorry, Sia."

"Don't be, Litsa," said Fotini. "She's not yet five."

"Sia," said Litsa, "We will one day, then you can give it a cuddle, Ok?"

Sia peeked back at her, nodding and wiping her tears. "Ok."

"We better go." said Hariklia.

"Bye, Nectarios." said Litsa, smiling at him.

"Bye, Litsa."

Rita sat through and absorbed everything. At thirteen, she was picking up the snippets of conversation and reading the cues. She got up and pointed at her brother. "You don't really love her, do you?"

"What do you mean, Rita?"

Fotini allowed herself to smile among the chaos of the situation.

"Well?" Rita insisted.

"We will get to know each other better in time, little sister."

"You better," Rita snapped back, "she is as good as you will ever get. And her Father is rich."

"Ok, bossy girl, enough. Take Sia outside and play." said Fotini.

She looked at her son. He was taller than her now, and she looked at him with a fresh pair of eyes.

"*Do* you love her, Nectarios?"

"I guess so, Mother. All that was hormones, and I'm sorry-"

Fotini stopped him with a raised hand. "That ship has sailed. We are not going to punish you forever. Your Father has asked us to trust him. He has never let me down before and I trust him with this. What will be will be. Again, I ask you, do you love the girl, beyond being naked with her? Life is hard, and you need much more to make a life together, much more."

"I cannot say for sure. Who can at this age?"

Nectarios wondered about life here, whether he married Litsa or not. What opportunities did he have here? Would he just live and die in the same house he was born in? What was beyond Tavroniti?

Twenty-seven days to go he said to himself.

CHAPTER 23

Sicily, 1967

Sister Malena's death was written off as pure bad luck.
Dottore Fulmino's instinct was to return to Zafferia to
investigate, before seeing the doctor's report - asphyxiation
due to an allergy to almonds read the report. No sign of
strangulation or blunt trauma. Just a nun who died of a rare
indulgence.

Fulmino touched base with Mayor Maresca. Father Damiano
was popular and life went on in Zafferia.

In Messina, Tino and Vanna found work faster than they
expected. Tino's handyman skills were snapped up by the
local council after being recommended by Pasquale Brinto.
He was sent to various blocks of apartments to repair
anything from leaky taps to putting in new stairs. He hit the
ground running and being occupied agreed with him.

Vanna's cooking got her a job in a local trattoria. She walked
in off the street, addressed the owner, a gruff rotund man
with a tic; a sequential scratch of his bald pate, his nose then
chin.

"I am a man driven to my wit's end by *deficient*." said the
man, counting the number of underwhelming cooks he went
through on his fingers.

"Tell me signora, can you make *pasta chi sardi*?"

"Bucatini or perciatelli?"

The man smiled wider than he had for ages. "Gianno Bacano, signora."

"Vanna Liverani."

"Please, Vanna. Come and see the kitchen."

The kitchen made her head hurt. Gianno saw her wince and asked "Problem?"

"It is clean, but everything is everywhere and nowhere. How do you function like this?"

"You make me *pasta chi sardi* and you can rearrange it the way you like."

"Gather everything and wait outside."

"Can I not watch?"

"Why? Do you get your kicks from watching women cook? No - if the taste is to your satisfaction, why should that not be enough?"

Gianno raised his hands, acquiesced and gathered everything for her. She smelt the fennel and approved.

"Are the sardines fresh?"

"Fresh from the market this morning."

Vanna smelled them. "Ok, go." she said, shooing him away.

Fifteen minutes later, his eyes lit up as he devoured the result, slurps and appreciative mmm sounds.

"Where and how did you learn to cook so well?"

"Ah, there have to be some secrets."

"The last cook ruined this by putting fucking saffron in."

"*Sti cazzi polentoni.*" she said, laughing. Bloody northerners.

Vanna ate her small portion and told herself *fuck it's not bad.*

"When can you start, Vanna?"

"Tomorrow, but I want to make sure my family can eat here, or I can take some food home. Take it from my salary."

He smiled at his luck. "No freeloaders though, Ok?"

"Of course. We know no one here. We only moved in a week ago."

They shook hands. Vanna roughly added the money left over after food plus what Tino was earning and felt secure. She loved the sea breeze at night and adapted better than she thought she would to the smaller confines of their apartment.

They now lived in a first-floor apartment on Via Istria in Borgo Del Ringo, where apartment blocks clamoured over each other on the same ground where knights practised for tournaments in the sixteenth century, and where floods, fires and earthquakes forced the city to take stock of life and land. The apartment had three bedrooms and although small, the living area was generous, the kitchen ample and a sizeable balcony where clothes dried in short time with the warm prevailing breeze. Vanna cried at the sight of the brand-new washing machine. She sat with Tino to learn how to use it.

"No more rubbing clothes in the sink, Vanna mia."

She surprised the family the first time she arrived home with dinner from the restaurant.

"Arancini, pasta chi sardi, risotto with squid ink; what the hell is going on here?" asked Tino.

"I got a job cooking at Bacano. These are some of the benefits."

"Bacano? What Bacano?"

"A trattoria three blocks away."

"Vanna, we do not need the money."

"I want to do this out of enjoyment, not necessity. I love cooking."

Claudio and Lidia clapped. Tino kissed her and said, "if it gives you pleasure, go ahead, cook!"

"We are not complaining," said Lidia, "are we Claudio?"

"No, I'm content with this arrangement, Mother."

Lidia found Claudio happier since the move from Zafferia. He took her out to the beach, for gelato and explored their new city, finding interesting monuments and shops wherever they went. After Zafferia, every day was a novelty.

A month after they left the farm, excavating vehicles marched across the farms formerly of Crudelli and Liverani. Posts were dug and lines were drawn with red string for new streets and a new suburb.

Filipo Maresca watched them scratch their tentative markings from the highest point of his property, smiling as he imagined the houses paying him rent into perpetuity. The *Romeo y Julieta* cigars Pasquale Brinto brought to celebrate agreed with him. He puffed the first one to its end and went inside for a nap before dinner.

CHAPTER 24

Sicily, 1967

Al più' potente ceda il più' prodente.
It is better to bow than break.
- Sicilian proverb

Tino sweltered as he repaired the concrete balustrade leading up the apartment block. The hot mixture of concrete powder and water was setting quicker than he expected, forcing him to work fast to fashion a nice even result. A strong bond replaced the cracked damage, but the colour was different to the rest of the curved structure. The woman leaning over the balcony above was giving running commentary to a friend across the street in another apartment block.

"Looks different."

"No cracks. Of course it's different."

"The colour is different, you can tell."

"The concrete is new. What do you expect?" The woman opposite said 'ignore her' to Tino, adding "I've got cracks you can repair in my apartment anytime you want".

"Floozy." called out the first woman.

Tino ignored the patter, smoothed and shaved off the excess sludge, rounding the area dry with a trowel and sandpaper. He washed the concrete of his hands and wiped his brow.

"You deserve a drink."

Fuck, Brinto. Tino turned as if he didn't recognise the voice, feigning surprise as he saw him.

"Is Messina treating you well, Tino?"

He shook his hand and nodded. "Yes, Pasquale. We cannot complain."

"Come on, let me get you that drink."

They walked to a cafe a minute from the apartment, the owner bringing a granita for each of them.

"So, all is well then. I'm glad. Your wife has found work I see. She didn't appear to be a lady of leisure."

"No, Vanna is a cook at Bacano."

"Bacano. I know Gianno well."

Is there anyone you don't know, thought Tino. He was well versed in *quid pro quos* now. He recognised the set up and leaned in. "I, we are very appreciative for the trouble you have gone to in helping us resettle here. Is there something you are asking me to do for you?"

"Only if you are inclined to do so, Tino."

Brinto offered Tino a cigarette, which he declined. He lit up and blew the smoke over his shoulder.

"Some people, a group of seven owners near San Cataldo, near the Alcantara River are being less than cooperative about selling their land. Smaller farming blocks than yours, but the land sits on the side of a mountain and poses a risk."

"What risk?"

"Our engineer's opinion is that the foundations are weakening. One day they will all fall and damage houses we have built on the land below. The development has cost quite a lot to complete, and as owners, their stubbornness to sell puts our assets in jeopardy."

"And they won't repair their footings to strengthen the foundations?"

Brinto wagged his finger. "Too much money for them and they are not obliged by law, and so, we are at an impasse."

"How can I help? I am no engineer."

"Not in the sense you imply, but you are someone who has seen the logic of being cooperative for mutual benefit, are you not? Your wife works because she wants to, not because she has to, your children are free to explore this wonderful city, and you are working miracles everyday with your handyman prowess. The council is very impressed with your contribution. A managerial position is a certainty."

"You exaggerate my abilities, Mr Brinto. What can I say to them? They sound very firm in their position."

"Tomorrow we'll drive down and meet with them. Just say that your compensation for selling your land was very reasonable, nothing more, nothing less. They will not get a deal like yours, Tino. That was a one off; and may I say, well played. I turned a blind eye to you selling off most of your assets and livestock before we agreed. Very savvy the way you left just a little bit behind," said Brinto, tapping his head. "We just ask that you do this as a gesture of thanks to us."

Though blown by a gentle see breeze, Tino sweated, his palms clammy. He took a deep breath and said "Of course."

Brinto smiled and shook his hand. "I will be out front of your building at eight a.m. Don't worry about work, I will handle that for you." He slapped him on the back and dropped notes on the table for the granitas.

Once Brinto drove back past him with a wave, Tino pushed his drink away, waiting until he opened the door of his truck before vomiting on the road. He poured himself a glass of grappa at home and sat outside on the balcony. He had a second and showered before collapsing onto the bed, snoring within minutes. He didn't even wake when Vanna lifted his long legs onto his side when she came to bed.

Lidia appeared at the door. "Is Father Ok?" she whispered.

Vanna shrugged. "Probably tired."

The drive to San Cataldo gave Tino some cool morning sea breeze to snap him out of his lethargy.

"You look hungover."

Tino nodded.

"That home-made stuff you farmers make is stronger than the lolly water we drink." said Brinto. "Listen, Tino. I know

you're conflicted, my friend, but one hands washes the other,
no? This could have turned out far worse for you and your
family."

Tino nodded, the car turning back inland at Naxos to the
windy approach up the mountain to San Cataldo, the villages
dotted against the slopes either side of the Alcantara river.
They stopped outside a white brick school, faces showing at
the window. "Do well and follow my lead, Ok?"

They walked in, the talking coming to a dead stop. Brinto put
his briefcase down and addressed the group, varying from a
young couple to middle aged and older farmers whose
families lived here for generations.

"Thank you all for coming out this morning. As you are all
aware, the company I represent-"

"The Sidero standover family." interjected a bearded man
from the back of the room, towering over the rest of the
group.

"The Carnaso Group wishes to make a proposition to you, as
a group, that will benefit you all in the long run. Alongside
me is Augustino Liverani, a man who has aided the great
island of Sicily by selling his land so that the timber on it
could go towards the rebuilding that the *baracca* district
needs. He was paid well and with his family has made the
move to Messina. His wife and children are happy. But I will
let him tell his story. Augustino?"

"Thank you, Mr Brinto. My decision to sell my land was a
simple one. I had no use for the hardwood on my farm. My
children were not the farming type and we wanted to give

them opportunity in the city, so we moved. The Carnaso Group was very reasonable in their valuation of my land and our negotiation was smooth."

He saw the faces, blank, sceptical, some angry. An old lady near the front banged her walking stick onto the wooden floor, the sound echoing against the bare walls. She stood up and pointed her stick at him.

"You, you are an *ominicchio*! You may be tall, appear gentle, but you are small, playing in a game that bigger men, men with more power than you play. You may have gotten a deal from these people but do not try and fool me. I have no one else here with my blood. I will die here as my blood has for generations. No small apartment for me, no jail for to die in where no one will even know I am dead until my body is rancid." The woman walked closer to him, stood on her tippy-toes, laid her right hand on his shoulder and spat between his feet. She looked up at him.

"*Salvati figghiu.*" she whispered. Save yourself.

She shuffled to the door, oblivious to Brinto and walked home with her dog, a slow and old Alsatian. Brinto wasn't often spooked, but the woman made him uneasy, his left ear suddenly hot. He smiled and addressed the gathering, asking for silence.

"Ladies and gentlemen, we are happy to discuss a reasonable offer. But remember this, the offer you will receive if you all agree will be much greater than if only some of you agree. I encourage you to meet me, one by one to look at our offer and discuss with your family before deciding." Brinto suggested to Tino that he have some lunch at the local café, and he would collect him when finished.

The remaining six owners asked to hear their offers as a group. "We have nothing to hide from each other." said the bearded man who interjected earlier. Brinto unrolled a map with each property, taking out a red marker and writing a figure on each one, the anticipation palpable. With no figure to compare with, having owned the land for a minimum two generations, even the bearded man considered his options.

"The amounts you see on your properties will buy you a comparable property in the nearby area, or an apartment in Messina if you wish for a move to the sea." He turned to the bearded man as he seemed to be the most vocal. "Let me reassure you, Sir. While the Sidero family has some interest in our construction company, they hold a minority share. Companies need funding and with Sicily moving ahead, we cannot always be too picky when looking for investor capital."

"The offer is a reasonable one. We need to sit down and talk among ourselves."

"No one expects you to make such an important decision right here and now. That would be unreasonable. All I ask is that we set a time to reconvene. I will let you discuss a suitable time frame." Brinto walked out and waited in his car, lighting a cigarette. *I give them fifteen minutes* he said to himself. In ten, the bearded man came out to meet him.

"Elio. Elio Sciortino," said the man, extending his hand. "Can we meet here again in two weeks?"

"Same time?"

"Same time."

"Until then."

Tino was finishing a rustic penne pesto *al trapani* as Brinto joined him. Peckish himself he ordered the same.

"How did you go with them?" asked Tino.

"We did well; meeting again in two weeks. Make yourself available."

"What if the six agree and the old woman sits tight?"

"We can talk to her."

"Signora Alba?" asked the waiter, embarrassed at eavesdropping. "I wish you well. My apologies."

"Don't be shy, why do you say that?"

"She has a history that one. Only child, never married after her parents died. Many tried to woo her, but she just loved her own company, well, her and that old blind Alsatian of hers. She once shot a man in the leg when he was looking for his cat. She was convinced that he was trespassing with bad intentions for her dog and she fired. She still says she meant to kill him, but he escaped with a graze and a limp. Likes a drink, too."

"Did he find his cat?" asked Brinto, laughing.

"He never left home. The fucking thing was hiding."

"We will work on her." said Brinto once the waiter went back inside. "You did well. I thank you. You always find a spooky one like that Alba. Too much is made of superstition on this fucking island."

Brinto's left ear still felt hot after the old bat walked past him, and superstition was all that Tino could think about on the drive home.

CHAPTER 25

Crete, 1966

By all means marry: if you get a good wife, you'll become happy; if you get a bad one, you'll become a philosopher.
- Socrates

Hariklia looked down on most of the women in the town, but her respect for Fotini was growing as she observed her as she measured Litsa with care and precision. Litsa smiled at Fotini in a way that made Hariklia jealous. The material took a week to come from Athens. Hariklia was sceptical of Fotini's process, more of ignorance than knowledge; looking at the mass of satin and lace and how she would create the centrepiece of her only child's wedding day. The template was based on simple calico, fine-tuning the adjustments in the chest area, waist and measuring up for a high neck-lined bodice Hariklia insisted on. Rita and Sia looked on, laughing as Litsa made funny faces at them.

"Nectarios is lucky to have you." said Rita.

The colour drained from Litsa's face and she asked to sit down. She sat and cried. "Why am I crying, Mrs Fotini?" Hariklia rolled her eyes.

"I'm sorry." said Rita.

"No, Rita, don't be." said Litsa.

"You are going through an emotional time, my child." said Fotini.

"Ok, let's keep going." said Litsa.

"We're almost done."

Fotini sat from two in the afternoon till midnight, only breaking to feed and bathe the children, Sia refusing to have a bath without her. Her eyes ached as she hand-stitched the ends of the bodice and skirt together, placing the garment against the body form before sewing the section in between with the sewing machine. She laid out the back piece and drew the length of the split with a fine pencil and cut the length, before turning the front and back pieces inside out and stitching the ends. She then sewed the sides, before carefully turning the material the right way. The dress sat on the hanger and swung with the gentle breeze coming through the window. Nikos stared at the wall, pretending to be asleep as Fotini slumped into bed, exhausted beyond belief.

Hariklia tossed in bed, dragging the blanket off Stelios.

"What's eating you?" he said, rubbing his eyes with his palms.

"You haven't slept better since the day Nikos agreed the boy would marry Litsa. Can you tell me why?"

"The boy had to marry her after what he did. You agreed. The custom has always been the way of this island, a custom. Either that or he gets the gun. Anyway, she is damaged goods for anyone else."

The shove caught him off balance and his fat, round form fell to the floor, his elbow catching the sharp corner of the bedside table. Hariklia leant over the side and compounded his pain, connecting with a punch to his ear with a fist, Stelios' eyes rolling back before he felt the pain in his elbow and his ear throbbing. He rode the initial pain and tried to sit up, his balance failing him.

"How dare you-" he said on his knees. Hariklia leant over the edge of the bed, her neck muscles straining, her chin pointed at him.

"How dare I? You speak about our child like that and expect nothing? She is the only good thing to come from us, and you speak of her like she is fruit. You are no man, you are a cheat, full of your own vanity. VANITY!. You inherited all of this from your parents, but you have not added anything. You make us move to Chania, to a shitty little apartment so you can fleece tourists with boat rides as you wear a ridiculous Captain's hat, because no one else has thought of this caper before, tapping your nose like some wise oracle because real work is beneath you. Then we come back here, and you redeem your male pride by making the boy marry Litsa. What a tough man you are!"

Stelios stood, grabbing a pillow. He glared at Hariklia, still shaken. *You stork of a woman,* he said to himself.

"Are you done?" said Stelios.

Hariklia cackled. "You want more? GO! Out of my sight, go sleep in the spare room, the balcony, anywhere but here!"

The next morning, Nectarios sat in the back of Mr Pandelis' car as his father and Mr Pandelis spoke.

"Why did you agree?" Mr Pandelis whispered to Nikos.

Nikos shrugged. "What can we do? She's a nice girl, and it's the way things are done here."

Nectarios drifted away and off to sleep as the car rolled towards Chania. Mr Pandelis knew an excellent tailor who was expecting them. Nectarios liked Chania, but at the tailors, he slumped as Thanassis Matrakis of Matrakis & Sons measured him up, peering up at him with impatience over his shallow glasses.

"Stand up tall, boy." said Nikos, laughing at his posture. Nectarios stiffened up and complied, waiting until every measurement was taken.

"Give me ten days." said Thanassis.

They had lunch, treating themselves to a *pilafi* with fresh seafood, the men sneaking in a finger of *raki* before heading back. Nikos allowed Nectarios a sip, the rocket fuel burning his lips before the warmth travelled to his extremities, the light-headedness bringing on an easy sleep as they left the outskirts of Chania.

Nikos surveyed his work bench and sighed at the mountain of repairs.

"All this in one morning?" he asked Fotini.

"The weather's turning better. How was Chania?" asked Fotini, making a drinking gesture with her hand.

Nikos smiled. "We had one *raki*, one."

"Was he as handsome as you in his suit?"

"You tell me in thirteen days."

"What else will we see in thirteen days, my husband?"

"What do you mean?"

"Please, I don't know you? You have been elsewhere, like a movie is playing in your head, scenarios. I trust you, but at some point, you need to let me in on what is going on."

"I will, I promise. But not here. Once the children as asleep. Now let me start on these."

Fotini squinted at him. "You're not getting out of it."

Nikos worked on without rest until Fotini, now impatient, called him for dinner. Only one pair of shoes remained. He recognised them as Mr Pandelis' boots. He quickly turned them over; the stitching was strong, unbroken, and wondered why he dropped them off. He shook them and a small slip of paper fell out. He unfolded it with care and read the message to himself: *a package arrived for you from Australia.*

He sat to dinner and afterwards walked the shoes back to Mr Pandelis.

"Your shoes are done, Pandelis."

"Oh, thank you, Nikos."

Anthoula went inside and he took Nikos behind the counter. He pulled out a box the size of his hand and opened one side enough to see two envelopes.

"I better take this back, Pandelis."

"As you wish, Nikos. Goodnight."

He hurried back into his workroom and took out the envelopes. The thicker one had cash, the other a letter. He hid the cash in a drawer and opened the letter. Rita rushed in and jumped on his lap.

"Father do you love me or Sia more?"

"What a question to ask me," he said, tickling her until she almost peed. "You are my first princess, Sia my second. I have no favourites, understand?"

Rita kissed her Father on the cheek. "What does the letter say, Father?"

"Nothing - a receipt for a customer."

"Ok, bye Father. I love you."

"Not as much as I love you, angel."

He opened the letter and turned on his lamp. His Uncle Gerasimos' hand was impeccable.

From Port Melbourne (Australia)
Dear Nikos
I hope you and your family are well. I have been struggling
since your Thia Ilya left this earth, but I battle on. Sixteen

*years since I left you, and you will remember my promise - to
bring you over.*

*Well now I can. Unless some rufiano has sabotaged this
package, you will find some cash with this letter. You have
probably hidden the cash away and are reading the letter
first before you count the money. Trust me when I say I sent
enough to take you and your family to Athens by boat from
Souda, stay in a hotel and cover any unexpected expenses. A
friend of mine will meet you and arrange your ticket on the
Patrts to Australia. You may be waiting two weeks, at most a
month before you can leave, but my friend (his name is
Prokopis Papazoglou) will put you up and arrange the right
documentation. He is peculiar to some tastes but he is
someone you can trust.*

*Make haste to gather what you need and leave behind what
you do not. Bring your repair kit and your lovely wife's
sewing materials. Much money can be made here by both of
you with your skills, and a better education for your children.
I can not wait to see them and spoil them.*

*Papazoglou will tell me when you leave and when I will
receive you in Port Melbourne. The trip is long, about 30
days, and you will need to be strong for your family. This
country has been kind to me and will be to you too. Do not
respond to me. If you have made contact with Papazoglou
(his phone number in Athens is below) he will tell me the
process has started.*

Please join me. You will not regret the decision.

With love

Your Uncle Gerasimos
(they call me Gerry here)

Nikos shoved the letter in his draw with the money under a hessian cloth. Though only seven years older than Nikos, Gerasimos enjoyed teasing him about being his uncle. He was thirty-three when he left, taking his bride Ilya with him against his brother's wishes, Alexandros threatening him never to return if he boarded boat in Chania, wagging his finger as he hopped on Sifi's boat.

"I demand you stay here as your older brother. Once you leave, you cannot call yourself Cretan. You're not one of us anymore."

"Go to Iraklion and tell that to Kazantzakis." the last words he ever said to his brother.

They stayed in Athens for two weeks before boarding the *Patris*. They conceived their only child as they passed north of Socotra in the Arabian Sea. When the boy was born, Gerasimos and Ilya laughed to the confusion of the doctors, telling them he was so dark because he was conceived in the Arabian Sea. They named him Saki after *thalassaki*, the sea infinite as the boat sailed to Australia, no sponsor, no plans, only suitcases and open minds. He learned English on the boat, enough to convince the fourth mechanic he walked into to give him a job, a gargantuan man called Keith - swamped with cars and relieved not to have a pisshead working with him. He worked hard, learned more English and shared the occasional Greek swear word with him. *You bloody malaka*, Keith. Ilya made friends, Greeks and Italians sharing stories, minding each other's children as they worked to get by. When Saki was thirteen, Ilya had trouble breathing and chest pains, Saki hailing a taxi to Royal Melbourne, where she experienced further chest pains as a pulmonary embolism overworked her heart. Ilya died in the corridor as they

154

wheeled her into emergency, trying everything, but in vain. Now fifteen, Saki took his Father fishing any chance he could, the solitude and company giving him peace until the clouds lifted. Gerasimos no longer saw just Ilya's face in Saki but Saki's as well.

Nikos craved a cigarette and snuck outside with one. He craned his neck up at the stars and wondered how the hell his Uncle and his departed Ilya pulled it off; the journey, the new life, how they had the guts to go. The snap of fingers broke his thoughts.

"Come on, stamp it out and tell me what is in the letter."

"What letter?"

"What else has made you reach for a cigarette?"

He smiled. "Rita, Rita."

"She's not a baby anymore. What is going on?"

Nikos walked up close and whispered. "My Uncle Gerasimos is providing for us to go to Australia."

Fotini asked him to repeat himself.

"Is this the plan you had in mind when you said trust me?"

"Not exactly, but I knew something was going to come along."

"Come along and do what? Break a promise? Our son is about to be married. You stood up and agreed. How strong is your word?"

"Woman, my word is strong to those whose respect I have and whose love I crave; yours and the childrens'. Litsa is going through the motions, and the light has gone out of Nectarios' eyes. They are both unsure and the only person happy with all this is Stelios."

"This is too much. Pick up and leave? And leave them, her at the altar, to lead them this far after saying yes, no matter how bad an idea we think this marriage is?"

"We would be on a boat, to Australia, with other families like us. We can make this work. Your dressmaking skills, my shoemaking and repairs, Uncle Gerasimos says we can make lots of money, educate our children."

"Leave this behind?" reminded Fotini, slapping her hand on the house.

Nikos put his finger to his lips. Shh. "Mr Pandeli has wanted a house instead of two small rooms behind his shop as long as I have known him. It wouldn't go to waste." He waited as Fotini's mind ticked over.

"I'm afraid."

"Stelios will not realise we have gone."

"Forget Stelios. Litsa? Does she not deserve to know what is going on? We skip town like criminals? Easy for you men. Imagine you're being left at the altar. I need to sleep on this."

She went inside before coming back out, grabbing his left ear, yanking hard. "If I catch you smoking ever again, you're dead. Now come inside."

CHAPTER 26

Crete, 1966

Litsa stood in front of the mirror, the calico template of her wedding dress sitting perfectly on her. The bodice sat against her chest perfectly. Her breasts were firm and contoured but respectful and not straining hard against the material, and Hariklia approved. Fotini estimated the amount of give.

"The real one will sit a little firmer, Litsa. What do you think?"

"Beautiful, Mrs Fotini, beautiful." said Litsa, holding back tears.

Litsa stood unsure if she was emotional about the vision of her in a wedding dress or the life to come. Thinking about it twenty-four hours a day only served to muddle the two.

"Hariklia?" asked Fotini.

"So far, so good, but I'll hold my judgement until the day," said Hariklia, her long index finger poised as a judgement over her lip.

"How did I come from her?" whispered Litsa to Fotini.

"Now now, she's your Mother."

The dress was half off when Nectarios walked in.

"Hello Litsa."

Fotini stood between them, shoving him towards the door.

"Go inside - bad luck to see her in the dress." said Hariklia.

"Bye Nectarios." said Litsa, her eyes staying with his for a second. She waited for a spark, anything, but nothing came.

She walked back with her Mother, seeing the houses around her as drab prisons, living out her life here, the same-same greetings, the obligation, the love she didn't feel replaced with children, a life unfulfilled. She wondered how she got here, how they got here. Hariklia walked ahead in her long strides, oblivious to her daughter's fears and questions. The war left people in Crete happy simply to wake up, work, eat and sleep without the fear of terror; base needs to survive. Fear was replaced by insecurities of living a life devoid of true love, of boredom. The images came to her and tears streamed heavy down her face.

Hariklia ushered her inside, shut the gate before anyone else saw them and slapped her across the cheek, Litsa's face stung by her Mother's bony hand. The rough outline of her bony hand showed as the blood rose to her face.

"Do you think you're the only one locked into marriage without knowing, without being sure if he's right for you? What makes you so special?"

Litsa pushed her away. "You who have accepted this life, a life with a man so vain. Isn't that what you called him the night you kicked him out, vain? I can see this is not true love. Unlike every woman who accepted and settled without it, I don't want to!"

Hariklia smiled, a curled nasty smile as she leaned in closer.
"What a pity this insight came after you opened your legs
like a slut for the first boy who flashed his eyes at you."

She sipped the horror on Litsa's face, then strode up the stairs
and calmly made herself a coffee. She sat on the balcony,
waiting for the satisfaction of hearing her daughter's tears as
she came into the house.

Instead, Litsa sat on the garden chair. She decided to stare
down tradition, her parents, promises and the expectations
and not go through with this, even at the cost of saying no! at
the altar, wearing the embarrassment. *Nectarios would
survive*, she thought. Her Mother's silhouette was clear
against the afternoon sunlight, her outline sharp and bony.

No tears for you, Mother, she said to herself.

After dinner, Nikos and Fotini sent Sia with Rita across to
help Anthoula, though Rita knew they were going to have an
adult's talk and shook her head at them.

"Come on, Sia."

Nikos glanced at Fotini. "Well?"

"The children are safe here; they are loved, and they are well
provided for. We have no war to flee like our parents, Nikos.
We are being indulgent."

Nikos bowed his head.

"But," she continued, "what remains for them once their
schooling is finished? Manual labour, hard work like ours?

This world is changing. We take a risk, a big risk." She closed her eyes. "I had a dream last night, seagulls flying, some calling out to those on a beach to come with them, but they would not fly. My grandmother used to say dreaming about birds meant courage, taking risks and looking for something better. I am ready to take this chance for these three children."

"And Litsa?"

"Nectarios will have to tell her, in secret. Today I got the impression she is reluctant. Her Mother, that cactus, she showed no emotion, nothing. But Litsa, she is owed an explanation, for her sake, not her broken parents."

Nectarios took all this in from outside as he crouched under the window. He crept in around the front and knocked to announce his arrival.

"Ah, Nectarios. How were deliveries today?"

"Hard work but all done. What are we talking about, where are the girls?"

"Nectarios, sit down please."

"Don't trouble yourself, I heard everything."

"Everything?"

"Are we going to live with Uncle Gerasimos are we?"

"We have a lot to do, but yes, God willing."

"I will tell Litsa," said Nectarios. "I agree, she deserves to be told."

"Not before I tell you to," said Nikos. "I have to plan this properly. I am not worried about the Father or the Mother, but I want to be clean away before they realise we are gone."

"Mr Sifi could take us to Chania on his boat." said Nectarios.

"I know. Leave the details to me. You will say nothing, do you understand? We have one chance, no mistakes. Are you scared, son?"

"Yes, but I am more excited than scared."

"Let the past bury itself and the future provide." said Fotini.

"Amen." said Nikos. "From here, we go forward, no looking back. The wedding is five days away. We pack everything on the last night in case Stelios drops by."

Fotini unpicked the calico proforma of Litsa's dress, two hours of patient unpicking, her patient hands taking care not to shred any calico and create an imperfect template to guide the satin pieces. Precious little satin and lace to waste and she took her time, pinning and cutting each piece against the calico template. She made herself a coffee and began the slow process of guiding the butterfly stitching, passing the inverted margins of the front satin pieces to sit just under Litsa's rib cage. *The easy part is done*, said Fotini aloud. She began the long process of sewing the sides of the front and back pieces together, a cruder process than what professional dressmakers used, but in Fotini's hands the result was beautiful. Nikos marvelled at the result, with only a few scraps of satin curled up on the table below.

"What a shame, Probably the best dress you have ever made."

"I spent more time on this one than any other."

"This one was personal. I hope she has the chance to wear it one day and be happy."

A wind blew the front door wide open, threatening to lift and whirl the dress off its hanger. Nikos grabbed it as Fotini shut the door, pushing the rod into the hole in the concrete floor. Outside, debris flew in cyclonic patterns in the air, helpless. And Nikos wondered if the weather would thwart them and leave them helpless too.

CHAPTER 27

Crete, 1966

'Ήθελα να 'χα μια αγκαλιά
σαν θάλασσα μεγάλη
να χανεσαι μα οπου κι αν πας
κοντά μου να 'σαι παλι

I'd like to have the embrace
Like the mighty sea
To be lost, but no matter where I went
You'd be close to me

George Xylouris

Nikos approached Sifi's house. The lights were off. Nikos reflected on their time together and saw Sifi as a second Father. The time he nearly drowned stayed between him and Nikos.

You're crazy to want to fish in this weather.
Please, Mr Sifi.
Ok, a short trip.

A short trip alright, thought Nikos. Barely half a mile off the shore, the wind turned and almost turned the boat over, Nikos knocked off balance and not holding the mast as he navigated his way around to cover, the boat catapulting him headfirst into the water, swallowed up and dragged under. Only darkest blue wherever he turned, no idea which way he was facing. Only by flailing around did he feel a rope, the relief of a mighty pull as Sifi dragged him from under the boat and over the metal railings, landing on his shoulder with a mighty thump, heavy from the water he absorbed. Nikos did not board a boat since. When Sifi offered to take Nectarios fishing, Nikos only let them fish off the wharf and Sifi didn't push the issue.

Nikos tapped the window next to Sifi's bed and waited for the creak and the grumble.

"Come in, Nikos."

"Thanks for getting up."

"You wouldn't tap for something unimportant at this hour. Is this about Nectarios?"

"A lot of things." said Nikos.

Sifi got up and brought over the *raki* and two small glasses. "A week before your Uncle Gerasimos left, he came to me. Your Father got drunk three, four times where you are sitting right now after he left. And now, you are here too. Tell me."

In spite of himself, Nikos smiled. "Funny that you mention Gerasimos. He has sent money for us to go to Australia with him."

"What?"

"He says we can make a life, educate our children, and Fotini has agreed to go."

"And how do I fit in here?" Sifi poured the raki and handed one to Nikos.

"The children, Nectarios and Litsa, they are not so sure-"

"Stop. You are thinking of leaving before the wedding and breaking your word?" Sifi rifled his drink down and poured another.

"We will tell the girl."

"But, if I understand you, not the parents."

"Yes."

"You are not unaware of the consequences of doing this are you? You are known as a practical, principled man here, Nikos."

"I am not worried about reputation, Sifi."

"That man Stelios is a fat, wind-filled braggart, all puffed up." said Sifi, blowing himself into a ball. "And that woman who married him, what a sour creature she is. And yet, what you leave behind, the ill feeling, that has to go somewhere."

"Are you suggesting we would be cursed if we left, Sifi?"

"What curse? I don't believe in any fucking *katara*, Nikos. I'm simply saying that, I don't know what I'm saying. If the girl is not interested in marrying your boy and vice versa, getting married is a curse in itself."

"Sifi, I want you to take us to Chania."

"Say that again?"

"Two boats leave Chania for Pireaus before the wedding. Today is Tuesday. The boat leaves Chania early morning on Thursday and Saturday, and I was hoping-"

"That I smuggle you off the island to Chania?"

"Yes."

"Rough weather is forecast tomorrow night, and who knows what happens on Friday night?"

"Does that mean you will take us?"

"Nikos, when Gerasimos sat here, he pleaded his case to me like he needed my approval. Alexandros never knew he came here. I will tell you the same thing I told him - go with your heart but beware of what you crave. And give me that glass back, you have too much to do."

Nikos held back tears. "Sifi-"

"Shh. Save the tears for when you hug me before I leave Chania to come back. Now go. Promise me the girl is let down easy."

Nikos grabbed the glass back and took the raki in one shot. He hugged Sifi and walked back home. *May your shoulders be broad* Sifi said to himself, unsure who he was saying it too.

Wednesday morning, and all shutters went up throughout the town as the northerly wind, the warm *voriá*, blew without mercy, the waves crashing over the road that ran along the beach, wand waves a mile off the beach over two metres high. Historically, the *voriá* in Tavroniti lasted anywhere from two to five days in summer, but in autumn it was a lottery. Nikos tried to take his mind off the weather, but with everyone inside and little work on his bench, he was tempted to sneak another cigarette, before thinking better. Fotini was similarly at a loss, the dress completed and no alterations waiting. The time had come to return to Chania to collect Necatrios' suit and the charade had to continue. Mr Pandeli drove them again, the trip silent. Nikos nursed a headache. *Absurd,* he thought, after only one shot of Sifi's *raki.* Nectarios moved wondered how each step would work; the stealing away, the trip to Piraeus, the long boat to Australia. He drifted off to sleep at Daratsos before his Father woke him with a slap on the knee as they parked outside Matrakis and Sons.

"Wake up, you're about to wear a suit."

Thanassis Matrakis assessed Nectarios and checked the pants, tugging at the front. "Yes, bravo, waist fit is fine." The shirt sat a little bunched, Thanassis reassuring him it would settle once the jacket sat on his shoulders, Nectarios was developing a nice V-shape torso now and the jacket followed it to the approval of his Father. After being to forced walk and turn, Nectarios was happy to take the suit and pants off. He took the thin black tie, a black belt and black shoes. Nikos paid Thanassis, who bowed and thanked them for their patronage, wishing them the happiest of days for Sunday. The wind found another gear as the turned off the main highway into Tavroniti.

"You have visitors." said Mr Pandeli, pointing to Stelios' car, parked right outside their front door.

They walked around the back and Nikos bristled, Stelios sitting at the head of the table. Despite the glances from Hariklia and Fotini, he stayed put.

"We thought we would drop in before the momentous day Nikos."

"Maybe one day we can visit you at your lovely house."

"How about we celebrate at our house?"

"Well naturally, Stelios," said Hariklia. "After all, we have more room."

"That sounds fine, Hariklia," said Fotini. "We will each bring some food and have a great afternoon. I'm excited, aren't you?"

"Yes, of course." said Hariklia, digging deep to find some enthusiasm.

"Mr and Mrs Sfirakis, do you mind if Litsa and I have a word by ourselves outside for a moment?"

Stelios glanced at Hariklia, who shrugged her shoulders. "I don't see why not."

Nectarios led Litsa outside and sat her with her back to the window. He held her hand.

"How have you been?" he asked.

"I am scared and unsure."

"Your parents are happy."

Litsa contorted her face in disgust. "Hariklia is making us play happy families. We had a row when I told her I wasn't sure about this."

"I'm not sure either. When you looked me in the eye the other day, I felt-"

"Aroused at seeing my body?" Litsa laughed nervously.

"Yes, obviously, like I had never seen your body before. But is that enough for a lifetime together?"

"Exactly! How do we know what life will bring or how we will be in five or ten years? How would we be with our own children without true love from the start?"

"Are you saying we wait until we are older?"

"No. I am saying we do not marry at all." Litsa tried not to sound mean but could not help sounding bitter.

" I understand."

"You do?"

"Yes. Actually, this is kind of strange, but-"

"Tell me."

"My Father's uncle, well, he's only a few years older than him, he lives in Australia and has given us money to live with him."

Litsa's face went pale and her hand limp. Hariklia called out to them but Litsa heard nothing, fixated on Nectarios' eyes.

"One moment, Mrs Sfirakis." Nectarios called out.

"You're leaving?"

"Yes."

"Well at least you're telling me, so thank you I suppose."

"I didn't want to leave you at the altar and not say anything."

"Litsa!" called Hariklia again.

"We better go in before she suspects something." said Nectarios.

"Meet me around the corner from my house at seven tomorrow night. If you don't see me - wait. Please."

They walked back in. "The lovebirds," said Stelios, beaming. "I cannot wait to walk you down the aisle, my little angel." Sia and Rita swarmed Litsa with kisses.

"Me too, Father."

The wind had let up for an hour, but Nikos knew it would swing around again in the late afternoon. After the Sfirakis family left, he walked across to Sifi.

"What do you say?" asked Nikos, optimistic.

"Not tonight - the flags are as still as a rock. But the *voriá*, she will return. Friday night should be calm enough. Meet me here at two a.m. Saturday morning. I usually go fishing at three anyway so if we are quiet, we won't raise any alarm. We will need two trips from here to the boat. Pack and pray for calm seas."

Barely an hour later, the wind picked up again, measuring nine beaufort in Chania and on Thursday, eleven before dropping to a gentle three by the evening. Nikos and Fotini spent the day 'cleaning up' as they told the girls, deciding what would stay and what would come with them. Neither of them were hoarders, and the job was done by dinner, each suitcase full of possessions laid out ready to be packed. Nikos and Fotini listened for the wind as they went to bed.

"This will all turn out well." said Nikos, squeezing her hand.

"I hope so." said Fotini.

"Remember the seagulls, my love. Goodnight."

On Friday morning, Mr Pandelis drove Fotini to Litsa's house to deliver the dress. Hariklia was watering the back garden. Litsa opened the door, eyes sunken and hair a mess.

"Your dress is here, Litsa."

Litsa hand shaped her hair, embarrassed at opening the door in an unkempt state. "Sorry, Mrs Fotini."

Litsa was unprepared and tried her best to feign delight, holding her hands to her mouth and opening her eyes. "It is so beautiful, Mrs Fotini! Thank you." She took the dress, holding it up to the light and for a moment wished she was getting married. She sensed the presence of her Mother walking in and turned to show it to her. "Mother?"

"Yes, lovely." she said, with a quick glance up and down and a cursory smile. "I presume you will be at the *esperinó* tonight so the children can take communion before Sunday?"

"Of course."

"Oh, one more thing - do you have a best man?"

"Yes, Sifi. He has been a close friend of the family."

Hariklia raised her eyebrows. "Curious age difference, but we are where we are. I am glad we divided these preparations up between us. My husband is quite the proud man, but I was not going to allow him to fleece you. I am not the friendliest of people, but I have principles. We will have a nice dinner here after the wedding. You have done a lovely job with the dress." Hariklia wondered if a tear would escape her eye and when nothing came and the moment passed, she returned to her gardening.

"That is as close as I have seen her come to showing emotion." said Litsa.

"She is who she is, my girl." Fotini hugged her, Litsa hanging on for an eternity, Fotini letting her cling as long as she needed. She kissed Litsa on the forehead and walked back to the car.

"Strange family that one." said Mr Pandeli.

"As God made us." said Fotini.

Fotini found Nectarios when she walked back into the house. "What did you tell her?"

"Who, Litsa?"

"Yes, Litsa. She looks like she has seen a ghost."

"I am meeting her tonight to tell her."

"Tonight is the *esperinó*. How will you tell her?"

"I was going to meet her around seven."

"What did you two talk about outside when they were here?"

"I, I -nothing."

"Son, you are a bad liar."

"We agreed that we weren't ready to marry."

"And?" she asked, coaxing the rest out of him.

"That we were leaving to go to Australia."

"Did you tell her when?"

"No. I promise."

She believed him. "Probably better that you don't."

"Why?"

"The baby wasn't the only thing that died inside that girl. She is suffering, and won't survive in that house, not with that insufferable parents God gave her. How that beautiful flower came from that soil I will never understand."

"What can we do, Mother?"

Fotini shrugged. "Nothing, we can only control what we have to do. Say whatever final words you need to, but do not tell her we are leaving tomorrow morning."

The *esperinó* commenced at six p.m., the small church two-thirds full. Litsa sat halfway down on the left with her Mother, two rows in front of Fotini and the girls. Stelios sat spread legged in the front row, while Nectarios and Nikos stood along the side next to the icon of the Prophet Elijah, his pensive form peering up at the raven who fed him. Pater Manousso scanned the congregation as he recited the Lord's Prayer. As he offered communion, Litsa lined up early with Hariklia, Stelios joining them.

"Ready for Sunday, Litsa?" asked Pater Manousso.

"Yes, Father." said Litsa, with smile.

"Hariklia, Stelios, so happy this has been sorted out so maturely between your families."

Nikos and Fotini waited until the end to join the line and take communion. When they left the church, Litsa was being ushered away by her parents, keen to evade the gossip outside.

Litsa nodded for confirmation and Nectarios nodded back, flashing four fingers twice at her, waiting for her to nod back. Nikos did his cross, meeting eyes with the icon Saint Nikolaos for what he thought was the last time.

They rushed home and began packing after the girls fell asleep, grateful that they did the hard work the day before. It would have been impossible to pick and choose in the night without waking them. Nikos picked up some of the equipment from his pile to be discarded, and fondly held up a pair of pliers he had replaced.

"We don't have time for nostalgia, Nikos. If it has not been used in six months, say goodbye. Come on, we are running out of time."

"He scooped the pile into a hessian bag which he dumped into the bin outside. Fotini's assortment of needles, threads, everything but the now outdated sewing machine was neatly packed into a suitcase of its own.

"I'm off to say goodbye to Litsa." said Nectarios.

"Remember what I said." said Fotini, pointing at him.

"Yes, Mother."

It was ten past eight when he made. Litsa was waiting, cross-armed and tapping her feet.

"What time do you call this?"

"I'm sorry, we're-"

The scowl on her face made her unrecognisable to Nectarios.
"Packing?"

"Well, yes."

"So, when do you leave?"

"Depends on the weather."

"How are you getting to Chania?"

"By boat."

"Sifi?"

"Yes."

"Ok. Well, I better go back before they realise I'm out. A
grand adventure, all of this. I curse the day I teased you from
my balcony, Nectarios."

"How did we know this would happen?"

"You're right. I deserve to stay here in this hell hole while
you explore new lands. Perhaps you'll impregnate another
girl and things will turn out rosy next time."

"Why are you being so bitter?"

"Bitter? That's a heavy word for a little boy."

"Ok, you know what? I'm going."

He kissed her on the cheek. "Have a good life, Litsa."

He walked ten steps and turned around. She was already gone.

Nikos saw his face first as he walked back in. "Stop, talk to me. What happened?"

"She was rude and bitter. I was happy to say goodbye to her."

"She's jealous of us leaving, not because the wedding won't happen."

"How was I so close to marrying *that*?"

Fotini gave him a slap on the cheek. "Show some respect. We have names. Now go pack your things, make a final pass over your room and stop sulking."

Nikos exhaled in relief that he had everything he needed, and a heavy knock startled him. Sifi walked in and smiled.

"So, you're finally ready. Destiny awaits." he said with his arms spread out above in an exaggerated manner. His breath stunk of *raki* and Nikos' eyes opened in horror.

"Oh no, Sifi. When did you start drinking?"

"Ooh, about three hours ago."

"Fotini, coffee, lots of coffee."

"I'm sorry, Nikos. I was thinking of you, your family, and I started. One, two, eight, I lost count. Can I sleep here?" he asked, knocking his head against the concrete wall as he fell onto the small couch in the workroom.

"What in God's name is this?" yelled Fotini.

"What you see." said Nikos.

"How are we going to go now?"

"Start the coffees going and I'll sort him out."

"Already on. Make sure he doesn't wake the girls."

Nectarios laughed as he walked in. In the chaos, with time ticking down faster than time, there it was; the sadness, humour and emotion that made this island. But he stood here, laughing, as the man who would take them on the first leg of their one-way journey to the unknown was drunk, unable to walk straight yet alone operate a motorised fishing boat.

They decided to let him sleep until ten. They woke him and he stared as if transported to another land, before his vision cleared and he smelled the thick coffee. Fotini blew it cool for him and coaxed him to drink it like a child taking medicine.

"*Metrio?*"

"No, unsweetened."

"I prefer *metrio*."

"Drink this and the next one I'll make *metrio*."

"That sounds fair." Sifi said with a stifled laugh, aware of Fotini's glare. He sipped it, screwing his mouth up.

Three coffees later, he tried walking to his house and back. He smiled at the moon, nodding with approval at the waning crescent. *Perfect for snapper* he said to himself. He managed the return trip without swaying and declared *I'm ready!* as he walked back inside, before going shh to Nikos and Fotini.

Nikos set the alarm to his tried and true clock to two a.m. Nikos slept on the floor of his work room while Sifi tried in vain to sleep on the couch, wired from the coffees. At two, they both sat bolt upright. Nikos woke Fotini and Nectarios and they assembled their suitcases by the door. Sifi brought his truck around and with Nectarios loaded up. They finally woke the girls and told them they were going on holiday, Sia jumping for joy but Rita mute and hesitant.

"I'll take the girls and Nikos first." said Sifi. The girls sat in the rear tray, the suitcases shifting with every bump and turn, Sia loving the movement of air through her hair. The night was cool with the brutal *voriá* gone, replaced by a gentle breeze. The drive to Kolymvari where Sifi's boat was moored took seven minutes. The wharf was empty, and Nikos sat the girls on suitcases as Sifi went back for Nectarios and Fotini.

"Father, this is a lot of packing for a holiday." said Rita.

"There's no fooling you."

"What is going on?"

"We are moving to Athens, and after, Australia."

"Australia? What is Australia? What about the wedding?"

"There is no wedding, Rita."

"I'm confused."

"We all are, my girl."

"So where is Australia?"

"A country where families like us have moved to, for a better life."

"But we weren't having a bad life here." she said, shrugging.

"No, but everything will become clear with time."

"How long will it take?"

"A few days." he said, his eyes giving him away.

"Another country will take more than a few days, Father. Why are you lying to me?" Rita started crying, and Sia went out in sympathy with her.

"I'll be with you until Athens." said the voice. Litsa stood a few metres away, a suitcase in each hand.

"Litsa?"

"Yes, Mr Nikos. I'm coming with you, to Athens that is."

"But your parents-"

"Forget them. I have. I have my own money. Well, I borrowed some from them. I worked out that they owe me for the way they have treated me, so I won't be imposing financially on you."

181

"You can't come with us. What will they think?"

"Are you worried they will think you kidnapped me? Far from it. When Nectarios told me you were leaving, I thought it was unfair, he gets to escape this place while I am punished. So, here I am. Accompany me to Athens, and I will take care of myself."

Nikos lost track of time and was confused when Sifi's truck returned. Fotini peered in the darkness.

"Litsa?" said Fotini, glaring at Nectarios.

"You told her what time we were leaving didn't you?"

"No Mother, I swear on my life."

"How else would she know?"

Litsa crossed her arms, defiant as Fotini walked towards her. "You better take me, or I will walk all the way back to my house and raise the alarm. My life is already worth nothing if I stay, so either take me or you won't go either."

Nikos placated her with a gentle arm on the shoulder, her breathing rapid. She burst out in tears as Fotini put her arms around her, her bravado gone.

"She is coming. No discussion." said Fotini. "Now we had better go." said Fotini.

"I'm unhappy too." said Rita, holding Litsa's hand.

Sifi helped them onto his boat, Nikos backing away. He let him work up the courage as he asked Fotini, Litsa and the girls to sit on the bench seat at the stern and asked Nectarios to help coax his Father onboard.

"Come on, that only happens once in a lifetime." said Sifi, smiling.

Nikos put his arm out, falling onto the boat with Sifi and Nectarios grabbing an arm each, his daughters giggling as he grabbed the mast for balance. He walked to the covered area near the wheel for safety. Nectarios gathered in the rope.

"And we are off!" declared Sifi, starting the diesel motor, the splutter giving way to a steady hum. Sifi pulled in the rope and took the wheel. Sifi's truck shrunk as they moved slowly past the flatness of Tavroniti's beach. Lights ran into each other; landmarks indistinguishable. Nikos lost his bearings until Sifi slowed to pass between Ayia Marina and Ayi Theodori, the boat gliding smoothly across the calm dark blue.

Sia huddled against Litsa for warmth. "Can you come to visit us in Australia?" she asked, pronouncing Australia as As-alia.

"Maybe a bit far to me to come, Sia." said Litsa, squeezing her cheeks, the pinch coming up red in the cold.

"Why don't you come live with us?" asked Rita.

"I wish I could, Rita, but I don't want to make this situation any worse."

"Don't your parents love you?"

"In their own way, yes."

Nectarios sat next to her and held her hand. "I understand now."

"When you told me you were leaving, I was heartbroken. Not because of you though." she said, smiling.

"Thank you." he said, laughing. "But I understand. This has changed us."

"Oh, I am changed, I can tell you. You, not so much. I don't think you will change, Nectarios. You are a sweet boy and you will become a sweet man, a man I would love to be with, in ten, fifteen years, but you love women and have no self-control. Once you settle in Australia, you will find trouble again, mark my words." Nectarios shivered as the words sunk in.

Litsa fell silent as she recalled her conversation with Pater Manousso the previous night. After the tense exchange with Nectarios, she walked around to the church, where the Priest was closing up. He turned the key the other way again when he saw her face and invited her in.

What is wrong, child?

What I tell you is private and confidential, correct?

Yes, Litsa. What bothers you?

Nectarios, Nikos, Fotini, the girls. They are leaving the island tomorrow morning. Going to Athens and Australia.

And you want me to stop them?

God no. I want to go to Athens with them.

For what purpose, child?

To find my own life. I am eighteen and I know living with these people will be a slow death.

That is a harsh judgement of your parents, child. Every parent does what they can.

And now I need to make my own way.

What is that? I'm all ears.

I will find that when I reach Athens.

If you think I am going to intervene and stop you, you can be certain I won't. I have known both of your parents since they were born. If we are being honest, to this day I cannot understand how you came from them. But-

But?

In theory you are doing the wrong thing. But we live in times where these things are possible. No one has our island under their thumb, and we are free to consider such choices. Will you choose wisely or choose whatever comes your way? With being eighteen and being in charge of your own affairs comes responsibility. Me, I am responsible for showing up

*tomorrow at two p.m. expecting to conduct a wedding
service, knowing full well that you will not even be on the
island. Your parents will know before that you have gone.
What you are leaving behind is a mess. Good luck my child
and may God guide you.*

Thank you, Pater.

Litsa kissed his hand and walked out into the night. She
made sure her parents heard her bedroom door shut and
started packing. She walked to Kolymvari once, the walk
taking over an hour, but she was eight. At one a.m., she
walked fast until she reached the small wharf, and seeing
Sifi's boat, found a spot behind some bushes. The adrenaline
drove her at a fast pace, and only as she sat in wait did her
legs ache. Sifi came with Nikos and the girls about ten
minutes after she did.

They were alone on the water until the bright lights of Chania
came into view, the boat slowing and drifting as Sifi scanned
for a spot in the Old Venetian Bay. He guided the boat,
drifting past the ancient lighthouse and alongside the
concrete jetty closest to the Guardhouse. It was a longer walk
but he was less likely to be moved on by anyone. They got
off and made the slow walk along the concrete walkway that
arced towards the town, passing no one on the way.

"What now, Sifi?" asked Fotini.

"I have a friend who will give you a room to rest until you
leave. The boat leaves from Souda Bay at eight a.m. You
need to have your ticket 30 minutes before to board."

They walked past the first block of cafes and taverns, pitch
black inside and out, turned down between two buildings.
Sifi stopped and knocked loudly on the glass pane of a door.
They waited for over a minute until a barrage of cursing
travelling down the stairs got louder.

"Who the fuck is it this time I swear to Christ himself I will
lose my mind one day and they will finally put me away,
fuck!"

The door opened and the thin man's heavily bearded face
changed from a terrible scowl to welcome surprise.

"Sifi!"

"Fanouri!"

They hugged, Sifi crushing his freshly woken friend before
Fanouris led them inside. He switched on the light and
checked the alley to be sure no one was watching, a habit he
couldn't shake.

"So, lovely family. I am Fanouris Herouvim."

"Herouvim?" asked Nikos.

He held up two fingers.

"Two Jewish groups existed in Greece; the *Romaniotes* and
the *Sephardi*. My family was from the Romaniotes. They are
the true Greek Jews, here for centuries. Most settled in Corfu,
Athens, Ioannina but my Father's Father came here and set
up business, a restaurant. My parents died when the Nazis
surprised us, but they had time to hide us - my sister and I -

under the house. They never found us, but we heard the two shots." He mimed a pistol shot to his head. "One bullet each. Some local resistance fighters took us in. My parents were part of the community, and I remain so. But I must apologise for the swearing as I came to the door - a reflex. They came at night too."

In spite of their collective fatigue and the hour being nearly four a.m., the family was speechless, until little Sia broke the silence. "You are very hairy, Fanouris."

Fanouris hugged the girl and said, "And you are very cheeky, little one. Come, let me show you to your rooms. You are leaving tomorrow from Souda, yes?"

"Yes." said Nikos. "Thank you for your generosity, Fanouris.

"Anything for this island, this man I call Uncle Sifi even though he hates the Uncle, I owe it everything. Please, rest and I will wake you at six. We will have a proper breakfast and some coffee. You don't want that shit they give you on the boat to Piraeus."

The beds were neatly arranged in two rooms. They all collapsed as one, the waiting and skulking taking its toll.

Nikos jumped at the knock at six. A breeze crept under the windowsill, a shrill whistle he remembered. He jammed the edge of the curtain in to muffle the noise. He touched Fotini's shoulder and thanked God she was not yellow and hot.

Fanouris waited patiently, sipping his coffee in the corridor. Sifi stirred in the couch, releasing a loud fart as he stretched out, much to Nectarios' amusement.

"Wait till you're my age. Air escapes from everywhere."

Fanouris led them the short walk to some tables outside a cafe. "Quick, sit down and I'll have you fed fast."

"This is his place." said Sifi.

Fanouris came out with a jar of crushed olives and a jug of iced water with wedges of lemon. "First, eat a spoonful of olives and wash down with the water," he said. "Stops motion sickness, I promise you."

The girls screwed their noses up before Litsa took the lead, eating them and going *mmm, yummy*. The girls followed. After some fried eggs with butter cream, toast and coffees, Fanouris tapped his watch. He went to bring his truck around and Sifi addressed them.

"This is hard, so I am going to walk back to my boat. I am going to go fishing as I was supposed to so nobody has any idea what has happened. I love you all, and I wish you all well. May God treat you well, may you work hard and be rewarded. You are the last of your line that I will ever see. I will never forget you."

Nikos cried as he hugged him, before Sifi pushed him away. "Your ride is here, go." Litsa, Fotini and the girls hugged him. He pulled Nectarios in tight and whispered into his ear. "Next time, if you are going to pull out, pull out you little bastard." He cried and laughed as he took a look at his face. "Go well and live like the mountains behind us."

Nikos loaded the truck and walked back to Sifi. He reached into his pocket and gave him an envelope. Sifi raised his hands in protest.

"No, go fuck yourself. I will not accept anything, Nikos."

"No, you hard-headed bastard. Give this to Mr Pandeli - in secret, under his door. I ran out of time."

Sifi shook the envelope, heard the jangle of keys and smiled.

"You are a decent man, Nikos. He will appreciate it and understand."

"When all hell breaks loose, remember to tell them you were going to be Nectarios' best man."

He smiled. "Thank you. I will." They took a last long at each other, before Sifi walked to his boat.

Fanouris drove them to Souda Bay, directing them to the ticket office. Nikos turned to Litsa.

"Are you sure about what you are doing?" *Hurry up* came the shout from the back of the line.

"I have never been so sure in my life, Mr Nikos."

"Four adults, two children please." he said to the cashier, huffing at Nikos for holding up the line. The bell sounded and they lined up. A woman approached Nikos as they neared the front of the queue. He was aware of her odour before he saw her. She was old and short, her teeth yellow, one gold and uneven like broken bricks. Her hair was strangely black for a woman her age. Her jowls moving as she spoke.

"You are fleeing something, are you not?"

"What are you talking about?" said Nikos, her foul odour hitting him a few seconds later.

"So obvious, and this girl," she said, pointing to Litsa, "she is not your own. You can flee the land, but the sin will follow." She walked backwards a step and turned to face Nectarios.

"And you, you shielding your body - you are the cause of this mess, aren't you? Shh, don't answer, your face is tight with guilt." She paused. "May you never have a son to carry your shame into the next generation."

"Ok gypsy, move on." said a man in uniform, placing his hands on her shoulder.

"Do not touch me!" yelled the woman, adjusting the scarf over her shoulder. The man walked back and apologised. "I'm sorry Sir. She tries to hustle passengers for money. She curses them and asks for money to reverse them with stupid incantations. Pay no mind to her. Have a pleasant trip."

Nectarios followed the woman the whole way until she disappeared out of view, mingled with the now swollen crowd of people of the concrete walkway. "Ignore the witch," said Fanouris. "I better go back to work. I wish you all well and may God's hand guide you safely." They hugged him quickly and were ushered onto the gangplank.

Nikos spotted two rows of four seats facing each other near the back. They shoved their suitcases underneath their seats. A movement from outside the boat caught Nectarios' eye. The witch stood and waved, a crooked smile showing her crooked yellowed teeth. He recoiled and sat back, his heart beating fast. A minute later, the large vessel vibrated, the huge motor coming to life, churning the water behind, before jerking forward sending the girls' legs in the air, accompanied by laughter. Litsa smiled at Nectarios, which Nectarios registered as pity. Fotini did her cross as they passed the church of *Panagia* at Kera, the others following suit. They settled back as the boat picked up speed over deeper water.

About a mile off Tavroniti beach, Sifi sweated the *rakí*, laughing at his luck, plundering, snapper and cod willing and abundant, a four hour catch taken in little over an hour. "Thanks be to God," he said. A final reward came with a large octopus that fought above and below the water. This one's for you, Penelope he said aloud. He sailed back and was relieved to see nothing and no one on the wharf except his truck. His watch said eight-thirty.

All hell would break loose in time, thought Sifi. That could wait.

CHAPTER 28

Sicily, 1967

*Tante cose sono dolorose in una
famiglia: il fornello che fa fumo, il tetto
rotto che piove, la moglie che urla e il
marito ubriaco.*

So many things can be painful in a
family: a smoking oven, a broken roof
that lets water through, a screaming
wife and a drunk husband.
- Sicilian proverb

Vanna ran her eyes over the pans she had going; *polpetti in sugo*, squid ink risotto and the *pasta chi sardi*. She managed all three, adding white wine, parmigiano and seasoning, a flurry of hands as her assistant cook looked on in wonder. The dim-witted nephew Gianno let into the kitchen was more of a hindrance than a help to Vanna, feeling she had to babysit him through basic preparation and techniques. She was better off on her own. Yet, her arrangement was one she would not find anywhere else, and her position was as safe as houses. Gianno needed her more than the reverse. Vanna was not inclined to leverage the situation; she was comforted knowing she was on the right side of the ledger.

"Quick, Rocco, give these to Gianno"

The busy kitchen was given the all clear after nine-thirty, Vanna exhaling with relief as Gianno walked through the double doors with a smile. He held out a note for Vanna.

"I usually kept the tips, or to be honest, the food never attracted much. But tonight, we have tips, so please, enjoy and keep it up." He turned to his nephew. "Learn from her *scemu*, keep your eyes open."

"He *was* helpful today."

"Don't lie to make him feel better. If he opened his eyes and listened, one day."

"One day what, this? I'm only here as a favour to your brother." said Rocco, his hair covering his eyes.

"Tell me what you really think." He smiled at Vanna. "Look, things have never been better here. I hope nothing changes. I'll clean up with Rocco, you go home."

"Absolutely not. Cleaning is part of my job."

"Ok, as you wish, but I'll help so we are all home sooner."

"Gianno, is there a Mrs Bacano?"

"No," answered Rocco, smirking. "She made Uncle Gianno choose between a failing restaurant and her."

"And you chose to stay?" asked Vanna.

Gianno shot a glare at Rocco. "I am a *testa dura*, Vanna. I thought if I made this work, she would stay and be proud of me, but instead I lost her and came close to losing this as well. There is still a lot of work to do-"

"Stop! What about your wife?"

Gianno raised his finger. "*Ex*-wife. Paola. We are not divorced, but she moved out. She lives a block away, but she never crosses this street."

"So, either she holds out hope or she is mentally torturing you."

"Please, Vanna, she mentally tortured me when we were happy."

Vanna walked the tables, the lighting dark, walls bare and bleak. "What if we gave this place a once over?"

Rocco clapped. "I told him to freshen this place up. A Funeral Parlour has more atmosphere than this place."

"Shut up, you ignorant twit!" shouted Gianno, hurling a chair in his direction, the chair falling well short.

"Can you paint better than you throw, Gianno?" asked Vanna.

He shrugged. "I suppose."

"My husband is a miracle worker with maintenance. He will work out a price we are all happy with."

When Vanna walked in, she found a note on the kitchen table.

> We have gone for a gelato. Back soon.
> Claudio & Lidia

Claudio and Lidia embraced the city move without difficulty, familiarising themselves with Messina, learning where not to go and both amazed at the way the city rebuilt itself after the catastrophic earthquake of 1908. They made a list of things to see and discovered hidden gems. Lidia and her brother discovered a love for antique furniture, Lidia appreciating the style, colours and finish and Claudio imagining how the piece was put together. Vanna smiled as she read the note again, the bond of her children strengthened with the move and Claudio's protective, loving nature.

Lidia caught the eye of many men already in Messina. Claudio's now more subtle look was no less effective at warding off any protracted ogling. Lidia didn't see her brother as a murderer, but a protective brother, blood who protected blood. With time, his ultimate act of protecting Caterina took on a sense of nobility to her. She was relieved that he was more mellow here, and sometimes she forgot what happened in Zafferia, as if they had all passed through a door through time; the act being in a previous life.

Tino snored, again diagonal across the bed and a glass on the bedside table. She sniffed the glass, her eyes watering at the fumes of the grappa rushed up her nostrils. She sat outside to enjoy the sea breeze. It was after eleven and Lidia and Claudio would be back soon. She liked watching them walk up to their apartment, the view of the Madonnina del Porto di Messina clear at the end of the curled natural bay to her right, the lights of Reggio Calabria in the distance. Vanna felt Tino's presence behind her and she moved her chair to accommodate him.

"How was work?"

"Busy but fine," she said, "but work doesn't worry me. What worries me is what you are replacing with the foul shit you are drinking."

"What I am replacing?"

"Are you deaf, Tino?"

"What do you want from me, Vanna?"

"The truth. What is in your head?"

"You have all thrived since we moved here, but me, I am lost."

"You tell me you enjoy your maintenance work. You engineered this whole move to make us comfortable here, to stop you from having broken ribs like Crudelli. And now you are unhappy?"

"The Sidero family has been using me to convince people to do what I did."

"What?"

"Brinto - he took me to San Cataldo to convince some landowners to sell up. Brinto's family have some houses in the land below and he's worried their older houses will cause damage."

"Well Etna is not far away from there. Maybe he has reason to be worried. But back to the question. Why are you numbing the day with booze? You never drank at the end of a hard day on the farm and you worked much harder there than you do here."

"I am conflicted and compromised."

"You have delivered a future to me and the children. You work less than you used to, and we lack for nothing. And for the few times Brinto may use you as a bargaining chip you are conflicted? I never saw you as fragile, Tino."

Fragile, thought Tino. He recalled the efforts he put in to keep them all fed, the times he saved lambs from the cold, carrying their shuddering bodies across fields avoiding certain death, ploughing acre after acre.

"Who the fuck are you calling fragile?!"

"You! And don't take that tone with me. You never have before and you have no reason to now. What moment made you turn to drink, tell me!"

He got up to walk back in before Vanna grabbed his arm and pulled him back to his chair. "No avoiding, we are going to talk."

Tino looked out onto the bay, the lights. "I know I should be happy, but the other day, there was this haggard, wrinkled old bat in San Cataldo, at the meeting. She called me an *omminicchio*, spat between my feet. At that moment I felt my life amount to nothing more than the blob of mucous, as is nothing I have ever done has amounted to anything. Ok?"

Vanna smiled. "Tino, your life has been the most productive and unselfish, hard-working one I know. We got caught up in this business and you chose to manage things to get the best outcome without any harm. Do you wish you fought them on principle like Crudelli, broken ribs and unable to work again?"

"Part of me wished I had."

"And for what, to ruin our future so you can tell yourself 'at least I stood up to them like a man'?"

"I am lost here, Vanna, lost. I say nothing because the three of you love it."

"We do, and we all appreciate your leadership, how you steered us through that uncertainty. Don't ruin your life with booze. It's a whirlpool I won't save you from I can promise you. You cannot say you weren't told. Have a wine with me here and there, talk to me, but being alone drinking gasoline, no. Promise me."

Tino smiled as he cried. "I promise, my love."

"If you need a project, I have something for you, a favour." She described the trattoria. Tino liked big projects and he agreed to go and have look, ramping up his enthusiasm for Vanna's benefit. Seeing her pleased was like nectar to him.

The laughter on the street below caught their attention as Lidia teased her brother, Claudio taking her jibes with humour.

"Angela likes you, brother." said Lidia, prodding Claudio hard in the arm.

"Ouch! Stop, will you?" said Claudio with a smile.

"So, will we go out again for ice cream with them?"

"Well I do have to chaperone you, little sister. You may run off at any time."

"I'm eighteen, not eight."

"Unfortunately, I have to accept that."

Tino smiled at Vanna as they let themselves in.

"Never forget we love you." said Vanna, getting up and patting him on the cheek playfully, before kissing him on the lips.

At three-thirty, Tino still lay awake, unable to put his finger on the moment his dread was pointing to. He would not have to wait long to find out.

Tino parked outside Bacano after his jobs the next day and met Gianno. He was secretly relieved. He posed no threat; a short, squat bald man with a wisp of hair hanging on for dear life. Sweaty too and that ridiculous tic, thought Tino. The threat displaced, he shook his hand heartily and surveyed the drab interior Vanna described.

"Bad?" asked Gianno, his tic in overdrive.

"Some brightening up would help."

Vanna came out of the kitchen. "See, I told you."

Tino tried being diplomatic. "Let's not exaggerate, Vanna. Better lighting, pest control, a new counter, paint, freshening up the tables and chairs, but nothing which cannot be achieved fairly quickly."

"Sounds like a lot, Tino," said Gianno.

"You do your thing and I'll measure up." He measured floor and wall dimensions, climbed a ladder and poked his head through a ceiling tile. A large rat scurried a metre away. "Jesus Christ." muttered Tino, ducking his head below the ceiling. He proposed the job be done on the slowest two days of the week until the job was finished, something Gianno agonised over at before accepting.

"And money wise," said Gianno, rubbing his fingers together, "what do you want?"

"You pay for the materials; paint, wood, electrical wiring, globes etc and I will do this as a gift to you. Vanna is very happy here and this pleases me. Are you Ok with that?"

"More than Ok. You name the days and I will close for you to do the work."

Tino approached his superior at work who told him to take as much time as he needed. He achieved so much in the brief period he worked with the local council, he was in front and putting many others in maintenance to shame. After seeing the rat, he covered the kitchen as soon as the Sunday evening trade was over, nailing a canvas sheet into the ceiling and walls to catch anything that fell. He mixed two solutions; a borax solution to wipe out all insect life and a dilute peppermint oil mix he used with success on the farm, in which he soaked cotton balls to repel the rats and mice. He climbed up into the roof space and crawled carefully along the ceiling joists, spraying every square inch with the borax solution, taking care to cover his mouth with a face mask. He soaked as many cotton balls as possible in the peppermint oil solution and scattered them into the far corners and around possible entry points. He heard scurrying from three different parts of his of the roof as the scent created the desired effect. Satisfied the whole space was treated, he backed down the ladder and gasped for air as he stepped outside. He treated the dining and kitchen areas sparingly and marked red any suspicious holes where pests made their way in. He made a rough concrete paste, blocked up the holes and at a tick past midnight, walked home a stinking mess.

Pasquale Brinto waited for the phone to be answered. As always, he answered on the fifth ring.

"Speak."

"Always the fifth ring." joked Pasquale.

"Life needs established habits, Pasquale. What news do you have for me?"

"Good news; six of the seven have already made contact with me and are willing to sell as a bloc as long as our offer is satisfactory. The last one is an old bat of a spinster. A local waiter says she's crazy and not afraid to use a gun."

"Take the farmer for continuity and close off the matter one way or the other. Do what you have to do. Call me when it is done." The phone went click.

Brinto peeked through the door at his daughter and knew she was pretending to be asleep, her twitching nose and a smile giving her away.

"Giulia you can't fool Daddy."

"One day I will." she said, giggling.

"Well you need your rest so you can become an expert at fooling Daddy. Ok my little doll?" He kissed her on the forehead and tucked her in.

His wife Saveria sat up in bed, adjusting her long hair into a bun as always before sleep. She curled her mouth into a cheeky grin and spoke with a low voice.

"Away again tomorrow, Pasqa'?"

"Yes, amore. Two, maybe three days. And then a week at home."

"No late-night phone calls?"

"No."

"No trips using your skills of persuasion outside of the home?"

"And you will be home persuading me to do something truly illicit?"

"If you keep talking like that, we can be illicit now."

"That's my boy." she said, pulling him close to her. "Give me something to tide me over."

"Whatever the lady wants." said Pasquale, inhaling her scent, the bun now unfurled and Saveria's hair covering his face.

CHAPTER 29

Sicily, 1967

Fatti i cazzi tuoi, ca campi cent'anni
Mind your own business and you'll live a hundred years,
- Sicilian proverb

Tino thought the vibrating shrill of the buzzer was from a dream, until Vanna jabbed him in the ribs. He walked to the balcony. Brinto smoked outside his car.

"Give me five minutes and I'll be down."

"Vanna, I'm off to San Cataldo again. I'll keep going at the restaurant later."

Vanna grunted and rolled back over to sleep.

Brinto explained the scenario in the car.

"You are going to talk to her. Tell her if she doesn't leave, doesn't take our offer, then we can't be responsible for any damage to her house from the works on the land nearby. She would be forced to leave with her mutt she loves so much. She already thinks little of you, so drop the pretence and tell it to her straight."

"I thought that was your-"

Brinto shot him a glance which sent a shiver through him.

"I mean to say, I'm not intimidating."

"I'm not asking you to stand over her, just tell her she will be on her own with no neighbours to lean on. At her age, this will make her life harder."

Tino tried to think from Brinto's perspective and his head hurt. "Aren't we better off trying to enforce some council regulation on her to either stump up the money to repair her house or move out?"

"And have her barricade herself in? She would love nothing more than a siege. She has nothing to lose. If she takes out a leg or God forbid, more, she would die happy. All old people have something that makes them vulnerable."

The weaving last leg up along the Alcantara River didn't make him as sick as last time. They arrived at the hall again and shook hands with Sciortino, who introduced the other five owners, their faces eager to make eye contact as they shook hands. The feeling in the room could not have been more different.

Brinto took six sets of paperwork from his briefcase and handed them to the owners, standing in a horseshoe pattern around him and Tino. "Ladies and gentlemen, I think you'll find the offer fair and reasonable. Please have a seat and read through with your wives. The details are straightforward; no traps. Take all the time you need as we are here all day. Obviously if we can all come to an agreement today, the amount you read stands. Any individual negotiations would weaken your overall offer."

"What about Alba, the one who spat at his feet?" asked Sciortino's wife, a short, thin woman.

"We are meeting with her later today."

"With respect, she isn't the kind to make appointments."

"We know but we will give her a chance to hear what we have to say. After this, she and her dog will be on her own, so I'm sure she won't want to be vulnerable."

"So, you're waiting for us to sign before you meet her."

"Please, read your documentation and we will discuss further."

Brinto waited for the first signed document to kickstart some momentum. He would stay and put up Tino if he had to, but he always aimed for the most expedient option. Sciortino smiled as he approached Brinto, putting his hand out.

"Signed, Mr Brinto."

Brinto smiled, signed and separated his copy, giving Sciortino's to him. "Thank you, Elio."

Within an hour, four others had signed. Only Dino and Lorenza Desantino dithered. Tino approached them after a further thirty minutes and asked if anything needed clarification.

Lorenza hesitated before she spoke, placing her hand on Tino's arm. "The price is fair, but we do not want to move to Messina. My sisters live in Siracusa."

Tino gave her a reassuring smile. "Understood."

"Siracusa, not Messina." whispered Tino to Brinto.

"And for that they're making my balls sweat? Of course, I'll arrange the move myself."

"Done." called out Tino to the couple, smiles spreading over their faces as they signed. Brinto placed his copies in his briefcase and shook Tino's hand.

"You did well."

"Your offer was already to their liking, Pasquale. I'm not sure I added anything."

"Don't be modest. You'll do well from this, trust me."

Brinto addressed the group waiting outside. "Well, I am pleased we could come to an agreement. You all have requested a month to pack and make arrangements, and we will be in touch to help you all move to your new apartments."

Sciortino cleared his throat. "And on behalf of my neighbours and my wife, I would like to thank you for your reasonable approach."

The scatter of pellets from the shell against the hall's terracotta tiled roof didn't register for a few seconds, except Brinto.

"Inside!" he yelled.

The blind Alsatian barked in fright at the noise, as Alba, her knees resting on towels, crazed and near blind herself,

reloaded her double barrel shotgun and prepared for another
crack at the group about fifty metres away from her balcony.
By the time she reloaded they were inside. She fired again,
shattering a window on the front of the hall by luck more
than by good aim, shrieks filling the hall at the sound as Alba
cackled.

 "Traitors! Sons of whores." she cackled. She reloaded, and
as she fired, a pain ripped through the left side of her chest.
The cracking of her right collarbone from the stock recoiling
didn't register, her crazed form now limp, her companion of
fourteen years howling, running laps around the balcony
before trying to lick and nuzzle his mistress back to life.

Senior Station Inspector Pietro Ignazio from Taormina drove
up two hours later and was met by a confused Mayor Pirottu,
a small man barely reaching his shoulders. *Must be a genetic
thing with these mountain dwarves,* thought Ignazi. He read
through the sketchy report from composite witnesses and
screwed his eyes up at the disjointed chronology in front of
him, trying his best to make sense. Pirottu wondered who
called him. He hadn't.

"So, six of the seven owners of the houses on the side of this
hill were gathered in the hall. They agreed to sell their
properties to the Carnaso Group, and as they were gathered
outside, this-"

"Alba."

"Alba, started firing at them?"

"Yes."

"And someone saw her fall as if she appeared to have suffered a heart attack. And the dog?"

"Barking like mad when I went to the house, so I don't think he has had a heart attack."

Ignazi took a breath and counted backwards from five, a ritual instilled by his Mother who still lived with him and his family.

"Just take me to the house please."

Ignazi followed the Mayor as he drove at walking pace up the side of the mountain. At the house, Ignazi stopped the Mayor from opening the front door.

"Let me sort the dog out first."

He picked out two slices of mortadella from his lunchbox and approached the door. He pushed it, unlocked, and he heard the nuzzling of the dog and a short anxious bark before he took the meat from Ignazi's hand. He opened the door enough to grab the collar from the top and led the dog to a rail, tying it securely, the dog whimpering but calmer with the mortadella and a series of pats to the head.

"You're a good boy, aren't you? Probably have better teeth than anyone else here too." he whispered.

The house reeked of damp and piss. *No wonder the dog slept outside,* he thought, seeing the wooden doghouse on the balcony next to the body of Alba Rabazzari. The shotgun sat precariously half on, half off the balcony. Ignazi moved it with a towel to one side, He noted the displacement of the right collarbone, before seeing the blood oozing to a trickle from a gunshot wound below her left collarbone. *Fucking hell, Brinto.*

"All Ok, Inspector?" called out Pirottu.

"Yes, please remain outside so you don't contaminate the scene."

Ignazi rushed to find two towels and wrapped them around her upper torso. He soaked the other in warm water and bleach from the laundry, holding his nose at the stench. He soaked up the blood congealed on the wood on the balcony, relieved the wood was a dirty, dark brown.

"Ok, Pirottu. Let's lift her into the trunk of my car." He took care to keep the towel firmly aound her upper body. The body flat and well covered across his trunk, he turned to Pirottu.

"Any next of kin?"

Pirottu shrugged. "She was an only child, never married. Wouldn't be surprised if she left everything to the dog. She loved that thing," he said, impressed with his own joke, before Ignazi's stern expression stopped him.

"You can go now. I will be in touch soon." He watched the Mayor walk to his car.

He undid the leash and handed it to Pirottu. "Take the dog with you, too."

"Me?" asked Pirottu.

"You want me to take this dog to Taormina, get ridiculed by the whole station? Yes, you."

He waved to Pirottu as the Mayor left, the dog barking at the unfamiliarity of the motion. *Cretino* he said to himself.

Alba never created a will, mostly due to her distrust of anyone in a position of power. She thought of doctors as charlatans and lawyers the devil. Ignazi held his nose, gagging as he saw rotting food on plates from the stench of food left on plates as he walked through the kitchen. He found a deed of sorts, a note with VOLANTA' E TESTAMENTO in big, crude writing nailed to the kitchen wall. He removed the nail and took the deed and note outside, sucking in clear air.

VOLANTA' E TESTAMENTO
Tuttu a cana quandu moru- chi cazzu mi sposa mo?
All to the dog when I die - who the fuck will marry me now?

She had a point, said Ignazi to himself.

He drove the covered body back to Taormina, shut the door to his office and called Brinto.

"Pasquale, why do you do this to me?"

"The bat had to go. An associate followed me and waited behind her house. When she went crazy and started firing, he took the appropriate action. To fire at the same time as she did, that would have been unpredictable."

"I applaud his timing and marksmanship. But I am left with a problem which is also unpredictable."

"Did she have a will?"

"It appears not. Now, the body?"

"She left everything to the dog?" joked Brinto.

"Fuck off, you too?" said Ignazi, exasperated. "Look, you take the body. No one else knows she is fermenting under blankets in my trunk and soon will stink. I cannot move her, no one in San Cataldo has a clue the body has been moved so move her - tonight."

"Relax, Inspector. Leave that to me. Now, to more pressing matters. She died intestate then?"

"I told you, yes."

"Tomorrow you will go back to San Cataldo - tell the mayor the deed defaults to the council, and given the circumstances of the adjoining properties, the Carnaso Group would probably make a suitable offer above the odds to take the land off their hands. Fair trade?"

"The body Pasquale - when and where? Please."

"Leave your car unlocked along the foreshore of Letojanni. We will make sure no one breaks in. Have a nice dinner at *Osteria Mazzeo* - they do a great marinara. Park by seven-thirty and we will be done by eight-thirty."

Ignazi hung up and poured himself a drink, reaching for the bottle of Averna on his desk and wolfing a glass down. He drove the ten minutes to Letojanni and found a spot opposite the restaurant. He requested a table with his back to the view

of the beach so he would not be on constant lookout. He
enjoyed the marinara, the freshness of the seafood taking his
mind off things, even drinking the broth, something he would
never be caught doing in a restaurant. He had stopped feeling
conflicted years ago but having the woman's corpse in his car
bothered him. Being told the bill had been paid though did
not, the waiter shaking his hand, smiling and bowing as one
would to a man of importance.

The demolition team sent out by the Sidero family a month
later worked fast on the seven houses in San Cataldo. Once
the ground was bare, nothing happened for three weeks, until
monster trucks with *Italestra* on the side, carrying machines
with drills, rolled slowly up the winding roads.

If the house owners had only asked Alba, she would have
told them of the huge sulphur reserves trapped under their
land. Fumes escaped from rock formations at the rear of her
family's farm since she was a little girl.

CHAPTER 30

Sicily, 1967

Cio' che Dio fa e' ben fatto.
What God does is done well.
- Sicilian proverb

Tino whistled as he finished his last job for the day. Unblocking the plumbing in the top floor apartment was easier than he expected. Seeing Brinto was pleasant, and his assurance that the San Cataldo business was over came as welcome news. The envelope of cash, equivalent to two month's wages, was especially appreciated.

He opened up Bacano with his key and braced himself for the clean-up in the roof cavity. He gently shook the canvas suspended below the kitchen ceiling first, listening for the rustle of dead insects as they settled in the base. More insects collected in the canvas than he expected, but Gianno had no concept of maintenance. Tino shook the dead matter into the bin outside and took up a bucket, brush and dustpan to clear out the roof cavity. Despite his mask, the scent was overpowering. Starting at the furthest point, he gathered copious dead insects, spiders and rancid piles of rat faeces. Once all the matter was collected, he crawled backwards towards the roof opening,

As he lowered his left foot through the hole to the ladder, his shoe snagged on a cable hanging over a joist and he slipped, planting his foot but missing the ladder. He fell against the ceiling joist to his right and clung with his left, only able to grasp a wire. The live wire burned his hand, the insulating rubber torn open by the gnawing of the rats, current surging through him, convulsing before the life left his body, smacking hard against the ladder and falling with a thump to the floor, his eyes still wide open in shock as the ladder collapsed and clanged on the hard floor next to him.

Vanna looked up at the clock and frowned.

"Claudio, Lidia - let's go and surprise your Father."

"How long does it take to collect insects?" asked Claudio.

"You know what your Father's like. Perfectionist."

Claudio pushed the door open and he adjusted to the light.

"What's that smell?" asked Vanna, "like singed hair." Claudio didn't hear her and ran to his Father's body on the floor. He felt for a pulse - nothing, pressed the other wrist, rolled him onto his back and beat his chest and turned to his Mother, eyes frozen, Lidia trying to restrain her, Vanna screaming, hurling chair after chair into the dark until she collapsed, bellowing and pushing Lidia and Claudio away.

A couple walking by ran to the nearest police station at the commotion. A seasoned officer of twenty years burst in and checked the body, knowing already the deceased had been electrocuted. He stood the ladder up and checked for himself, poking his head through the ceiling opening with caution, grimacing at the spliced and burnt out wire, its insulation covering melted and disfigured, smoke still emanating from the spot where Tino grabbed in desperation.

He climbed back down and sat next to Vanna, her mind not in the same hemisphere as his let alone the same place, blankly staring ahead. He got up and pulled Claudio and Lidia in and hugged them. *I'm so sorry, children.* He ran out and grabbed Gianno,

"Throw something on Gianno, quick." He waited and grabbed him by the ear as he shut the door. "Do you not take your responsibilities seriously?"

"What do you mean?"

"Walk."

He pushed Gianno through the front door. "This," he said, pointing to Tino's body. "He touched a live wire and was electrocuted."

Vanna lunged at Gianno and was too quick for the policeman, scratching his face and tearing his lower eyelid with frenzied swipes.

"You killed my husband, you took his goodwill and you killed him, you son of a whore!!"

Claudio stepped in and hugged her, walking her away from him saying *get out Gianno, go*. Vanna struggled to free herself from Claudio's tight grip.

"Let me die with him, Claudio, please. Let touch the wire and go too. You and Lidia will be Ok, just let me go with him please."

Gianno walked outside, holding his eye leaking blood and tears onto his cheek and the concrete.

Vanna's heart settled to a normal rhythm; her adrenaline expended. She sat, spent and empty. She kneeled on the floor and called to Tino, rubbing his burnt hand over her face. She turned to her children and whispered *take me home*.

The officer took Claudio aside. "You have to step up, take responsibility. Take care of your Mother and sister." He drove them home, Claudio and Lidia helping Vanna up the stairs, her body drained of energy. They put her to bed in her clothes. Vanna asked Lidia to sleep with her. She held her Mother and settled her back to sleep every time she burst into tears. Claudio lay a towel on the floor and slept next to them. At four-thirty and unable to sleep, he sat out on the balcony. The strengthening wind made the light of the Madonnina on the bay blink in and out till he fell asleep, the combination of ship horns, braking cars then a knock on the door waking him. He braced himself for the discussion with the funeral director but was surprised to see Pasquale Brinto at the door.

"Mr Brinto."

"Claudio, I am so sorry for your loss."

"Mr Brinto, how did you-, this is a bad time. My Mother is still asleep." whispered Claudio.

"I know and I will not be long. I wanted to pass on a token of my condolences; to help with your arrangements. Your Father was a good man. He set your family up well and this terrible accident has robbed you of valuable time with him." He handed an envelope to Claudio and shook his hand. "A friend of mine has agreed to take care of your Father's funeral, as a favour to me. I hope you are agreeable to this. He is very professional and will take good care and respect

218

your wishes." A short but sincere smile, and he was gone. Claudio placed the envelope inside a coat pocket in his wardrobe.

Considerate of Pasquale Brinto to suggest that Lina Faila accompany her funeral director husband, Nuno. Her presence calmed Vanna as Nuno expressed their condolences. In spite of her acute grief, Vanna was pleased Claudio broached the subject before they arrived, taking some solace in his maturity under the circumstances. He went through Vanna's expressed wishes with Nuno; a simple family service at the *Chiesa di Gesu' e Maria del Buon Viaggio*, followed by a simple burial at the *Cimeterio di Pace*, a relatively small cemetery where she could take the bus. Lidia shoved her grief deep as she concentrated on her Mother. She was surprised she had the presence of mind to think these details through. She held her hand and smiled.

The next evening, they went to view the body. Lidia and Claudio led Vanna into the room.

"Children, I need a minute or two alone with your Father, please."

Vanna was unsure if she should be angry at Tino or herself; for getting him involved in that fucking restaurant or for him not paying attention and dying in such a senseless way. She was used to hearing Tino's side after she pushed him to talk, expressing hers, then everything settling with an embrace in his tall, strong arms and a kiss. *It wasn't always that romantic,* she thought, but she remembered those discussions now with a fondness that killed her.

"You're not here for me to tell you how angry I am at your carelessness. But I am angry at myself," she said, thumping her chest at the words myself, "angry for getting you involved in that dump I wanted as a stupid fucking project. Why? Why?" She slumped over his body, and cried a high-pitched cry as she rubbed his cheek, hard and cold when she was used to warm and yielding; much to get used to being without, and she spiralled, thinking about all the little stupid things she would never sense about him again.

Be calm and accept said her Mother when she was young.

Then her other mantra - *cio' che Dio fa e' ben fatto*. What God does is done well.

If this was an act of God, vaffanculo said Vanna, now breathing and reasoning again. She called in her children and stood at Tino's feet to let them stand close to him. They stood in silence.

"Bad enough we never got to tell him what we thought of him when he was alive. Tell him everything here while he resembles your Father. Go on."

Claudio nodded for Lidia to go first.

"Father, you protected me and loved me for as long as I can remember. You taught Claudio to be as protective as you were, and you loved Mother, you adored her. I hope I find the love I saw in your eyes for her. I will miss you every day." She hugged her Father's torso and lingered. Tino's pale face was a shock to Claudio, remembering his Father's immense strength, hoisting sheep and pigs over his shoulder and driving fence posts a metre into the ground for fun,

getting him to try his best and encouraging him. He always
thought he would find him dead on the farm in some remote
corner, his heart giving out to overexertion at a ripe old age,
refusing to retire. Instead, here he was, dead from a mistake
he wouldn't possibly make on the farm in a million years.
The city made him soft, if not physically, mentally, and the
work was too easy, without graft or duress, the arduous effort
removed from his days. He acceded to the bastard's veiled
and tacit threats; and the three of them were beneficiaries, of
what exactly he struggled to understand.

"Augustino, my strong and silent Father. I wish we never left
the farm. You were happy there. Your love for us will stay
with me for the rest of my days." He wanted to say love and
lessons, but he would be lying; his Father would not have
condoned his murder of Father Di Pardo to protect Caterina.
Rather, he would have seen Claudio as culpable as the
deviant priest, something he could not accept, albeit in this
moment of grief. He did his cross and kissed his Father's
hand.

They stood at Tino's feet, Vanna calling for Nuno to come
back into the room.

"Remember - a closed coffin, Ok?"

"As you wish, Vanna."

The service was booked for two days later, wedged in
between the morning liturgy and a remembrance service. The
day before the funeral, Claudio walked past the trattoria for
therapy (or was it curiosity?), not telling Vanna or Lidia, but
making sure Lidia stayed with her. The inside was dim, but
the ladder stood as before, the natural light passing through

the opening in the ceiling. A piece of paper was stuck to the inside of the door, with a notice crudely scrawled in capitals, the pen tearing through the page at the sharp points of the As.

CHIUSO A CAUSO DELLA MORTE DEL PROPRIETARIO. CLOSED DUE TO DEATH OF OWNER.

The door yielded with a squeak when he pushed. He called *permessso* out but got no response. He read the note again and went inside. A faint creaking sound came from the kitchen, and Claudio walked to the kitchen door, knowing what to expect. Through the round glass panel, Gianno, newly dead, swung limp from a noose, eyes bulging from his last-ditch efforts to breathe. Claudio walked back out, wiping the door handle with a handkerchief, certain he had not touched anything else.

In the time between leaving the apartment and the church, a storm rolled in from Reggio Calabria, the rain hitting the hearse and the following car at right angles. They waited until the downpour eased and took their chance, Claudio and Lidia helping Vanna up the stairs to make sure she didn't slip. Gloops of rain landed on their heads from the statue of the Madonna above the door.

The Priest welcomed Vanna and gave his condolences. They sat with the priest in the few moments before the funeral service and waited for the liturgy congregation to leave.

"If you are waiting for more people, don't worry yourself. It is just the three of us, Father. You can start when you are ready."

The priest raised his eyebrows at the closed coffin and presented a minimal service as requested. Without the burden of others' expectations, Vanna was relieved. The sun emerged as they left the church, Claudio assisting Nuno with the coffin, along with the priest and a kindly man who stayed behind the liturgy to pay his respects. They drove to the cemetery, Vanna insisting to the priest he only do what he needed to do so he wouldn't be late for the remembrance service. The priest committed Tino's body to the earth and wished the family well. The three of them stayed another ten minutes in silence, another belt of rain hitting the cars as they made their way back down to Borgo del Ringo. They entered the apartment and sat around the table, staring at each other. Claudio spoke first.

"I'm hungry but let's go out to eat."

Vanna nodded. She opened the refrigerator and took out the remaining meals. She expected to be thrown into shock at the sight of them but calmly stacked them on the countertop.

"Claudio, take these to Signora Bruna upstairs will you? Say it's from the wake or something."

The old woman had diminished vision from dense cataracts and was untrusting about visitors but recognised Claudio's voice.

"Oh, Claudio, I am truly sorry for your loss. Far too young. Yet people like me ready for the scrapheap, we are allowed to live out our days." she said, catching herself. "I'm sorry, how insensitive. I wish your family strength through God."

"No need to apologise signora. Thank you for your kind wishes. I have food from the wake - on your kitchen table, Ok?"

"Very generous of you. *Buon anima* and thank you."

"Thank you."

Days passed more quickly. When they thought they could leave Vanna alone, Claudio took Lidia by bus to visit Tino's grave.

"I haven't seen you cry, Lidia."

"We've been looking after Mother, Claudio. What do you want? How about you show some emotion?"

"I have been organising the funeral, Lidia."

"So now we can both cry." said Lidia, running a finger down a fresh tear on his cheek. Claudio put his arm around her. They stood holding hands at his grave, shifting leaves, though the wind would bring others. Vanna smiled on their return.

Gianno's neighbour came two days later to check in on him at the restaurant after he didn't answer at home, and found his suspended, bloated body.

Vanna overheard two older women gossiping at the market a few days later.

"Awful about Gianno."

"The trattoria?"

"After the poor man got electrocuted, the owner started drinking and hung himself in his kitchen. Imagine the guilt. At least he leaves no one behind."

"Just as well. Imagine having to face that every day, forever."

Vanna walked home. She recognised when a neighbour had lost someone. People came and went in black, holding containers of food as an offering, the husbands staying outside to smoke and make small talk. No one came to Vanna, and she preferred it that way.

CHAPTER 31

Crete, 1966

Sifi wondered how and when the fat bastard would react, point his sausage fingers at him demanding where everyone was. Until then, he was content to tenderise the octopus in his hands, bashing it on the concrete, the tentacles still contracting. The fire behind him crackled and he placed the *skara*, the metal grid above the glowing wood, sizzling as the water burnt off. He removed the beak, cut off the head and turned it inside out, pulling out the muck inside. He soaked the octopus with the tentacles in olive oil, lemon, salt and pepper until the fire was ready.

Penelope licked her lips as she enjoyed the last piece, Sifi wiping his bread through the fragrant juices left behind.

"More tender than usual." she said.

"What about the octopus?"

"Ha, hilarious. On a serious note, how are we going to deal with Stelios?"

"We are shocked as you are, Stelios. I was supposed to be the boy's best man too!"

"Hmm, convincing. Save it for when he comes."

Anthoula went to open up the shop and swore as the door caught.

"Pandeli, what the devil have you done to the door?"

"What are you talking about?"

"It's stuck, oh-" she spotted the problem and picked up the envelope catching under the door. She took out the keys and a small slip of paper fell out.

The house is yours.
I hope you can forgive me.
If you do, destroy this note.
Love always, Nikos, Fotini and family

She read the note again and glanced across the road. "Pandeli!"

He came out in his robe, half his face unshaven. "What's wrong, woman?"

"This." He read and a smile spread over his face.
"Why are you smiling you idiot?"

"Nikos once told me one day a letter would come from his Uncle in Australia. He took his chance; *he took his chance.*" He took the letter from his wife's hand, lighting it with a match.

"You knew this was going to happen?"

"No." he said, arms up in protest, "but he mentioned his Uncle often. A package arrived two, three weeks ago - must have been money, a letter or something. I didn't peek, pry or ask. I had no idea they were going to leave overnight. Sifi was carrying on from their house at about ten. I thought they were getting drunk with the wedding coming up. He was going to be their best man."

227

They walked across to the house and unlocked the front door. Only the sewing machine remained in the front room, already larger than their living quarters at the back of the shop. Mr Pandelis inhaled at the expanse of space in the family room and kitchen, table and chairs in the centre and began to feel giddy.

"That bedroom is yours," said Anthoula, laughing.

"I hope Litsa gets over this." said Mr Pandelis.

"She used her allure on him. This is her fault as much as his. And don't think of repeating the line about the ocean liner or I'll smack you up sideways." she said, shooting him a warning glare.

"Hell will break-"

The screech of Stelios' car interrupted him, followed by a loud slam of the door.

"WHERE IS SHE ?!" Stelios yelled, his shotgun pointing out in front of him, Hariklia close behind, hearing the echo of his voice and noticing the emptiness of the front room.
"They're gone, Stelios, gone!"

He pointed his gun at Mr Pandelis.
"No!" said Anthoula, standing in front of her husband.

"Where have they taken her?!" spluttered Stelios.

A strong hand shoved Hariklia into the room and the other held his harpy knife to Stelios' throat from behind.

"Let's all settle down before someone gets hurt, Ok? Now gently lower the gun to my left hand. Like that, good. No need to do anything you might regret. Let's all take a seat, Ok?"

Sifi put the gun on the ground, removed the shells and put his knife away. He sat at the head of the table and glared at Stelios.

"Well?" he said, eyeballing Stelios.

"I'm sorry, Sifi."

"Not me you idiot, to Mr Pandelis."

"I'm sorry, Pandelis. We woke and found her gone, and now this house empty. I am distraught."

"I told you, she has left," said Hariklia. "I am not surprised after what I said to her."

"What?" asked Stelios.

"She didn't want to marry Nectarios. I told her she shouldn't consider herself to be so special. Lots of us married without knowing what life would be like." she said, looking at Stelios. She left out the part that stung Litsa. She could not repeat those words.

"You were both close to Nikos and Fotini. Neither of you honestly had no idea they were going to leave?" asked Stelios.

"No," said Mr Pandelis, arms raised. "I found the keys under my door this morning."

"No note?" asked Stelios.

"No." Stelios turned to Sifi.

"I had no idea. To think I was supposed to be the boy's best man."

"Well they have either gone to Chania or are already on a boat to Athens." said Stelios. "We need to find them fast," said Stelios, his arms waving in front of everyone.

"What do you mean *we*?" asked Mr Pandelis. "I have a community to serve here. I can't just close my shop or leave Anthoula on her own."

"As I do," said Sifi. "Drive your flashy car to Chania and search." He paused to put the fear into Stelios. "And one more thing, do not ever let me see you brandishing a gun anywhere in this town again or I will skin you like a goat. Do you understand me?"

Stelios nodded.

"Let's go Stelios." said Hariklia.

The car left with a screech.

"Hope the fat bastard gets pulled over for speeding." said Mr Pandelis.

"So, what happened, Sifi?"

"Nikos told me about a package from his Uncle in Australia; enough money to get them there. They decided to leave before the children were tied down in something only Stelios wanted. I took them to Chania by boat and soon they will be in Piraeus."

"And Litsa?"

"She caught us by surprise. I dropped off Nikos and the girls and when I came back with Fotini and Nectarios, she was there, demanding to come with us. She threatened to tell her parents everything if we didn't take her, so, we took her."

"To do what?"

"Her parents; wouldn't you want to be away from them if the opportunity came up? Nikos and Fotini will make sure she is settled there. They are good people; they will not leave her to the streets."

They nodded. "And the keys under the door were Nikos' gift to you. For years you have lived with cans and jars above your heads in that storeroom. He wanted to tell you but ran out of time."

"What are we going to do with all this space?" said Mr Pandelis.

"Live." said Anthoula, pinching his cheeks.

Hariklia said little on the drive to Chania, looking out the window and leaving Stelios be. No use berating him for his bravado, entering the house with a gun. He knew he had been deflated. Her brutal dismissal of her daughter had tipped things over, but in truth this was the inevitable result of two people who should have never crossed paths in life creating life of their own.

Stelios accelerated on the flat, straight stretch of road going through Daratsos. Officer Vangelis Dourakis was woken by the rush of wind as the saloon whooshed past, and he caught them as they slowed to turn left at the Vamvakopoulo turn off to Chania.

"Well done." said Hariklia at the sound of the siren.

"You're enjoying this, aren't you?"

"Not half as much as you think. Think with your brain when you talk to the officer and not your ego."

"Sir," began Dourakis, "do you have a reason for driving thirty miles over the limit?"

"My daughter has been kidnapped."

"Excuse me?"

"She left our house and we think she has left the island for Athens."

"So, which is it? She left home or was she kidnapped?"

"She left. With a family and their three children."

"Who?" asked Dourakis.

"That bastard Nikos Petrakis took her."

Dourakis remembered the name and asked as flatly as possible. "From Tavroniti?"

"Yes," said Stelios, encouraged. "You know him?"

"I once caught him speeding a few years back when his wife was in distress, around when their youngest girl was being born. Haven't seen him since." *And if he's escaping you, I'm buying him some time.* "Step out of the car please, Sir. I need your licence, too."

"Officer, I'm in a hurry."

"Licence please." said Dourakis.

He fumbled for in his wallet and unfolded the paper, nearly tearing it. Dourakis nodded and gave it back.

"Officer, our daughter."

"All in good time. Your wife's manner assures me we are not dealing with a kidnapping and right now, I am inclined to believe her. Your driving though bothers me. Stick out your tongue, please Sir."

His breathing more rapid now, Stelios struggled with this basic task. Dourakis smelled his breath and detected no alcohol. "Back in your car please, Mr Sfirakis."

They waited for an eternity before Dourakis returned with a fine of one hundred drachmas. "Do you have that much on you at the moment?"

"I do," said Hariklia, reaching into her purse, producing the
money.

"Your driving is that of a madman who cares nothing for
society's rules, Sir. Are you that madman?"

"No, Officer."

"Then be more careful. I will be watching for your car on this
road. You don't see many like this. Now go slow with the
grace of God; ease up on the gas. What will be will be. Have
a nice day." he said, tipping his hat.

By the time they reached Souda Bay, the six travellers were
passing Aegina to their left, the mainland and Athens still not
in view. Litsa slept most of the way, leaning on Fotini and
then on Rita as she too slept, Sia nestled against Nikos'
shoulder, Nikos drifting in and out of sleep as Sia's little
body jerked at regular intervals.

Only Nectarios found sleep elusive, the image of the haggard
gypsy waving from the edge of the wharf appearing every
time he closed his eyes. With the fatigue came the questions,
and for the first time in his life, he questioned his own worth;
was this what I will be forever, a man who gets himself and
others into trouble? Am I cursed? Litsa's eyes opened. He
liked the idea of waking to her every morning, the minutes
and hours in between were what proved difficult; the
conversations, the promises and compromises he found
difficult to define, his mentality still lagging behind his
biology. Awake now, Litsa questioned his facial expression
with a silent what?

You are beautiful he mouthed back.

She smiled and whispered back a bit late but thank you.

Nectarios was still unaware of this truth, but what had happened only served to make her more beautiful, more self-assured, enough to know he couldn't and wouldn't be part of her life. Yet without the fumbling awkwardness, the ill-conceived night where fate delivered opportunity to act on their impulses, she would not be here, in charge of whatever mess of a destiny she would follow.

When land appeared, the boats coming and going from Piraeus by the dozen, Litsa woke Rita and showed her, Nikos and Sia fast asleep. Fotini chose to keep her eyes shut, conserving her energy for the frenetic days ahead.

As the ship began to slow, Nikos sprung to life and asked the others to lean in.

"We must stay together. This is not Tavroniti or Chania. Do not trust anyone here except the six of us. We will call our contact and go from there, understood?"

Everyone nodded, as rain came sideways, splashing over the deck outside their window. They stepped onto the gangplank and walked fast to find cover.

Stelios and Hariklia sat in the small office at Souda terminal, waiting for a figure of authority to come and talk to them. A small, thin man emerged from a door at the rear of the terminal.

"Mr and Mrs Sfirakis?"

"Yes." said Stelios.

"We had sixty-seven people board the ship to Piraeus this morning. I have rung the Piraeus terminal and the ship arrived an hour ago at six p.m., sixty-seven people disembarked. Onboard were five, six people the cabin crew classed as around the eighteen-year-old mark. As we do not ask for identification for our family tickets, we cannot be sure if your daughter was on the ship."

"When is the next ship leaving?"

"In three hours."

"What are you planning to do, Stelios, scour the whole of Athens for her?"

"Arrange two tickets, please." said Stelios, ignoring her.

"Of course."

"Stelios, she is gone. We, you and I, we have driven her away."

"Pah! We are not perfect parents, but she needs to be held to account."

"You did not see her with Fotini. The way she interacted with her; measuring her, fitting her, asking the kind of questions only a real Mother would ask. There was more togetherness between them than I ever had with Litsa. I have to live with that. She has gone to find her happiness, Stelios. Which part are you refusing to understand?"

"Very well, be the martyr and blame yourself, but on principle she has to come back and face what she has done."

236

"Face what, the high crime of embarrassing Stelios Sfirakis? What would be her punishment, I mean, apart from enduring life with us?"

Stelios rolled his eyes. "Two tickets or one? Because I will go on my own if have to."

Hariklia snatched the keys. "When you return, whether with her or alone, we will be living in separate bedrooms, living separate lives. Perhaps Litsa is the wisest of all of us."

"Come on Hariklia. Don't be like this."

"Like what? One of us has clarity. The other one is about to conduct a deluded search for a single person in a city of three million people."

"I will find our daughter and-"

"Oh, shut your mouth you gasbag! She is the only thing we have achieved together. The rest has all been about you, you and you. Go to hell." She strode off and drove away, stopping a few times, unsure of how to navigate her way to the other side of Chania. She stopped at a periptero, the square street kiosk stocked with snacks and newspapers. Hariklia got the attention of the small lady hidden behind the small opening.

"How do I leave Chania?"

"That's the eternal question, isn't it?"
Just what I need, a philosopher said Hariklia under her breath. "Which road do I take to Tavroniti?"

"Here, a street map. The tourist bureau makes us give them out for free."

Hariklia took the map, disoriented as she ran her finger over the streets. "Where are we?" she asked, dreading the answer.

The woman came out and pointed to the spot on the map, threading the route out of Chania with a red pen. "Drive safely, and be careful, the policeman in Daratsos catches speeding drivers like you and I swat mosquitoes."

"So I hear." said Hariklia. "Thanks."

She followed the streets and in half an hour passed Officer Dourakis, travelling well below the limit, earning herself a thumbs up. She got home, fatigued from the drive and walked past the photo of Litsa taken when she was twelve. She met her eyes and felt nothing, no resemblance to either herself or Stelios, as if she had been dumped on her doorstep by the stork as a test.

"I was not fit to have children." said Hariklia aloud. She tried to name a good quality Litsa had taken from her and struggled to name one. She wondered how she would react if she received bad news of her daughter and chided herself for thinking of such things. Exhausted, she collapsed on the bed and cried herself to sleep.

CHAPTER 32

Athens, 1966

Though late winter, steam rose from the closely huddled on the crowded bus from Piraeus to Athens, making the uninitiated feel claustrophobic. They alighted, the Acropolis directly in front of them, the faded lights shining up the columns. Nikos had no idea where they were. Across to his left he saw a string of shops close together and guessed one would have to be a tavern. They walked across the chaotic intersection, dodging the taxis oblivious to the pedestrian crossing.

A man showed them to a table in Taverna Asteri, collective relief as they finally sat.

"Bring us enough for a small meal, please." said Nikos to the waiter, a tall, thin man called Aris with a flinty voice. Aris got on the girls' good side by bringing out chips to calm them, winking at them as they smiled. Nikos called the waiter back over.

"Aris, is there a public phone here nearby?"

"Not nearby. Use ours."

"Are you sure?"

"Please, for the love of God. I'm not going to make you walk the streets looking for a phone. Come."

He dialled the number on the letter and waited an eternity until a rushed voice answered.

"Speak."

"Is this Prokopis Papazoglou?"

"Who will receive you and where?" said the voice, the words rushing into the crescendo of *where*.

"Gerasimos Petrakis, Australia." Nikos felt uneasy at the formality of the tone.

"Where are you now?" asked Papazoglou, the tone now more friendly and rounded.

" Taverna Asteri, near the Acropolis."

"Don't labour yourself. I know where it is. Walk down *Cheiden*, and after three blocks you will see Hotel Centro. I will call them and book for five-"

"Six."

The silence that followed bothered Nikos. "Six? How are you six?"

"We had an unexpected passenger. She is staying in Athens."

"Ok, I will book for six under Prokopis. You have money from Gerasimos, correct?"

"Yes."

"Spend wisely – it is so easy to blow it quickly in Athens and you have to make six go into five. Sleep well and I will find

you tomorrow in the hotel cafe at nine a.m. Don't sleep in."
Click.

Nikos steeled himself for a string of bizarre encounters and unpredictability before he left Crete, but the conversation made him think he was part of some clandestine operation. He made a mental note not to talk too much.

The aroma of meat and seafood greeted him, cheerier faces smiling as he returned to the table. They ate heartily and made the fifteen-minute walk to the hotel, where a large man with dark hair, dark rings under his eyes and a pockmarked face showed them to their room, a large single with three double beds. Sia refused to sleep unless Litsa slept alongside her, meaning Rita had to sleep with Nectarios. After some protestation and a firm word from Nikos, they slept, tired but full.

Litsa moved as she dreamt.

She felt her wedding dress, smooth and perfect over her breasts and abdomen and she lowered the veil over her face. Stelios smiled at her as the church door opened. Hariklia stepped in front of them and lifted the rifle, firing at point blank range, Stelios' head a bloody mess as he lay on the ground, droplets of his blood scattered on her dress and rolling down the smooth satin, dripping onto the wooden floor, the church now empty except for Pater Manousso, chanting may his memory be eternal. Hariklia whispered you were right child, you can do better, now go, go and live your life before he wakes up.

Sia shrieked as Litsa's cries woke her. The light came on Fotini walked to her. *Ok, child, you had a nightmare. Shh, it's Ok, just a dream.* Sia ran to her Father's bed and curled up close. Fotini held Litsa until she fell asleep again. At eight thirty, she woke everyone to get dressed.

Prokopis Papazoglou's parents came as eighteen-year-olds in the forced mass migration from Smyrna in 1922, months before the signed population exchange of 1923. His Mother Pipina came across with her uncle and aunt, his Father Fontas accompanied by his Mother after brutal attacks claimed his Father, who fought against his Mother's wishes. They grew up five minutes apart in Smyrna, and even closer in *Nea Smyrni*, the settlement constructed by the Greek government to house the refugees. They knew each other by sight but were introduced at a community dinner. They married six months later by the arrangement of their parents, keen to keep their families together by any means possible. They had difficulty conceiving, living under the same roof as Pipina's uncle and hectoring aunt, before Fontas got a job as a baker with an early refugee from Smyrna called Basili and they could afford a small two room apartment. They fell pregnant two months later, and Pipina insisted on the name Prokopis whether boy or girl, the Greek word for progress and industrious, so the child would remember his Father's hard work. When he was ten, Fontas took over the bakery from Basili and taught Prokopis the trade. He rose and came home with his Father, his proud Mother smiling at her working men. At sixteen, Prokopis shot up to six foot two, and attracted the attention of many female customers young and old alike. Fontas died of a stroke at fifty-six, and Prokopis lived in the same apartment with his Mother ever since, the bakery doing well enough to leave it to staff he trusted and treated well, introducing bonuses for good days. No one asked about the horrors and trauma of Smyrna, and he was

happy to be Athenian with everyone else inside and outside
of Nea Smyrni.

Now forty-two, he stood and scanned the cafe for the family
of six, spotting them easily from the Cretan accent being
spoken. Nikos got up and introduced himself.

"You didn't sound tall on the phone." said Nikos, introducing
him to the family.

He shrugged and sat down. "So, we're here. How did we
sleep?"

"Mostly well." said Fotini,

"Let me explain how I work. I run a bakery in Nea Smyrni,
about twenty minutes away. I have an apartment with a
kitchen; cosy but secure and no one will ever find you."

"Find us?" asked Nikos.

"Do you think you haven't left trouble behind?"

"How do you know?"

"He's right." said Litsa, explaining her situation. After
hearing her story, Prokopis thought and said, "I presume your
Father will already be on the way here and will ask the police
for help. Athens is big, but small at the same time. It only
takes one lucky break and he could be less than a block away
from us. So, follow my advice, stay close and I'll have you
on the *Patris* as soon as possible. As for you Litsa, we need
to discuss what you're going to do here, but I already have an
idea."

"How long will this take, roughly?" asked Fotini.

"With no passports, no ticket and only a sponsor, we are looking at ten, maybe fourteen days. Please try to be patient."

"How did you get into this?" asked Litsa.

"This… what?"

"Arranging passage for people."

"Well, my ancestors were forced to move without any chance to make arrangements. Call it a public service, but not too public. Some authorities would not like what I am doing. Have you heard of Dionysios Ross?"

"He is in theatre or something?"

"My Father changed his passport from Rossoglou to Ross. With that surname, he got into America without any hold up."

"And my Uncle Gerasimos, how do you know him?" asked Nikos.

Prokopis was used to answering questions and became tolerant to them. It was necessary in this second occupation.

"I was about nineteen when he walked into the bakery with his wife. A man stood in front of him, nervous, sweating bullets and he asked my Father for a Vienna. A Vienna? he said, yes, *a Vienna* repeated the man. My Father took him inside the back office. Two policemen came in, asking if we had seen the man who walked into the back with my Father, described him perfectly. They asked Gerasimos, got up close, checking for a lie in his face, and he became aggressive *No, and I have been waiting forever for a loaf of bread, and now when it is my turn, how lucky am I to be involved with some missing persons investigation!*" Prokopis laughed so hard that his eyes watered. "The Cretan *moustaki*, the attitude, it threw them, and they left."

"Then what happened?" asked Nikos.

"He asked if there any Viennas left after the man with my Father bought his. Out of gratitude, my Father arranged his safe passage. When your uncle got his feet on the ground, he started sending money, small amounts but very much appreciated. My Father said he would do anything for him, And, here we are. We better go. I only have two vans and my boys will need mine to deliver the rest of the bread."

Prokopis drove them in his three-wheeler delivery van back through the snarling city traffic, fumes, the honking of horns and abuse filling the air, the luggage sliding on the smooth, floured floor, Nikos and the children holding on for dear life. The door opened and they slid on their bottoms onto the bitumen. Buildings rose all around them and Sia marvelled at the number of apartments and windows.

"Come this way." said Prokopis, opening the glass door to the building. He opened the first door on the left of the first floor and showed them in.

"Ok, we have two bedrooms; one with a double and three singles in the other. You will have to sleep on the couch." he said, pointing to Nectarios.

"That's fair." he said. The Acropolis made another appearance, this time to the right. "Now, if anyone knocks, you only answer if you hear my voice saying Vienna, understand?"

"Got it."

"No one in this building knows about what I do, so it is not as if this is a holding pen or anything. Nikos, give me all of your identification so I can go to work."

Nikos inhaled as he handed everything over and took a set of keys from Prokopis.

"I feel vulnerable, Prokopis, I can't lie."

Prokopis smiled. "You would be lying if you said the opposite. Trust me," He shook his hand and kissed Fotini on the cheek. "If you need bread, I'm on the other side of this building on *Odos Artakis*. You will find an excellent butcher and greengrocer two doors down. I'll be in touch."

As the door closed, Sia pointed to the Acropolis. "Can Litsa take me there, Mother?"

"No one is going anywhere far, little one." said Fotini. We may be here for a while, so we need to shop and stock up. No more eating out. Litsa stared out into the vastness of the city beyond the balcony.

"Litsa?" said Fotini. "Now while we have a chance, we need to talk."

"I know, Mrs Fotini."

"So, what exactly are you planning to do with yourself? We cannot leave here until we are one hundred percent sure you are safe and can make your way once we are gone."

"Well, Prokopis said he had an idea."

"Child, until ideas amount to something, they are nothing but smoke. What do you want to do?"

Litsa flung herself into the couch pillow, bawling her eyes out. "I just wanted to leave Tavroniti behind, and now?" Rita and Sia comforted her, Sia scowling at her Mother for upsetting her new best friend. "Mother, you are mean." she said, wagging her finger.

"Litsa, sit up like the adult you are supposed to be and look at me."

She wiped her tears and matted hair away. "Put some thought into what you think you are good at. You are here without a formal education past primary school, no experience; this city will swallow you up if you're not careful."

"You are more of a Mother than mine ever was."

"Litsa, please, your Mother loves you."

"You don't believe it. That nightmare I had last night – it was her telling me I was right; I can do better."

"Better than what?"

"I don't know, better."

"Well, you're a smart girl so think about it."

Their conversation was interrupted by Nikos and Nectarios snoring in tandem, one in each room. Their spontaneous laughter broke the sombre mood.

"One day you can have this too," said Fotini to Litsa, kissing her on the head. "Come with me and the girls to buy some food."

"Of course."

Fotini walked the girls, holding a hand each as they approached the traffic with caution, now well versed in the random movement of vehicles and driver's agnostic to stop signs and pedestrian crossings. They bought enough meat and vegetables for a beef stew and some rockmelon for dessert, stopping past the bakery for a loaf and a chocolate each for the girls.

In Piraeus, a tired Stelios stepped out gingerly onto dry land, the cold air blowing his hair sideways, laughing coming from other passengers. He took out his faded picture of Litsa, and regretted not having a more recent one, remembering he didn't have one because he hadn't bothered, despite many opportunities. He rolled through the irritations in his mind; Hariklia, Sifi and Mr Pandelis. He was certain that in spite of him being the only one trying to find his daughter, they were all laughing at him behind his back.

After Hariklia left him in Souda, he became aware of the disgusting gypsy woman, approaching him pockmarked and reeking of sebum and *raki* as he sat on a bench.

"Who do you seek?" she asked him.

Stelios turned away fearing the malodour that would accompany her speech. He reluctantly showed her Litsa's photo, the recognition showing in an instant. She put out her hand for money, and he gave her a single drachma note.

"They left this morning for Piraeus. She was anxious to leave."

"And?"

"It will cost you more than that to know."

He produced a five drachma note.

"She left with a family of two girls and an older boy."

He nodded.

"Tell me something. Did you molest her?"

"Go to hell, you foul beast!" yelled Stelios, standing upright and calling out for any authority within earshot, before walking towards a cafe until time to board.

She cupped her hands around her mouth to propel her voice through the wind. "You won't find her; she does not want to be found."

Stelios stopped and let his murderous thoughts pass before walking on to the cafe.

Now in cold Piraeus, he walked to the sign of the police station and began making his enquiries, the baritone voice of the tall officer asking for clarification of whether she was kidnapped or left of her own accord.

"If she was kidnapped, Sir, surely some suspicious behaviour would have been noticed."

"Look, she left without telling us and she needs to come back."

"So, was she kidnapped, or did she leave of her own will?"

Stelios slapped his thigh in frustration. "Not this again! She is not where she lives."

"How old is she Sir?"

"Eighteen, I told you this already." said Stelios, exhaling.

"I understand you are agitated Sir, but aggression does not help your cause here in Athens. In Crete, maybe, but not here. Be civil and we will try to help."

"Do you have a daughter?"

"Yes, two. I have two daughter's worth of wrinkles. Now let's start over; can we see a picture of her, and we will start looking as best we can, Ok?"

"Yes, Sir." said Stelios, as he produced the picture of Litsa.
Directed to a seat, he sat and waited. He expected to do a lot
of waiting now.

CHAPTER 33

Athens, 1966

The Petrakis family were fortunate to have contacted Prokopis when they did. He often arranged two or more families' journeys concurrently. Delays were inevitable and patience sorely tested.

He would have them on the *Patris* within a week if not for Litsa. It left Piraeus every two months on average, so timing was everything. He remembered a customer, a Professor once telling him any chemical reaction was as fast as the slowest part of it, the *limiting step*. Here, this was Litsa. Nikos and Fotini were committed to helping Litsa settle, and treated her like their own, which helped. Prokopis considered all this as he waited at the same cafe his Father frequented, just off the central park of Nea Smyrni, the church of Saint Foteini prominent on the top of the shallow hill. A pair of hands covered his eyes.

"Guess who?" said a gravelly female voice.

He laughed and held the hands, the myriad of rings a dead giveaway, then got up and hugged his friend. Kyriakoula Sarantos stood taller than her five-foot four frame, her dimpled cheeks and short, mousy hair attracting looks wherever she went. But only her family and close friends knew her by this name. Since she launched her fashion house *Koukla Flora* with her friend Flora, she experienced early signs of success, not riches and excess but enough to live on and be creative, beholden to no one. Today Koukla wore a dark brown skivvy, a tan checked knee-high overall with large white buttons and white tights.

"You're looking more reserved than usual today."

"Mind if I light up?"

"Have I ever minded before?"

"So, to what do I owe the pleasure?"

"Apart from basking in your sunshine?"

"Come on, stop blowing smoke up my arse."

"A family from Crete has arrived and they have a stowaway girl, eighteen. Before they can leave on the *Patris* for Australia, I need to make sure she is settled."

"She can't go back to her family in Crete?"

He shook his head.

"And you want me to take her under my wing?"

"Well, you meet her and see what you think."

"Describe her to me. Don't over-sauce it."

"She's eighteen-"

"You said that already."

"She's beautiful and has a vulnerability about her."

"Ok, easy with the mayonnaise." said Koukla, getting up.
Head bowed, Prokopis got up to say goodbye.

"Don't be glum, Prokopis. I'm only leaving to pick up Flora.
We'll meet you in an hour."

Prokopis hugged her. "Thanks." He scribbled the address and
handed it to her.

"Don't thank me yet. It takes two votes from two to make any
decisions. But you obviously see something." she said with a
wink.

Litsa cried in the room she shared with Rita and Sia. Sia as
always sat with her, ignoring Litsa's wish to be alone, staying
like a limpet to her form as she cried in bed. Compounding
the guilt for holding back the family from moving on with
their lives, the possibility of being shipped back to Crete
scared the hell out of her. She would jump ship rather than
hear her parents tell her they told her so. She told herself the
hand of someone would place her where she needed to be in
the world so she could make her own mistakes and grow.
The knock on the door startled her. She overheard Fotini
talking to Prokopis and heard female voices. She sat up and
wiped her eyes.

"Do you know who they are, Sia?"

Sia shrugged. "Let me help you look beautiful, come on."

While Litsa washed her face, Sia grabbed her brush and
brushed as high as her little legs would allow, drawing
laughter from Litsa.

"I wish I had you as a little sister."

"Me too. Come on the ship with us. You hide and I won't tell anybody."

"You're too sweet for words." She checked herself in the mirror.

"And you are beautiful, like a princess."

Fotini knocked on her door and called for her out. Litsa emerged to see Koukla and Flora sitting at the table. They got up and introduced themselves.

"I'm Koukla, Kyriakoula actually. Aren't you a beautiful one?" she said, shaking her hand.

"Prokopis was right. She has something." said Flora, less flamboyantly dressed than Koukla in a short dress and her jet-black curly hair tied up in a bun. "I'm Flora, and that's my real name."

"Please, sit," said Koukla.

"Nectarios." called out Fotini.

Nectarios came out from his room and blushed as the women looked up at him.

"What's going on? Where's Father?"

"Your Father has gone to buy food for tonight. You're taking your sisters for some sweets. Bring back some change, Ok?"

Prokopis started, turning towards Fotini. "When I said I had an idea for Litsa to settle here, I thought, I didn't want her to be some waitress at a tavern, not because there's no honour in work like that, but-"

"You wanted to be sure she could make a life here once we were gone."

"Exactly."

"What do you two do?" asked Fotini.

"Koukla and I run a fashion design house, Koukla Flora. We do alternative fashion."

"Like this?" she asked, pointing to Koukla.

"Oh, that's tame compared to some of our designs. Women are tired of the same old clothes they are expected to wear. No disrespect, Mrs Fotini." said Koukla.

"None taken, and Fotini is fine."

"How do I come into this discussion?" asked Litsa. She wanted to be respectful, but they were discussing her future. Koukla nodded at Flora. "Up to now, we have either modelled the clothing ourselves and had photographers take shots or have used models and paid them for a single shoot. What we need is a face for our company, one people can associate with our look, an icon. I cannot speak for Koukla, but for me you would be perfect."

"Yes," said Koukla, smiling, "perfect."

"You are eighteen, yes?"

"Actually, nineteen in two days."

"So, you are old enough to determine your own affairs. We would offer you a contract, offer you full board, food, a roof over your head, and above all, safety with us, as," she said, looking to Flora for the right word. "Godmothers," said Flora. "We have seen women who go into fashion become manipulated by men, men who either want to bed you or work you like a slave. This is why we became partners. I found Koukla drinking from a bottle of some disgusting brew in the middle of Syntagma Square. I put her up for the night and we discovered we loved fashion. But men had forced us out if we didn't open our legs or work for nothing. We lived at my parents' place, worked seven days a week for two years, got enough money together to rent a small apartment and buy a sewing machine where we could design and create. Once we sold some pieces at a market, we got more cash together and slowly, slowly, here we are." She placed her hand on Koukla's and squeezed tight. "We have stuck together through some hard times."

Fotini pursed her lips at their hands intertwined and sat back. Koukla laughed. "You think we are, what, together as a couple, Fotini?" Flora joined in, then Litsa and Prokopis before Fotini placed her hand over mouth and gave in to laughter.

"This doesn't happen in Crete." she said.

"Not that you know of." said Koukla with a wink. "But no, we like men. And one day we hope to find men who love us for who we are and what we do. Until then, their loss. We

have a lot of work to keep us busy and much to achieve. But
back to Litsa. Tell me, angel, are you interested in fashion,
modelling?"

"How would I know? I have lived on an island where none of
this exists. This is all new to me, but I like what you have
both done, the sacrifice, the vision. Do you think I could do
this?"

"We are still sitting here because we want to welcome you
into our family." said Flora. "You are definitely a natural
beauty, and we'll make you a model, but we hope you can
help us with design as well, once you have worn our clothes
enough. And we promise to care for you until you can look
after yourself. Who knows, one day you could outgrow us."
Litsa held Fotini's hand. "What do you think?" Fotini turned
to Koukla and Flora.

"Where is your studio?"

"Kipseli. Come, we'll take you."

Koukla hailed a taxi and rode with Flora, Litsa and Fotini to
Kipseli. Fotini wondered how the locals got any sun, the
canopy of trees providing shade over the street.
Litsa drifted away with the smell coming from the opposing
apartment buildings, marble steps freshly washed by the brief
morning shower. Children played hide and seek around the
trees.

They walked past cafes with French and Italian names
unfamiliar to Fotini and Litsa; *Bistrot, Cinzano, Lavazza*,
machines whirring and grinding coffee offering the locals
more than the standard Greek coffee. Flora led them down a

narrow street, Atias Zonis. Between two tall competing apartment blocks was a shorter concrete building with an industrial grey door.

"And we're here." said Flora, unlocking the door, leading them up a narrow stairwell, into an equally narrow hallway, opening up into a wide room with concrete floors, low lamps and desks along each side. Two shallow windows let in natural light. A small balcony with a table and chairs sat behind the small kitchen.

Posters of varying sizes covered the dark grey concrete wall to their left; Jackie Kennedy, Brigette Bardot and Mary Quant, but Litsa's eyes were drawn to the enormous painting on the opposite wall. She walked fast towards it and stopped a metre away, transfixed as the oblique ray of sunlight streamed highlighted the ridges and valleys of the oil. Melina Mercouri sat outside a street café in Plaka on a wooden chair, cigarette in her left hand, her right hand cupping her angular chin, legs crossed as she wore a light, three-quarter sleeve printed summer dress, exuding chic independence. All this in the simple act of having a coffee and a cigarette.

"Brilliant isn't it?" asked Koukla.

"Stunning. Who did this?"

"An artist friend of ours painted it from a classic photo by Slim Aarons, the American photographer; 1961 I think. A child could have been standing with a toy camera instead of Aarons, and she would be the same." said Koukla.

"I can show you the original of you like." said Flora.

"I want to be just like her." said Litsa.

"Who wouldn't?" asked Flora, noticing the tears on Litsa's face, falling onto the hard floor. Litsa turned to them. "Where would I stay?"

"We have a small bedsit next door to us, but you would work and eat with us here. She would be under our care." said Flora, turning to Fotini.

"Show me."

Flora walked them into a small room with a single bed, small wardrobe, a tall boy and a small ensuite shower. She turned to Flora.

"Well, Prokopis has vouched for you, but I need to speak with Nikos. We are responsible for Litsa." She walked over to the painting and put her arm around Litsa, still transfixed by the painting. Litsa held her hand and squeezed it tight, crying.

Stelios grimaced as he got up from his hotel bed in Piraeus. *Four star my arse* he said as he rubbed his lower back. The cacophony of horns and chatter on the busy Polytechnio Road below hurt his head. He had heard nothing in two nights, and he was sick of just sitting in taverns and cafes waiting for the police to give him something, some hope of seeing Litsa again. He showered and took a taxi into Athens, asking the driver to drop him off in Syntagma Square, anywhere with masses of people. Punctuated by crude swearing and obscene traffic manoeuvres, the trip made

Stelios wish he had walked. He gave the driver the fare, tapping him on the shoulder to turn and face him.

"You should be tipping me for the stress you caused me."

"Get lost you idiot." said the driver, barely waiting for the door to close before he screeched off.

Stelios stuck out as an islander with his hat and tie, looking up at the tall buildings. He knew the chances of seeing Litsa here were slimmer than slim but walking around gave him something. The free time thrusted upon him gave him a chance to think things over. His Father was a strict, berating patriarch, showing love in short glimpses and mostly in the presence of others. When he fell into marriage by arrangement, he had no other template to follow. He wavered between his Father's example and allowing Hariklia's cold maternal approach to take over when he ran out of answers. *Is it any wonder we're at this point?* he said to himself, relief that he could say it. In the middle of this epiphany, he strode out onto the road and a taxi narrowly missed him, honking and the open-palm *moutza* hand gesture directed at him. He walked in ten-minute spokes outward and inward from Syntagma, and hailed a taxi in the mid afternoon as the cold set in. He rang the Piraeus Police Station from his room. *No news on your daughter, sorry.*

As she fell into bed, Hariklia cursed the phone. She ignored it the first three times but picked up the fourth.

"Have you found her, oh intrepid explorer?" she answered in a flat tone.

"No, but not because I haven't been trying." he said, slurring.

"Ah, the Cretan male's last refuge, *raki*."

"For your information, it's beer. I've had quite a lot of it."

"Are you showing your class by ringing me from a public phone?"

"No, from my room. I have standards."

"Like the festival of Saint Nikolaos. Ring me tomorrow when you're sober."

"She hates us, Hariklia. The gypsy said she didn't want to be found."

"Go to bed."

"I'm sorry, Hariklia."

"At last; you've accepted it too. I'm happy for you. Now go to bed and call me after breakfast."

Hariklia hung up. She reflected on her time with Stelios. Sure, he was arranged and she put up no resistance, but she loved him for a short window, as much as she was able to express love. Before she died, her sister Theodosia told her *'emotions didn't run in our blood.'* She wondered if an unexpected disappearance would have triggered some emotional discovery, and her trepidation about such a thing answered her question in the affirmative. Some things we were gifted or cursed with, and others we had the power to change. She hoped for good news about Litsa, hoping she did do better; and even more she hoped to never see her again, and be forced to face her sin of being a cold Mother.

Stelios got up early the next morning and took the first ship back to Crete, running to the amusement of onlookers wishing their loved ones a safe trip. He didn't bother dropping past to pick up Litsa's photo from the police station. He admitted to himself he didn't deserve it, and if she ever returned of her own will, he would be in her debt forever.

Litsa returned from Koukla Flora full of hope but checked her excitement when she saw Fotini wiping tears from her eyes.

"Mrs Fotini?"

"Yes, Litsa."

"If nothing came of this, I would have come to Australia with you."

"You're trying to cheer me up, which is lovely. It was bad enough we took you with us to Athens. But another country, hemisphere? We would deserve to be locked up."

"I love you, Mrs Fotini. You showed-"
Fotini tried not to sound cold. "Not this again, please. Your Mother and Father are probably worried sick about you. I showed you the same love any child should expect. You need to promise me something."

"For you, anything."

"Once you are settled, you will send a letter to your parents telling them you are Ok, that you are fed, have a roof over your head, earning money. Give them some peace. They are

263

not normal, loving parents, I know, but they are your parents.
Torturing them with no news is no way to act. Promise?"
She nodded. "I promise. So, you and Mr Nikos will let me
stay with Koukla and Flora?" Fotini winked. "Your face in
front of the painting of Mercouri. This is your destiny. Leave
it to me."

The conversation with Nikos and Prokopis was shorter than
Fotini herself expected.

"You don't want to meet them?" asked Litsa.

"I'll meet them when we take you. Prokopis and your Mother
approve. What else do I need? But one thing, Litsa."

"I already told her, Nikos."

"I will make sure my parents know I am Ok." said Litsa.

"Good girl."

Prokopis got up and slapped Nikos on the back. "The next
departure of the *Patris* is in two days. I have only one step
left for you and you will be on it - your medical clearance.
The Australian government is strict on this. Tomorrow
morning, I will pick you up at eight to see my doctor. He will
clear and stamp your paperwork and then we go to buy our
tickets. The road, well the sea, is clear."

"We should celebrate." said Nikos.

"No," said Prokopis firmly. "Let's not jinx ourselves. We will
drink and eat on the night before you leave, when everything
is complete. I insist."

After dinner, the girls collapsed into bed, tucked in by Litsa.

"Will you visit us when you are a famous model?" asked Rita.

"If I can afford it, I would love to see you, and you too, Sia." But Sia was already out to the world.

Litsa joined the others at the kitchen table.

"Strange how we have ended up here isn't it, child?" said Nikos to Litsa.

"Life is surprising." said Litsa.

"No one is to blame for what happened. After everything, I can talk more calmly about destiny and such things. When your Father made all those threats, I accepted Nectarios would marry you, and I had no idea my Uncle would show immaculate timing like he did, but here we are. Fotini and I have come to love you as if you were one of our own. Respect yourself, work hard and do not be tempted by distractions catching your eyes. This Koukla and Flora, they sacrificed and worked hard, and they are making their own path. You need to do the same."

Nikos and Fotini retired to bed.

Nectarios smiled at Litsa and put his hand out. She squeezed it hard. "You're a handsome man," said Litsa. "Make sure you stay out of trouble. Try and keep it in your pants."

"I'm confused by all this." said Nectarios.

"I know. But I still hold out hope for you. Be a brother for your sisters. They love you so much. You have parents who love you, but they will always need their big brother."

Prokopis knocked at a quarter to eight and drove them in his van for the second time. He parked down a cobbled laneway and walked them up three flights of dusty stairs at the rear of a building.

"This is a doctor's office?" asked Fotini.

"He doesn't need us coming in from the front." said Prokopis. He let himself in with a long key and led them down a long passageway. He counted seven doors and let himself in. They were in a waiting room at the end of a corridor and Prokopis asked them to sit. After ten minutes, a short, bearded man with round glasses emerged from a door. He spoke perfect Greek but with a Russian accent and introduced himself as Dr Alexi Sidelkov. He examined them in a small room off to the side of the waiting room, and in an hour, they left with fully stamped paperwork. Sidelkov placed the money handed over by Propkopis in the usual spot in his bureau drawer and called in his next patient from the waiting room that patients accessed from the front door.

Stelios hoped Hariklia would be waiting for him when he disembarked. Instead, the gypsy caught his eye, her head nodding, judgement vindicated, her ugly smile as she followed him with her eyes the whole way until Hariklia ushered him to the car.

CHAPTER 34

Sicily, 1967

Cu nesci arrinesci
Who leaves their own comfort zone - succeeds.
- Sicilian proverb

Vanna attracted glances and mutterings as she walked to the market to buy food.

"Only twenty days since he passed and she's back to wearing summer dresses." whispered one woman to another over the balcony to her neighbour.

The neighbour laughed and took the cigarette from her mouth. "Fuck off; as if you'd know. You've never been married."

"Thanks for the commentary." said Vanna, not bothering to lift her head. Claudio and Lidia flanked her wherever she went since the funeral but today she just wanted her own company.

At the market, she bought what she needed for the squid ink risotto, not engaging in any discourse in case anyone recognised her from Bacano. Squid ink risotto she could handle making and could not imagine never eating it again. She vowed never to make *pasta chi sardi* or *polpetti* again. That was a past life, and she had chosen to move on from it. Her second cousin Stefano was due to visit today. Upon hearing of Tino's passing, he wanted to pay visit and his respects. His train would arrive from Palermo in a few hours and she wanted to have everything done in time. The women were back inside when she returned. She fried the onion and garlic and chopped the squid into small pieces, adding it with the squid ink and some warm water, cooking it down slow with passata until the squid was tender. In a separate pan she toasted the rice in some butter, adding the wine. She enjoyed the *ttsss* of the wine hitting the pan, the alcohol burning off before she added the fish stock in ladle by ladle.

The process of making risotto used to irritate her, but now all she had was time, and little rituals like this gave her something between satisfaction and a thrill. She didn't need a clock to tell her when twenty minutes were up, the rice told her. She mixed through the squid, ink and passata from the other pan and folded it through gently, adding parsley and more butter. She left the fluid a few millimetres above the rice and covered it. Claudio and Lidia returned from La Chiesa Biblica Messina after hearing that they were collecting clothes for the impoverished. Claudio now drove a red 1963 Fiat his Mother bought now that the council had taken back the truck Tino drove.

"Did they take the clothes?"

"Yes." said Lidia. It bothered her that her Mother was so quickly able to pack her Father's clothes and move them on. Vanna picked up on her irritation.

"Lidia, do not confuse me giving your Father's clothes to charity with me somehow not grieving. I grieve every day, in here." she said, her fist making a noise as it hit her chest. "His clothes are just what he wore, and I do not need to see them to play out the role of a mournful widow to keep up appearances for those gossiping bitches or anyone else. Understood?"

"I understand, Mother. I'm sorry."

Vanna cuddled her. "You have been dealing with this too. I'm sorry. We all need to stay close and speak our minds, even when we're wrong."

Claudio beeped the horn from the street below. They drove to Messina Centrale and waited as the train rolled in. Stefano stepped out, well dressed in a white shirt and thin black tie.

"Zia Vanna, hello!" He smelled of some exotic cologne she had never smelt before as he hugged her.

"Call me Vanna for the love of God, we're second cousins."

"Vanna, Claudio, Lidia, my condolences to you. I only met him a couple of times, but Tino was a lovely man."

"Thank you, Stefano. We are coping as best we can."

"My goodness me, you bred them beautiful, didn't you?" He hugged Claudio and Lidia together. "I look forward to staying with you."

Vanna served the risotto and they spoke about him some more before turning to Claudio.

"So, what do you do here?"

"I'm about to start work in construction." After the funeral, Pasquale Brinto offered him some work at the timber mill, but Claudio baulked at going back to Zafferia, so instead he found him work as a labourer in some new apartments near Mili Marina, a twenty-minute drive along the coast. He only

had to be there from seven to three, so that he could spend
time with his Mother.

"And you, Lidia?"

"I want to be a chef like my Mother."

"That's news to me," said Vanna, trying not to sound terse.

"Well, either that or become a housewife. You looked for a
job where you could cook when we came here."

"Didn't that turn out well?" said Vanna, before apologising.
"I didn't mean that. Sorry, Lidia."

"That's Ok."

"I lost my Mother last year." said Stefano. "The pain is
always there, but it becomes easier to get through each day."

After dessert, Lidia emerged from her Mother's bedroom.
Stefano would sleep in the same room as Claudio and Lidia
with her Mother. Vanna looked up at her.

"Where are you dressed up for?"

"Claudio said he would drive me to Taormina for a coffee
with three friends."

"Coffee, at this time of night?" asked Vanna, raising her
eyebrows.

"I will look after them and it will only be coffee, I promise,"
said Claudio. "No alcohol. We'll be back before midnight."

"Did you ask your cousin of he wanted to come out with you?'

Lidia and Claudio looked at each other. "Of course, he's, you're welcome to come along."

"Your Fiat holds five people if you all breathe in. In any case, I'm tired and I'll stay here with your Mother. You have a great night."

"Thank you for taking us, Claudio." said Lidia in the car. She got out and her friends hopped in the back, squeezing in tight.

"Your brother's a cutie, what's his name?" asked the middle one, Laura. *Too much lipstick,* thought Claudio as he looked in the rear mirror. "I'm Claudio."

"Sounds like a *mafioso* name." said Saria, the girl behind Lidia.

"It does not." said Angela.

"While you girls have your coffee, I'll be at another table nearby. I'll wink at Lidia when we have to go, Ok?"

"Maybe you should wink at me." said Laura, blowing a kiss.

"That will do." said Lidia, her serious face breaking out into a smile as she pinched her brother on the cheek.

They found a table outside and ordered some coffee and dessert, while Claudio sat two tables away. He found it easy to hear them without appearing to eavesdrop and watched the passing parade of people. He ordered himself an indulgent cannolo and a short black. As the girls' conversation ebbed off, he turned and winked at Lidia, her view obstructed as three men approached them, greeting them with *what do have here?* They sat down in and around the girls, the tallest one locking eyes with Lidia, Lidia's pupils dilating, not with attraction, but with fear. "We're going sorry," she said, pushing the tall one's hand away from her thigh before accepting his handshake with the ends of her fingers, and they walked towards the direction of the car. The tall one turned to his friends and stuck his tongue hard against his cheek.

"That one," he said with a crude hand gesture, "I'd break her in half," the other two joining him in raucous laughter. They took the girls' table.

"Three *Amaro Averna!*" yelled the tall one to a waiter taking orders two tables away.

In the car, he turned to his sister. "Are you OK?"

"Yes," she said, "that man really put the fear into me. I didn't do anything to-"

"Shh – no need to explain. Some men are pigs, they think they can take what they want. Don't fuss yourself over him. I'm here." The girls in the back seat were also rattled by the sudden approach of the men and stayed silent all the way home. He dropped Lidia off first, waiting until the stairwell light was on before he left. He dropped off the other girls and turned back onto the road to Taormina.

He parked behind the row of bars, restaurants and cafes. Their banter was louder, their legs splayed out, leaning back as the multiple rounds of Amaro Averna took effect, calling out obscenities to anyone who looked their way. The manager walked over to them as Claudio sat with his back turned, asking them to leave.

The tall one dropped some notes at the feet of the manager, laughing as he and his other friends walked towards the park behind the cafe. Claudio got up and walked the long way around. The tall one bid his friends good night as they got into their car.

"Let us drive you home." said the driver.

"You? I'm safer driving drunk than putting my life in your hands." He slapped the roof of the car and continued across the park. The car sped away and Claudio shifted into the shadows of the trees bordering the park. Within a minute, he was ten metres behind him, the man stumbling, walking fast then slowing to regain his balance, then legs crossing over, his gait deteriorating. Claudio was at his side and startled the man.

"You like my sister?"

The man stopped and faced him. "Sorry?" he said, eyes wide open. Claudio's smile, equal parts congeniality and menace, unsettled him.

"Do you like her or not?"

"Sure, but-"

"But what? You got so close to her, it seemed that you liked her, really liked her. Come to my house and meet her. Come?" Claudio smiled.

"Ok."

"What's your name?"

"Vito, Vito Semola." He began to sweat, and things spun around him. He stopped the spinning by trying to estimate how far he was from the lights of the cafes from their brightness. He strained to hear the chatter of the people, but only got silence in return. The next sound was the strike of Claudio's wooden truncheon against the back of his skull, his eyes rolling for a second before the lights went out. Claudio carried him with ease to his car and drove to the Taormina clifftops overlooking the Strait of Messina with his lights off. A car was leaving, and he took the opportunity to drive onto a narrow patch of grass alongside a row of bushes. He slipped his shoes off and lifted the still comatose Vito from the car, took his jacket off and lay it on the grass away from the edge. He stood Vito up against the car and slapped him awake. Vito's eyes opened to halfway. Claudio walked him across to the edge, his footprints easy to see in the moonlight, before pushing him onto the rocks and foaming waves below. His body made a dull thud, coming to rest a metre from the water, waves now crashing over him. Claudio checked himself as he drove back to Messina, passing the apartment to see his Father. He walked with his torch to the grave and sat in the dark, level with where his head would be.

"With you gone, I have to look after Lidia, Father. Vanna is capable of looking after herself. I'm sorry and I am certain you wouldn't approve of my actions. You were always a decent man. But I will never apologise for looking after my family. I love you and miss you every day." A guard shone his torch in his direction.

"Have you been drinking?" asked the croaky voice.

"No, just visiting my Father."

"At this hour?"

"Yes, but I'm going."

"May his memory be eternal, my son."

"Thank you." said Claudio. He showered and crawled into bed. He was nearly asleep when Stefano said *psst*.

"What happened? You took a while after you dropped off Lidia. Was she nice?"

Claudio smiled. "Don't tell Vanna or Lidia. She was lovely."

Stefano tapped his nose. "Don't worry, our secret."

Claudio wondered if he would see the fright in Vito's eyes again in his dreams. He fell asleep easily from the effort and the driving before he had a chance to relive those two minutes and woke refreshed. He drove Stefano to where their farm used to be. The timber mill fumes continued to spew. Claudio had to shut the car windows to prevent the fumes from coming in. Hairs stood on the back of his neck as he drove past what used to be Crudelli's front gate, the stump still there where Sister Malena dropped dead. He slowed and wondered if he should bother driving any further. Crudelli's

275

land was an ant's network of dirt roads, with some houses already built. He drove on to the old farm and his eyes boggled at the number of houses already constructed and counted three excavators clearing further land for more. He drove past Mayor Maresca's farm. Cars sat at the top of the drive and he continued on home.

"It must have been difficult for you to move, Claudio." said Stefano.

"It was for Tino." he said, comfortable calling him by his first name now that he had passed. "But you can't stop progress, can you?"

They spent the next day at the beach at Vanna's suggestion, as Claudio was due to commence work the next day. Stefano watched as Claudio and Lidia swam out together to the first major wave, riding it as it came back in.

"Vanna, do you remember Uncle Elio."

"The one in Australia?"

"Yes, in Melbourne. I got a letter from him last week. He married an Australian woman who died last year. They had no kids and he wants to sponsor someone to come over and look after him. He is not well and says he does not want to die alone. He approached me because I am a lawyer. A favour for a favour."

"Are you thinking about going?"

"Me? No, no. I am very happy in Palermo. I have a job, a girlfriend. He asked me first and if I chose not to go, he says I am obliged to get someone else to fulfil that role."

"A guilt trip tipped with gold then."

"Yes. So, what do you think?"

"Stefano, I am forty-five, a widow at forty-five."

"Who cares what people will say?"

"I do not care about gossip, Stefano. I spent twenty-four years with Tino. I cannot just abandon those years and start a new life in Australia."

"I agree, it sounds confronting. Let it sit for a few days."

"My answer will still be no, Stefano. I am a little upset that you came all this way to unburden yourself of this wish."

"I came also because I wanted to pay my respects, but yes, I should have been more honest about that."

"We are happy to have you here, but I hope you won't be offended if I say no."

"No to what?" asked Claudio, towelling his hair.

"Nothing." said Stefano. "I just offered to buy you all dinner tonight and your Mother refuses."

Claudio knew better from the tone but let it be. His Mother's judgement was razor sharp and he didn't need to question her

277

further. They returned home and treated themselves to dinner at a trattoria overlooking the bay, walking along the promenade afterwards to digest before Vanna relented and let Stefano buy them all gelato.

Claudio woke early, dressed and drove to his first day at work. He made it in good time. He found the foreman, a short hairy man called Nando Pappalardo.

"So, you're one of Brinto's men, are you?"

"Claudio Liverani."

"Ok, pull on a hat and start moving those bricks to that pile over there."

Claudio's endurance was tested as he hauled load after land of bricks with a wheelbarrow. He came out from the toilet. A police car was parked outside the foreman's office. He continued with the bricks, watching the two policemen. At lunch, Pappalardo addressed the workers.

"I have some awful news. The son of our boss, Vito. He fell off a cliff at Taormina last night. He's dead."

"Probably drank himself to death, the entitled prick." said a voice behind him.

When he delivered the blows to Father Di Pardo, when Malena made her veiled threats, when he threw Vito onto the rocks and drove back to Messina, Claudio's heart rate didn't rise above eighty; but now it raced and it felt foreign. He was sweating and had to tell himself not to look around to see if he was being looked at. He sat in a toilet stall and willed his

heart to return to normal. He worked on until Pappalardo
called him in fifteen minutes before his clock off time.

"Here you go, pretty boy." he said, handing over a fat
envelope of cash.

"What's this for?"

"What do you take me for, an arse?" He smiled when he
realised Claudio had no idea what he was talking about. He
spoke slowly in a patronising voice. "Brinto will come past
during the week and collect his 'wage', understood?"

"Got it."

Pappalardo pushed across another, thinner envelope. "And
here's yours."

Claudio veered towards the other side of the road twice on
the way home, nearly clipping another vehicle both times.
Pull yourself together, he said aloud. He showered and had
hardly sat down when there was a knock on the door.
Pasquale Brinto walked in.

"You Mother, sister and cousin are out so I thought this
would be a good time. Sit down."

"Would you like a drink, Mr Brinto?"

"Just a cold soft drink, whatever you have, and Pasquale is
fine. Do you have something for me?"

Claudio handed him the envelope. "All there, Pasquale."

"You're not the kind to peek. You're an honest man, Claudio, like your Father. You didn't peek, did you?"

"No."

"So be honest again with me when I ask you this. And I will know if you are lying."

"The man you disposed of, Vito?" He made a downward motion with his hand. "I also had concerns. He deserves to rest on the Taormina rocks. He was disrespectful to my niece, felt her up and kept going when she said stop. My niece is not yet eighteen. He would've gone all the way if she didn't mention that I was her Uncle. I sent a colleague of mine to sort him out, but you got there first. He was very impressed with your work. Are you feeling Ok, Claudio?"

Claudio went pale. He dry-retched, his eyes bulging and the room spinning until Brinto lay him down onto the floor, coming back with a wet towel and placing it over his forehead.

"Don't worry. You have real balls. You did what I only considered doing, and I owe you. Must have rattled your cage seeing your sister hit upon uh? Did he proposition her? Just nod. That's what I thought. Just relax."

Brinto resumed his seat and spoke slowly. "Now this is what is going to happen. I'd like you to keep working there at Semola's construction site. You keep bringing me the envelopes that dumpy foreman Pappalardo gives you. He won't threaten you. I'll make sure he lets you off half an hour earlier than you leave now, and I'll call in when I need to. Even a couple of envelopes at a time. You won't be tempted to dip into them, I can trust you on that. If you need money, you know to ask me, don't you?"

"Yes, Pasquale."

"You need not worry about the Vito business. What you did was community service, saving how many young women from being violated by that son of a slut."

Brinto knelt down again by his side and checked his pulse. *How many times has he done this and felt no pulse* wondered Claudio. "Your colour has returned. Let me help you up."

He slowly got up and sat in the chair.

"I'm sorry." said Claudio.

Brinto chuckled. "You have nothing to apologise to me for. Now go have a shower so your Mother doesn't think anything is wrong. She's a canny woman that one, and you can't put anything past her. Go."

The door closed as he turned on the water. He let it run all over his face and wondered what was worse, Lidia knowing about Father Di Pardo or Brinto knowing about Vito. *They were souls, misguided souls but souls like the rest of us* he told himself. When he emerged from the shower, he heard laughing. Vanna, Stefano and Lidia were playing *scopa*. Vanna victoriously raised her hands in the air as she held the *settebello*, the seven of coins aloft.

"Vanna always gets the *settebello*." said Claudio.

"Come and play and make it a foursome. How was your first
day at work?" asked Vanna.

"Ok, uneventful."

They played on late into the evening, only stopping to eat
leftovers. Claudio went to bed, wondering if he was a
psychopath, able to overcome the fear Brinto put into him yet
play cards as if nothing had happened. He concluded that he
was, but it was different to Di Pardo and Semola. The priest
prayed on the vulnerable Caterina, and Semola touched who
he wanted on his own terms. How was he anything like
them? He fell asleep, calmed by this reassuring thought.

CHAPTER 35

Athens, 1966

Prokopis spread all the paperwork into neat piles on the Petrakis kitchen table; medical clearances, fresh blue passports, *Patris* tickets, all in order from oldest to youngest. He smiled with satisfaction.

"Sometimes I cut it fine, other times everything is ready too early, and I have to make sure the people don't do anything stupid out of boredom or impatience. This one is just right," he said, rubbing his hands before doing his cross. "The *Patris* leaves at midday tomorrow, so tonight we will have dinner together, drink a little, not too much. In the morning, we will take Litsa to Koukla and Flora then I will take you personally to the wharf by nine where my person will settle you on board before the rush. So, try and be up by six-thirty."

Nectarios' chest tightened up at the thought of being stuck on a ship for four weeks. Being cooped up in this apartment was bad enough, and the only times he left was to help shopping or take his sisters for a treat. Girls his own age made eyes at him as they walked past him babysitting his sisters. He would have given anything to go out and walk on his own before they left, before telling himself *that's how we got here, idiot*. Litsa was right, he was dragged by his penis and not his brain, the two forces battling for supremacy in his head. God help him if anyone half as beautiful as Litsa on the boat gave him the eye. Their two impromptu flings were chances offered by fate; the allure of the tryst as much about the smell of the air and getting away with it against the chance of being caught as much her natural beauty and the way she teased him. He caused this mess and now he had to move on and try not to repeat the mistake. As they sat in a tavern in Nea Smyrni, the autumn air slowly replacing the winter chill, he should have been happy, but instead he mulled over these things in a loop. A lady begged for money across the street, giving thanks as a man stopped and threw change at her, more to rid himself of her than from any sense of charity. The Souda gypsy, her curse, foul mouth and even fouler body odour.

May you never have a son to carry your shame.

He repeated the words to himself, her malodour filling his nostrils again.

"Nectarios are you Ok?" asked Litsa.

"He's already seasick." said Rita.

Prokopis lifted a glass. "I want to propose a toast, to your safe journey. To your new life in Australia; may you be prosperous and healthy. Litsa, may you find success and happiness here in Athens. Come and see me anytime. Just don't forget me when you're rich and famous."

"Thank you for everything, Prokopis." said Nikos.

"To your health." everyone said, their lives diverging from the last audible clink of the coming together of their glasses. A waiter brought out a white frosted cake while another lit the candles in a ceremonial manner, asking the diners to join in as they sang happy birthday to Litsa.

"We didn't forget." said Fotini.

Litsa beamed as she blew the candles out with Rita and Sia cheek to cheek with her. The tavern photographer took a polaroid photo of the family, giving one each to Litsa and to the family. She held their hands as they sang silly songs on the walk back to the apartment, a sadness filling her heart knowing she would not see them grow.

"Please visit us when you have lots of money Ok?" asked Sia.

"I will try my best," said Litsa, holding back tears as she squeezed their hands. "I love you both."

After tucking the girls in, Litsa joined Nectarios outside on the small balcony. The night had cooled but there was no breeze.

"You were quiet at dinner."

"The gypsy."

"That mouldy, smelly, foul piece of work?"

"That one."

"And?"

"May you never have a son to carry your shame, she said."

"She could have said 'may you never dance the *pentozali* again'. Who cares? She can't control whether you and your future wife have a son or not. Stop being so dramatic."

Nectarios laughed.

"What?"

"You're gorgeous when you're feisty."

"You haven't seen me angry or feisty."

"And sadly, I probably never will."

She pinched him on the cheek. "There's still time."

"Will you be Ok here?"

"Who can tell? I'll be better off here than back in Tavronit."
She placed a hand on his shoulder. "I was mean to you on the
boat about getting in trouble in Australia."

"No, don't apologise. I deserved it."

"I played my part; led you on, teased you until you couldn't
say no. We were both at fault. But I will say this - you were
sweet, and you'll always be my first."

She sat on his lap and kissed him on the lips, lingering for a
second. *Goodnight, Nectarios.* He sat alone, the Acropolis
staring at him until the clouds came over and he felt a chill.
He went to bed for the last time in Greece.

Fotini slumped into bed. Nikos turned to her and cupped her
cheek. "At last we're here. Are you ready?"

"I am, are you? The way you go all weak near water? It will
be like having a fourth child to look after."

"Prokopis told me to chew ginger."

"You hate ginger."

"True, but I hate feeling seasick more."

"So, chew away. How will we keep the girls occupied?"

"There are activities on board. I'm more worried about Nectarios. Ever since we left Souda, he has been spooked."

"Pfft, the gypsy is a fraud, don't give her any more thought."

"I just want to settle in the one spot when we arrive. All this moving and planning has upset my nerves."

"Aw, my man wants to settle down."

"We need to learn the language too. English isn't easy apparently."

"We'll manage. Dumber people have succeeded. We will too."

At six, everyone got up and packed, ensuring nothing was left behind. The drive to Kipseli was quicker at this hour, and a bedraggled Koukla emerged some five minutes after Prokopis pressed the buzzer, smiling warmly as she invited them in. Flora was already groomed and well dressed and poured coffee for everyone.

"You must be Nikos." said Flora, extending her hand.

"My wife assures me you will take good care of Litsa."

"We certainly will. Please, sit. Do you have time for a coffee?"

Nikos nodded. He may not have been familiar with fashion, but he recognised the workplace of a hard-working person. The desks were full, each desk had its own place in the business. He nodded with approval.

"We work hard here, Nikos. We can't wait to work with Litsa here. Like parents, we think we will be successful when she makes us redundant." said Koukla.

Nikos teared up and failed miserably to hide his emotions. "Litsa, you show respect and you will receive respect. We are going to miss you. We better get your things."

Sia paraded herself in a purple silk material, twirling around the floor, her free hand making flamboyant gestures through the air.

"Sia-" said Fotini.

"Leave her," said Flora, smiling, "it's an offcut anyway. Take it my little Princess."

Litsa returned with her two suitcases and stood before them. "So, this is goodbye."

The girls hugged her, Fotini struggling to prise them off her, Sia crying *come with us, Litsa, I'll be lonely on the ship.*

Fotini whispered in her ear. "I am happy for you and will miss you."

"Oh, I will miss you more, Mrs Fotini." said Litsa as she began blubbering.

Nikos kissed her on the forehead. "I wish you every happiness, child."

Nectarios held her in an awkward embrace, before Litsa cried into his shoulder.

"Oh my God, what am I doing here?" she whispered through tears.

"The right thing. Follow your heart, Litsa."

She wiped her tears and tapped him on the nose. "And you, try to remember what we talked about, Ok? Be nice to your sisters." She kissed him on the cheek, and they walked to the door.

Koukla and Flora waved the family goodbye as Litsa cried at the window. They comforted her after the van was out of sight.

The girls cried the whole way to Piraeus, Nectarios putting an arm around both of them until his tickling finally cheered them up.

Prokopis manoeuvred the van into a small garage a block away from the dock where the *Patris* was waiting. His Father got nabbed for suspicious behaviour the first time he organised travel for someone, naively parking on the dock itself. He escaped with a stiff warning. They walked across to the ticket office and showed their passports and paperwork to a short man with metal glasses and thick lenses magnifying his beady eyes. Nikos wondered why the official screwed up his face, looking from the tickets to the family, scanning each of them, and back again.

"Ok, here you go." said the man in a gruff voice, shoving the paperwork to the side, already looking past them to scrutinise the next family.

"Why the face back there?" asked Nikos.

"You'll find out," said Prokopis. "Don't concern yourself."

A tall man in white uniform approached them, looking stern before extending his hand to Prokopis, smiling.

"How goes things, Prokopis?"

"Good, Manoli. This is my family travelling to Australia."

"Leave them to me, my friend."

Manoli returned with a small trolley and loaded their luggage. Prokopis sensed Nikos' unease and pat him on the shoulder. "Relax, I have arranged everything. You're in good hands. Now, let's go eat. Enjoy the ground under your feet."

They walked past the garage where the van was, down a laneway to a cafe. The owner showed Prokopis and the family to a table in the kitchen he reserved for guests and friends. Eggs sizzled away and coffee brewed in multiple *brikia*, the kitchen hand taking each metal brewing cup off the heat as their foam surged to the top. *Rizogalo*, the sweet rice pudding was cooling in a huge pot.

"Eat lightly is my advice." said Prokopis. "Now a few things about the voyage. Today is the twentieth of March. The ship usually takes twenty-five days to reach Australia, not Melbourne, but the west coast, a place called Fremantle. After that, another five, six days until Port Melbourne, where your Uncle Gerasimos will greet you. I spoke to him late last night. He is expecting you and is very excited. Keep your children close at all times. Let them play with other children but keep your eyes open. The ship has some activities and fun things to do, but I won't lie; mostly you will be bored waiting from watching the sea."

"Prokopis, how can I thank you?" asked Nikos.

"I tell every family the same thing because I mean it from my heart - live well. As a Cretan, you will understand being free is above everything else in life. What is inscribed on Nikos Kazantzakis' tomb, do you remember?"

"Uncle Gerasimos used to read his books. He told me: *I hope for nothing, I fear nothing, I am free.*"

"Exactly. Be free in Australia, let nothing hold you back. Let your children spread their wings. Be free."

Relief came over Nikos, the guilt he felt about leaving Crete vanishing. No one could define who he was except he himself.

Prokopis paid the bill, waving away Nikos' protestations. "My final gift to you. One day I may make my own journey and I will need somewhere to stay."

"You are always welcome."

"Let's go."

Manoli motioned with his head to an empty gangplank.
Prokopis waved at them as they walked, shouting "I'm not
good with final farewells. God bless you and have a safe
trip," turning his back and walking back towards the van.
Nikos' feet shook at the sight of water below. "Come on,
scaredy cat, you'll be alright," said Fotini. When he turned
back, Prokopis was gone. Manoli walked fast and
encouraged the family to do likewise. He walked them down
two levels.

"Here we go, Doric Deck D, Cabin seven. They are thinking
about phasing out first class cabins to make more smaller
ones to carry more people. You're lucky to have a friend like
Prokopis."

"First class?" asked Nikos, stopping.

"Yes." said Manoli, showing them the generous bunk
bedding and the larger than normal bathroom. Nectarios
paced the floor and counted seven normal steps by ten. A
small lounge and an armchair took one wall, a thin table and
four chairs another. Two pairs of bunks occupied most of the
other two walls, Sia claiming the top bunk before realising
she and Rita would have to sleep top to tail.

"Just a little advice for free, don't advertise you are in First
Class. Jealousy makes people do strange things. And people
go a little strange on boats anyway, Ok?"

They sat unrushed in their cabin, quiet at last. Nectarios
sucked in deep breaths and swore the walls caved in as he
breathed in and straightened as he breathed out.

"I have to get out." he said, dashing for the front door.

"Imagine the other rooms." taunted Rita.

"Shut up."

He ran to the observation deck and took in the view of Piraeus for the final time. The vessel vibrated as the steam engine warmed to the task. Sweat poured down his neck, the breeze drying it cold on his back. He would spend many an hour on the deck. He laughed, he suddenly claustrophobic, his Father without sea-legs.

Back in the room, Sia asked if Nectarios was Ok.

"He's afraid of small spaces," explained her Father. "He'll be Ok. Are you Ok, my little darling?"

"Yes, Father. I will take care of you."

"Thank you, Angel."

"Let's go find Nectarios and wave goodbye to all the people on the wharf."

As they walked up the two flights to the deck, people ducked and weaved, suitcases smacking into other suitcases and people, kids being dragged like luggage and frustration on everyone's face. Doors opened then closed as belongings were deposited in rooms before the decks facing the wharf filled with passengers waving goodbye to their loved ones. The Petrakis family had no loved ones to wave goodbye to. They, the sum total of their lineage, were here on the ship, waving back at the land that circumstance and an offer too

good, too opportune to refuse, had pushed them to leave.
With the passing of years, the sentiment of those waving
goodbye to the passengers would transform from sad parting
to resentment. People sensed instability in Athens, the
occasional protests and military vehicles becoming more
frequent; but nobody expected an absolute coup and a
military junta to plunge the country into chaos a year later,
not even Prokopis.

CHAPTER 36

Sicily, 1967

Sergio Calderama walked into the Messina Police Station; slight, unshaven, poorly dressed, his shirt half out and yellow nails from chain smoking. Commissario Fedula walked him personally into his office and demanded no interruptions. The rest of the branch speculated on who he was, presuming he was a criminal about to confess a crime. but here he was being welcomed by the Commissario into his office.

"Calderama, where are we at?"

Fedula worked hard to insert him into the Sidero family without anyone suspecting. His voice and analytical skills were top notch, his knowledge of different dialects unmatched. He melded in well with his surroundings and had ice in his veins. As a single man, he was ideal in case his cover was blown. Fedula was pragmatic but didn't want a widow or God forbid, children without a Father on his conscience.

"The net is drawn, Sir. I have evidence of every tentacle the Sidero family has touched, with photos of meetings, recordings and documents."

"You have put yourself at enormous risk for this. Did anyone suspect you?"

"No, Sir."

"Ok, lay it all out for me." Fedula cleared his second desk of all clutter and called in his deputy, Bonvissuto to watch and listen, insisting Calderama not be interrupted as he showed his hand-drawn schematics of names, mayors, businessmen, Sidero family members and their links with each other. Fedula winced at the sight of Pietro Ignazi's name. *Merda, che peccato.* It was eight-thirty a.m. By one-thirty in the afternoon, the extent of the corruption and intimidation was clear. Police officers implicated by the investigation were rounded up that night, and by ten the next morning, thirteen mayors named in the investigation were arrested to reveal everything they knew about the Sidero family, each pumped for information with multiple threats held over them. This productive approach led to the next wave of arrests an hour later, with Pasquale Brinto dying in a shootout as he attempted to leave his house, his wife and daughter watching from the front window in horror, Brinto ramming his car into police and their cars until no more blood flowed to his legs.

Claudio slowed as he approached his work as four police cars parked in front of the foreman's office. He resisted the temptation to do a U-turn and drove past the site, turning left three minutes later and driving home another way. He ran up the stairs and gathered his Mother, Lidia and Stefano around the table.

"Mother, whatever Stefano was offering you at the beach the other day, well, we have to know."

"Why the urgency, what happened?" asked Vanna.

"You have to trust me on this. Tell me first and I will explain." He watched Lidia's head fall into her hands.

"What, Lidia?!" asked Vanna, now more urgent.

"Mother," said Claudio, " what is the offer?"

"Uncle Elio, the one in Australia. He wants someone from our family to go there to live. He will sponsor the family that goes as long as they care for him. He has sent some money, enough for the ship journey, and he has a house big enough for everyone."

Vanna grabbed Claudio by the sleeve. "Now, tell me what the hell is going on."

"The other night when I took Lidia for a coffee with her friends. A group of men sat themselves down and one, a man called Vito, he got very close to Lidia."

Lidia nodded, tears streaming down her face.

"He said something I won't repeat here about Lidia and after I dropped them off home, I went back."

"That far, back to Taormina? To achieve what?"

"I waited until the manager kicked them out. They were all drunk. I...I followed Vito through the park and attacked him." He drew breath. "And then I drove him to the cliffs at Taormina and threw him onto the rocks."

Vanna looked at Lidia, shocked at her lack of shock and her head shook uncontrollably. When Claudio didn't plead his case, Stefano said "There's more isn't there?" He nodded.

"What could make this worse?" asked Vanna.

"One of Brinto's men was watching him that night because
Vito had touched up one of Brinto's nieces. He witnessed me.
Brinto told me he wouldn't turn me in, that I had done society
a favour, as long as I collected his protection money from the
construction site, Vito's Father's construction site."

"This is too unreal to be true." said Vanna, no longer shaking
but stunned and pale. "So now what?"

"I drove to work and there were police everywhere. I think
they have busted the Sidero family, but the foreman will
surely tell them I collected money for Brinto, who may will
turn me in when they ask about Vito."

No one spoke as everyone absorbed the multiple bombs.

"I did not want to leave this house, this island, this country,
my husband, my dead husband!" yelled Vanna.

Stefano placed his hand in the middle of the table. "I think
we need to deal with this."

Vanna tried to speak softly so the neighbours wouldn't hear.
"How, Stefano, how? My son is a murderer and now the
police will be after us. Wait - how much money do you have
stashed away from the collection?"

"Two envelopes worth." said Claudio, indicating the
thickness with his thumb and index finger.

"And you think nobody will be after that kind of money?"
asked Vanna. "Stefano, how quickly do you think we can
travel to Australia?" She felt sick as she asked the question.

Stefano handled the occasional immigration case, and the answer came immediately. "The *Galileo Galilei* leaves on the fourth of every second month, but its sister ship the *Guglielmo Marconi* sometimes leaves a bit before or after, depending on demand. My suggestion - we pack what is essential and bunk in a hotel for tonight in case anyone, Sidero or police comes knocking. First thing tomorrow we find out and go from there."

"Go pack, both of you. Now!" yelled Vanna. She sat and composed herself, looking around the room to see what she could and could not leave behind. Once she had calmed down, she packed also, crying as she was forced to make decisions as she went. She stuffed photos, the cash from the farm sale that was left over and jewellery between layers of clothing and bid farewell to the rest. She stopped as Claudio walked into her room, sheepishly looking at her. She picked up a shoe and caught him hard on the forehead.

"Vanna!" said Stefano. "You can tear through him later. We don't have time for that. Let's move. Claudio, do you have the money?"

"Yes."

"Pack the envelopes between two layers of clothing at the bottom of your suitcase. Do we have everything? Lidia, are you Ok?"

"I'm packed. Let's go."

"Walk quietly one at a time with your suitcase meet me out the front. We don't need to raise any attention. Claudio, give me the keys."

Stefano walked out and observed the traffic. Nothing. He started the car and waited as they came a minute apart, Vanna last, locking the door quietly as possible. He drove them to a hotel north of Messina, the Elan, nondescript and quiet. They had to book two rooms and slept, waking at seven and driving to the port. They were the first to be served as the roller shutters of the ticket office went up.

"Timetable for the Galileo and Marconi please." said Stefano.

"The Galileo left three days ago, but the Marconi arrives from Genoa the day after tomorrow. Do you have passports?" asked the unshaven man, tugging at his Lloyd Triestino cap with importance, his eyes nearly covered by its peak.

"Yes, here."

He inspected hem over and handed them back. "So, you have passports. First class or tourist?"

"Tourist is fine." said Vanna, reaching for her bag.

"Good choice. There are no first-class cabins left. Now the important question. Do you have 570 lira?"

"We need to visit a bank and we will return." said Stefano, steering Vanna away.

"What are you doing? I have the money."

"I'm not paying your way, Uncle Elio is." he said, handing her an envelope that came with his letter. "You need to board at Genoa. If they look for you and see the passenger list leaving Messina, they will see your names."

"So now we're going to Genoa? What madness is this?"

"Vanna, trust me on this."

"And the car?" asked Claudio.

"You'll drive bigger and better ones in Australia; American made. Learn to let go. What you acquire there will make you forget what you left behind." He strode towards another ticket counter and bought them three one-way tickets.

"The ship leaves in an hour, at ten. Don't go anywhere," said the woman in a cranky voice, as if she would be inconvenienced. They sat with their luggage and waited.

"Are you hungry?" asked Stefano.

"Who can fucking eat at this moment?" said Vanna.

"Mother!" said Lidia.

"Leave me be." Vanna snapped. Claudio bowed his head and stayed quiet.

They presented their tickets at the first call. Vanna turned towards Stefano, crying, then laughing.

"Why am I laughing?"

"Your body is trying to cope. Here is my card. If you need anything, anything, you call me, even from Australia." He hugged them all quickly and ushered them up the gangplank.

"Claudio."

"Yes?"

"You're the man of the family. Act like it."

Claudio nodded and trudged upwards. Vanna pointed to an empty section of seating and slumped. She cried again as the ship blew a loud toot of its horn, the first thrust forward shifting them in their seats. *I've abandoned him* she told herself. She rushed to the deck facing where Tino lay at one with the soil and the worms, standing in a silent salute until Lidia coaxed her back inside. Exhausted, she fell asleep as Lidia softly ran the filaments of her through her hands, just like her Mother did to her. The ship powered on, Claudio watching from the stern deck until la Madonnina of Messina bay disappeared out of view.

Stefano adjusted the seat in the Fiat, refuelled and drove the four hours back to Palermo, earning himself a cramp as he got out.

Every room in Messina's police station was used, crooked police and those associated with the Sidero family who had not died by the gun interrogated in groups. Nello Mezzomarte, the young man sent by Pasquale Brinto to spy on Vito on the night Claudio threw him off the cliff was absent from the proceedings, departed from this world by his own hand as police ran up to his one-bedroom apartment;

and with him any suspicion of Claudio. Nando Pappalardo
sat with his boss, Augello Semola.

"Nun dir nu cazzu pri a busta." whispered Semola. Say
nothing about the envelopes; anyone left untouched when
this blows over will kill us if we do.

None the wiser about this turn of fate, Claudio sat on the
Mari Santi, looking to the left as the captain announced the
Corsican port of Bastia, its protective arm cuddling the bay
just as Messina's did. He walked outside to have a look.

"Smaller than Messina's," came a raspy voice a few metres to
his left. A man appearing every day of his seventy years of
age turned to him, leaning on the railing, cigarette in hand.
"My wife won't let me smoke anywhere near her. Are you
visiting family in Genoa?"

"Yes, an uncle. You?"

"Our daughter lives in Messina. She works for the
government. Married to her work, no children, but she is all
we have. She arranges two trips a year for us. We cannot
complain."

"That's nice."

"We old people don't need to be pampered. Some, they take
advantage. Not being ignored is all we ask." The man
stamped out his cigarette butt, shivering as the breeze picked
up and shuffled back inside. Claudio stared at the rhythmic
lapping of the waves going past. He raised his eyes to the
land, houses dotting what was once farmland. He thought of
Brinto and how he and that corrupt Maresca had forced their

hand. He didn't think of his Father as a coward for bowing before they broke him; it was an impossible situation, the momentum unstoppable. His only lament was that he didn't have time to square the ledger with Maresca.

He needn't have worried though. A day earlier, Palumbo fingered him under duress to whittle down his sentence, naming him and mayors of four other areas surrounding Messina in the glue; Tremestieri, Bordonaro, Contesse and Pistunina. He walked out to the back of his house, the grids of houses below, and shot himself through the mouth as the police approached his house, thankful in his final moments that Concetta and Matteo were not there to see him. The timber mill and the housing development ground to a halt as the investigation teased out the corrupt tentacles in both. A new mayor promising integrity and a new start was elected in a landslide, and long grass grew around the paved roads and houses without occupants, looters grabbing anything they could to improve their own homes. The void was filled by workers from the north, who came to reboot the mill.

To locals, events only confirmed their long-held belief; whether by corrupt locals or northerners, they would always be screwed.

Claudio went back inside to see his Mother stirring. She had slept for four hours nestled in the crook of Lidia's shoulder. She woke, only sea around her. Not seeing land in any direction panicked her for a moment before her children held a hand each and reassured her. The canteen finally opened, selling day old panini with mortadella and pale provolone. They ate, chewing slowly, in part due to the slight staleness of the bread, but also because they had time to kill, with Genoa still three hours away. Their life was like an accordion now; time moving fast to leave the apartment and onto the ship, now seemingly endless time before they had to rush to buy their tickets to come back the other way, and all that before actually leaving Messina. Vanna tried to think of the trip to Australia; twenty-five days at best on a ship scared her, even when she thought of breaking the voyage up into small chunks. But she had made up her mind.

She tapped the table and said, "Let's play *scopa*."

As a young girl, Vanna's Nonna use tarot cards, different from the traditional *Tarocco Siciliano*. Nonna's eyes and facial expression when she did pretend readings left an impression on her, and she always dealt cards quickly, as if the slow reveal of a card contained some portent for the future. When they played days earlier, it was harmless fun. Now every card held significance as if her Nonna was playing through Claudio and Lidia. *Turn them over faster please* she asked, ignoring her childrens' glances at each other. A few hands later, the foreboding washed out of her brain, and Claudio and Lidia relaxed and laughed as their Mother started laughing and teasing them as she racked up point after point, normal order restored.

Rounds and time passed until a passenger announced the faint glimmer of light in the distance, and relief showed on Vanna's face. They stood on the deck as the ship slowed on approach to the bay. The air cooled and picked up speed as the wind funnelled through between the mountain ranges that fed down into the city. Claudio sweated in spite of the cold; five carabinieri waited at the end of the gangplank, talking between themselves behind their hands. He shot Lidia and his Mother a look, mouthing *tranquilli*. They walked down and past them, and towards a general information counter.

Two of the policemen sprang into action as a young man stepped off the gangplank and made a swift dash to his right, lasting twenty metres before slipping and being brought to ground by the pair. The man was frogmarched past them. He locked eyes with Claudio and spat a globule that narrowly missed him, earning him a hearty backhander to the cheek from the largest of the policemen.

They approached the counter. The old man behind it was slumped, asleep. Claudio tapped the counter and the man slowly came around before falling asleep again. A policeman approached them and tapped the counter with his truncheon. "OH! Wake up, old timer. Forget him. What do you need?"

"The closest *pensione*, please."

"A block that way, Genziana."

"Do you know what time the Marconi departs tomorrow morning?"

"Nine-thirty. Ticket office opens at seven."

They paid for a room with a single bed and a double bunk. Claudio paid the clerk a five lira note to make sure they were up by six. Claudio's stomach churned again, and he spent the night between falling asleep and being woken by stomach pains. Lidia woke each time he groaned in pain. Vanna slept deeply, oblivious. The over eager clerk woke them ten minutes early.

After two incorrect instructions, they found themselves at the ticket office for the Marconi.

"When does the Marconi leave?" asked Vanna.

"For where?" said the woman behind the counter in a bored voice.

"Melbourne, Australia."

"Passports?"

The ticket officer peered at them more closely than the man at Messina, and took their passports away to a man at the other end of the counter, an imposing man who stood over the counter and speared Claudio with his glare while the woman, enjoying the tension, stood with her back to the wall.

"Are you being sponsored by someone in Australia?"

"Yes." said Vanna, handing him the letter. The man read it, smirking then leaving it on his counter and turning to the passports, back and forth, looking up, again focusing on Claudio.

"Are you the male of the family, are you?"

"Yes." said Claudio.

"Explain to me as the male of the family why you are boarding a ship to Australia from Genoa, when you are from Sicily? Boarding at Messina makes more sense no?"

"We came to visit our uncle before we left. He is invalid and unable to come to Sicily."

"Where does he live?" asked the man, watching Claudio's face with intent.

"Marassi, near the Stadium of Luigi Ferraris." replied Claudio, keeping a straight face.

"Is he a Sampdoria fan or Genoa?"

"Genoa."

Satisfied, the man softened his tone. "You must love him very much."

"We do."

He laughed. "Tell me something, what is it with you southerners always leaving things to the last minute? Say it was booked out, what then?"

The woman began sniggering behind the man, drawing a rebuke from him. "Go back to your station *ritardata* and serve - show some respect." He turned back to Claudio "I'm sorry about that. We just have to be on our guard in case of anyone suspicious. Three tourist class tickets?"

"Yes please." said Claudio, looking to his Mother for the money. She handed him the envelope and counted out the 570 lira. The man handed over the tickets, passports and the letter.

"They are very strict on not leaving the ship unless instructed. Disembark and you will have a lot of explaining to do if you try to get back on. Please be ready to board thirty minutes before departure, which is in two hours from dock C, about a hundred metres that way." He pointed to the right.

He continued in his rehearsed voice. "Do any of you get seasick? Because if you do, the pharmacy sells tablets that will help you. They make you a bit drowsy, but better that eh?" The man was all warmth and smiles now, and wished them well for their voyage as he handed them their tickets, paperwork and passports.

Claudio held on for two minutes before his stomach revolted and he lurched to the water's edge to vomit, bracing himself against a bollard, the offensive panino from the day before making an unsightly splash into the water, the small blackfish herding around the water dispersing before returning to feed on the new bounty. Vanna and Lidia shepherded him to the nearest cafe and got him to drink some water. They moved on in ten minutes, Claudio recovering quickly and found the Marconi, shorter than Claudio expected. People milled around the stern, eager to claim the best cabins, unaware that these were already allocated when they bought their tickets, but staff in dark blue from the ship waved them back. They heard the first boarding shout and decided to board and rest. The purser directed them to another staff member who led them around the other side of the boat and down a level of stairs. Their cabin was for four, and the man explained in a strong northern accent that they should be alone, but in case of overflow or a ticket mixup, they may be joined by a person travelling alone. Claudio produced a ten lira note.

"If you can make sure we have the cabin to ourselves, I would be grateful."

The man smiled nervously as he accepted the money and said *I'll try my best* before slinking away. The cabin contained two pairs of bunks in an L-shape and a two by three metre space of floor with a table and four small chairs and a small shower and toilet off to the side. One armchair sat in the opposite corner of the room from the bunks. Vanna made a noise her children recognised as satisfaction.

"At least it's clean."

They relished the opportunity to lie down and rest their bodies after the twelve-hour trip north to Genoa. Claudio had just fallen asleep when a loud knock sounded. *Everyone outside to wave goodbye* sounded a chirpy female voice through a megaphone. Exhausted, Claudio and Lidia wanted to stay in, so Vanna walked the way around to the port side where the number of passengers had swelled and the wharf was full, people from both sides waving with white handkerchiefs. As she walked back to the cabin, the boat rumbled and pulled away. An hour later, all three slept soundly. Vanna finding sleep seductive. Lidia slept in the top bunk above her and Claudio on the bottom bunk of the other pair.

Vanna moved as her dream played out, her arm outstretched as Tino, his eyes bulging, reached out for her, his pale body resuming normal colour as long as they maintained eye contact. The other hand held the live wire, the electricity a blue aura around his body. Don't leave me alone with the worms, Vanna, I beg you, stay with me until it's your turn, before the arm dropped, limp, and the body pale again, eyes closed.

CHAPTER 37

Tyrrhenian Sea, 1967

Vanna woke. Claudio and Lidia were still asleep. She opened her suitcase, brought out pen and paper and began writing. An hour later she read over her words, placed the letter in an envelope, then went back to bed. Her watch said nearly eleven a.m. She got up again before sleep could take her, deciding to stay awake until they reached Messina so she could say goodbye properly.

She hadn't thought about her brothers in Acireale for some time. They disowned her for not taking their arranged choice of husband, a doleful but dopey farmer called Fortunato, a decision made to offload her so they could marry. Their parents died young, and she was beholden to their wishes, until the day she and Tino locked eyes in Taormina as they visited their only living uncle. Vanna followed the gentle giant as he strode through the town, eventually catching up with him as he stopped, her reflection in a shop window catching his eye. He turned his long neck and made eye contact. He smiled and walked back to her, blocking out the sun so he could see her face better.

"Are you lost, signorina?"

"You presume I am single?"

"You have been following me for ten minutes. Won't your parents be worried?"

"My parents are dead."

"Oh, I'm so sorry - how stupid of me."

"These things happen, and you could not have known. I'm Vanna." She rested her hand into his large plate of a hand, her heart racing as he rubbed his thumb over her knuckles.

"Vanna – I have never heard that name before." he said, still holding her hand.

"I hated Giovanna, so I said Vanna, and Vanna stuck." She coaxed him for his name.

"Tino, as in Augustino, which I hate."

"So, we have that in common then. This cafe has a table." she said, pointing over his shoulder. "Let's have a coffee and share a cannolo until my brothers find me."

"How many-"

"Two," she said, "but I think they would cower in front of you. What do you do?"

"I'm a farmer, near Messina. I needed a break, so I came by bus to enjoy the smell of the sea."

"You could have gone anywhere, with beaches just as beautiful as here. And yet you came here, and fate has placed us here on the same day."

"Fate or accident?"

"Either way, are you displeased?"

"Not at all. In fact, quite the opposite."

They shared ten minutes together until a crude shout from her oldest brother Barbaro caught their attention.

"Donato! She's here," yelled Barbaro, a short, thin man who approached carefully, noting Tino's imposing frame as he stood.

"Your sister was lost."

"And who are you?"

"Tino Liverani. And I would like to marry your sister, if of course she does not object."

Barbaro turned to his brother, equally short but fatter and sweating buckets. "This cafone wants to marry Vanna. Five seconds and he fell in love."

"How sweet." said Donato.

"Do you think we're idiots?" asked Barbaro.

"We need time to answer that question." Vanna snorted, trying to suppress her laughter, before pulling her hand away from Donato's grab for her, his stumpy fat arms too short.

She continued, arm around Tino. "I'm not going anywhere. I like this man. This is the kind of man you should have found for me, not that stunted, cross eyed goat lover. Leave me here, and you can marry those dumb young tarts with the big tits you chase around. See how quickly they age when they realise their life is nothing but waiting on you hand on foot, and wonder why they don't love you in ten years when there are four shorter, fatter versions of you running around."

"Are you finished impressing this local...what do you do anyway?" asked Barbaro.

"I'm a farmer near Messina."

"And why should we consider this ridiculous proposition?"

Tino took a step forward. "Because we like each other and Vanna seems old enough to make up her own mind."

Donato stepped in front of Barbaro and lifted his chin as he spoke.

"Or is it because she is the first putana to give you a hard-on with a smile-"

The left fist of Tino caught Donato, the sound of his cheekbone breaking unmistakeable. Barbaro knelt down as his brother wailed in pain before rising up to face Vanna.

"If we walk away, you will have nothing. Nothing. We have not been complete bastards as brothers. We have put aside a dowry for you for your wedding day, but you will lose the lot."

"Keep the dowry. I will provide for Vanna. We will marry in our good time." His face hardened as he stared down at Donato, casting a shadow over his disfigured face. "Before you leave, apologise to your sister. Make this your good deed for the day."

"I am sorry, Vanna," the v sounding like a muffled f, the right side of his face comically swollen.

"Let's go." said Vanna, placing her tiny hand inside Tino's huge one.

"Where to?" asked Tino.

"Wherever you were going." she said, leaning in and rubbing her nose into his strong arm. They took the bus back to Messina and hopped off at the closest point to Zafferia.

"I'll need new shoes, Tino."

"And clothes, too. Are you up for the thirty-minute walk home?"

"Yes, my darling giant."

They got off the bus and began the walk to the farm. Tino was impressed with her stamina. After a few minutes, he stopped.

"Wait."

"What's wrong?"

"We won't be alone at home. With everything, I forgot to mention. My Mother lives with us." A slight pause as he waited for Vanna's reaction, and for a moment his heart sank.

"And?" she asked, smiling.

"I thought I should tell you."

"Let's go meet her," she said, Tino scratching his head. She turned around and walked back. "What is her name?"

"Lidia."

"That is a lovely name. And your Father?"

"My Father Domenico died three years ago." he said blankly, still rooted to the spot.

Vanna walked back to him and smiled, a pitiful smile. "I'm sorry to hear that." She tapped him softly on the cheek, before reaching up on her tippy toes to kiss him. He leant down and pecked her on the cheek, her hand moving his lips to hers. Yes, this is right, she thought to herself.

"What happened in Taormina is no different than when a man and a woman, strangers, are placed in a room and told they will marry. Don't be scared. I fell in love with you the moment I saw you walk. I hadn't even seen your face. I can't explain it, and I don't want to know why."

She tugged his hand and cajoled him to come along. They walked along roads and moved through fields. Despite his Mother being in a state of early dementia, declining, Tino couldn't wait for her to meet Vanna. Her eyesight was still keen, and her tall frame stood at the door as they approached, long grey hair cascading over her thin shoulders, her thin, frail arms out to greet her, her pale green eyes meeting Vanaa's.

*"Figghia mia, comu t'aspettavu," she said as she embraced
her. My child, how I've been waiting for you.*

Vanna stopped there. That was enough for one flashback and
she was tired. She would relive these memories over time,
nostalgia happy to occupy her thoughts until something (not
someone, that was out of the question) new came along to
ignite another part of her brain. The last thing that stirred her
passion was cooking at Bacano. She thumped her chest hard
twice as punishment for saying the name in her mind. Her
heart purely served now to keep her going until Tino got his
wish. Claudio and Lidia purred on, asleep.

Vanna paced laps around the ship's deck, walking away from
sleep, silently chasing her, always keeping up, her body
flagging, making an inevitable beeline to bed. The warmth of
the cabin hit her as she returned, and she succumbed at last.
Two vignettes of Tino filled her head, both in Brinto's car
leaving the farm. Tino's last words as they left came, deeper
and slower than his natural voice

*You only feel nostalgia well after you say goodbye to
something, not as you say goodbye, he said, alive before he
got into the car.*
*How true, said Vanna in the car, turning to Tino, now pale
and fixed, staring out the window, deep fissures spreading
across his face until he was unrecognisable. The car stopped
in front of their apartment, a bloodied Brinto turning to
them, the bullet hole oozing blood where Crudelli had hit
him. We're here.*

Claudio and Lidia let her sleep and they walked the deck to
see where they were. Reading their minds, a purser walking
past in dark blue uniform pointed to the island on their left

and said *Ischia, bella isola, e fra pocom Napoli*. They stayed and enjoyed the cool breeze in the shade as the ship turned to dock at Naples, staying only fifteen minutes before departing. Passengers boarded, and men passed and slowed their pace as they watched Lidia, both those alone and with wives on their arm. Claudio turned and warded them off with a warning glance which they quickly heeded. The dinner bell rang out, an unusual high peal of a sound but given the time the logical conclusion.

They went to find the restaurant. It was filling slowly so they returned to the room to wake Vanna. They walked together to the early dinner sitting, enjoying lasagne and salad.

"Are your insides feeling better?" asked Vanna.

"Much." said Claudio, eating his lasagne with gusto.

"I hear there is plenty to do on here to keep us busy," said Lidia. "Games, card nights, movies, theme parties."

"Just make sure Claudio is close by if I am not." said Vanna. "Do you not see eyes running over you, my girl?"

"Yes, Mother." said Lidia, rolling her eyes.

"Don't dismiss what Mother is saying," said Claudio, eating with his mouth full. "I know how boys think. Trust me."

Vanna walked over and poured herself a strong black coffee.

"Can you stop yourself if a boy wants to talk to me?" whispered Lidia.

"Depends what you mean by talking."

"I don't want you to be my shadow everywhere I go."

"I can't promise that." said Claudio.

"And if *that* happens again," she said, tilting her head toward Sicily, "you may not be as lucky. How can you be sure there won't be police waiting to board the ship and find you when we dock at Messina?"

"It's my job to protect you. If they find me, that is God's will."

"That man in Taormina."

"Vito Semola."

"He was creepy, all over me, smelled of aftershave. But what if another good-looking, *respectable* boy who I like wants to talk to me? Can you tell the difference, or do you think he's just after one thing? How will I meet anyone?"

"In Australia, we will go to parties and you will meet the right one, I am sure. But here, on this boat? All touched in the head. They would see you as an adventure, someone to be conquered without any consequences, to be forgotten."

Vanna returned to the table, Lidia getting up. "I'm going for a walk. I need some air."

Vanna shook her head. "Leave her. What did you say to her?"

"She resents me for protecting her, Mother."

"Well, after what happened, how would you be if you were her? Women start desiring to meet the right man at that age, ready or not."

"She's too young to meet that man."

"I met your Father at nineteen. How old is Lidia?"

"Nineteen."

Vanna tilted her head to one side to make her point. She wondered how she would have reacted to Claudio murdering that boy had Tino not died. She had been given to thinking about Father Di Pardo lately, and couldn't bring herself to ask him. She would tell from his face if she asked, but did she want to? Yes, she had to. Talking about one murder led naturally to the other.

"Father Di Pardo."

Claudio's face was unchanged, but his pupils dilated and gave him away. Vanna grabbed him by the arm, and they walked out

"He had her in the vestry, pinned against the wall with his pants down."

"Caterina?"

"Yes."

"How did you know?"

"The way he stared at her in bible classes. On the night of the festival I stayed behind. She was the only child who didn't leave the church, so I grabbed a rock and snuck in and hid behind the last row of seats. She was crying, and I went in, hit him at the back of the head, then finished him off above the ear."

They walked back to the cabin. The wind blew getting cooler and the sun was dropping fast. They stopped as the clifftop houses of Tropea reflected the last of the brightness westwards, shadows forming between them. Vanna struggled to erase the image of Claudio throwing another man off the cliff. They played some more *scopa* before Vanna got tired.

"The view of Torre Faro at night is beautiful," said Vanna. "Why don't you both have a look?"

"I'd like to. Come on, Claudio."

"Sure."

Difficult to tell whether the haze in the distance was Calabria or Sicily, but as the ship turned slightly starboard, the light of Torre Faro winked at them, and the Strait of Messina opened up. Five minutes later, the Madonna of Messina Bay made a reappearance.

"Are you Ok, brother?"

"Mother knows about Di Pardo."

"You're surprised?"

"I'm cold. We better go inside. Just in case."

Vanna's bed was made when they returned. *Vanna* called out Claudio. Lidia checked the bathroom and searched around the room as if some secret space existed.

"Don't stress," said Lidia, "she probably regretted not coming out and is enjoying the view. She will be back soon."

"I'll go find her if that will make you relax." said Lidia.

"No, you're right. She'll be back soon."

Ten minutes passed and they both decided the walk back to the hall.

"Maybe she went for the second sitting. She did enjoy that lasagne." said Lidia.

They walked back to the hall. People were filling tables and minding spots for their loved ones and friends they had met early in the journey. They walked past every table and panic began to set in. Claudio called out to Lidia.

"You keep looking here. I'll go back to the cabin."

Claudio look around the cabin, ridiculously looking under the bed. As he stood back up, the gap in the cupboard caught his eye. Her suitcases were missing. The tannoy blew static then announced in a busy male voice: *ladies and gentlemen, we are approaching Messina. We will be docked in Messina for forty minutes. We ask that you do not leave the vessel please. Dinner is being served for a further thirty minutes.* Claudio ran to the deck. He was facing the port and did a lap. He ran up the stairs and did a lap of the upper deck. *The dinner hall's the other way* said a man walking the opposite direction. Nothing. He kept running, returning to the room hoping he would see her eating with Lidia at the hall, finding neither there. A man in uniform stopped him, his hand firm on his shoulder.

"Please, Sir. No running. What is the problem?"

"My Mother, she's nowhere to be found." he said, his breathing fast and shallow, heart racing.

"Ok, let me make an announce for her to come to the dinner hall."

In two minutes came the announcement; *Signora Vanna Liverani to the dinner hall please*, repeated twice, ten seconds apart, followed by another announcement: *we are departing Messina in ten minutes, repeat departing Messina in ten minutes. Tonight, we will be showing a movie in the cinema on Deck B. Please present ten minutes early; first in, best dressed.*

Claudio shouted to Lidia on the opposite side of the room.

"I can't find her anywhere."

"Neither can I."

"Now what?"

"You walk back to our room this side. I'll go the other way and I'll meet you at the cabin. Cover as much room as possible."
Lidia walked the port side, people amassed near the water's edge, lit up by the Marconi's harsh light, waving their

handkerchiefs, past them. past the noise and caught a glimpse of her before she moved from light to dark on the port with suitcase in hand, her gait unmistakeable and quickening as the shadows swallowed her small figure.

Vanna chided herself with every step she took, slowing when her name came over the tannoy before her feet moved again, telling herself *don't look back*. She had abandoned her brothers and now she was abandoning her children; drawn inexorably to Tino, then alive, now dead.

I am living just to be dying by your side, amore, she said to herself.

The Marconi blew its loud horn in two long bursts. Vanna brushed past the man with his eye on the first taxi in the queue and got in, hurling her suitcases into the back seat.

"Where to, signora?"

"Home."